ALL THINGS
SLIP AWAY

Other books by Kathryn Meyer Griffith:

Scraps Of Paper

ALL THINGS
SLIP AWAY

•

Kathryn Meyer
Griffith

AVALON BOOKS
NEW YORK

Published by Thomas Bouregy & Co., Inc.
160 Madison Avenue, New York, NY 10016

Library of Congress Cataloging-in-Publication Data

Griffith, Kathryn Meyer.
    All things slip away / Kathryn Meyer Griffith.
        p. cm.
    ISBN 0-8034-9759-8 (acid-free paper)
    1. Serial murderers—Fiction. 2. Illinois—Fiction. I. Title.

PS3607.R5488A79 2006
813'.6—dc22

                                        2005028541

PRINTED IN THE UNITED STATES OF AMERICA
ON ACID-FREE PAPER
BY HADDON CRAFTSMEN, BLOOMSBURG, PENNSYLVANIA

For my beloved grandmother,
Mary Fehrt, who told me
my first stories . . .

Prologue

(Ten Years Earlier)

Frank Lester didn't have time to think, it happened so quickly. Think how dangerous it was rushing headlong and alone after the suspect in the dark. Think what he would do if the man he was jumping fences for and trampling through unlit backyards to get at, would turn and attack him. What if the perp had a weapon? Backup hadn't arrived but Frank's police instincts, honed by nearly twenty years of being a homicide detective, were hounding him to pursue.

Don't let him get away . . . catch him and lock him in a cell so he'll never be able to hurt another person. Catch him!

Because Frank's instincts also told him the lumbering shape ahead was the kidnapper who'd abducted and killed six people in the last month and a half. Frank wasn't about to let the man escape. He'd been close before, but the kidnapper had been clever and had eluded him.

It'd been a gut hunch, Frank guarding the latest victim's mailbox, waiting for the inevitable delivery, and it had paid off. The kidnapper, who Frank thought must be a frustrated artist of some kind, left clay figurines representing his victims as a personal signature to his crimes. Looked like little lumps of dried mud to Frank. The mud creations were tiny,

1

primitive, and barely recognizable as people. They were placed in a mailbox or somewhere else around the victim's house under cover of night and often in foul weather to prevent being seen.

The press had dubbed the serial kidnapper/killer the "Mud People Killer" after Frank's partner, Sam Cato, had called him that in an interview. This time, after hours of waiting and shivering in the snowy dark, Frank had caught the man in the act of delivering his tiny mud person to his latest victim. When yelling "Stop. Police!" failed to impress the guy, Frank had taken chase without regard for police procedures or his own safety.

Now he wasn't sure he'd done the right thing. The wind was like a stone wall in front of him, tossing shorn tree limbs at him or in his path. The icy ground made it difficult to stay upright, much less run. He'd already fallen twice, messed up his knee, and done something painful to his left hand while trying to catch himself.

Winter in Chicago could be brutal. It was the northern air off the lake that made it so vicious.

What was he thinking?

A bullet, then another, zinged through the air inches from Frank's face. The creep was shooting at him! It had to the kidnapper. Frank hurled his overweight body behind an underweight tree. As frigid as the weather was he was sweating underneath his coat, though shivering beneath that. His wife was right. He needed to go on a diet. Out of shape and out of breath, that's what he was.

He drew his Beretta 9mm automatic with frozen hands and switched it to his left one. He'd called in Sam and some backup right as he'd taken chase. He prayed they'd arrive soon as he concentrated on where the bullets were coming from. Concentrated on staying alive.

He wanted to catch the man he was chasing more than anything. It'd become personal, plain and simple. From the beginning the kidnapper had singled Frank out, of all the investigators on the case, taunting him in notes he'd send the newspapers or hand-written messages left in places where Frank could find them. In Frank's mailbox. Taped to his car window at the police station. Never the same place twice, though. Once Frank unrolled his daily newspaper and a note from the kidnapper fell out. Made him so mad. How dare that psychopath intrude like that into *his* life. The kidnapper had even called him once at home to taunt him.

If you're wondering . . . yes, I kill them. All of them. And you can't stop it. You aren't going to catch me, Officer Lester . . . I'm too smart for you. You dumb fat cop. I'm too smart for all of you.

The worse thing was, Frank was afraid that what the man said was true, though he preferred to keep thinking of him as a kidnapper. The realization that the suspect was also killing the people he was kidnapping was too much for Frank to stomach.

Regardless, the man was evil and had to be stopped.

But why was Frank getting all this unwanted attention from a soulless kidnapper? Probably had something to do with his being head detective on the case and being mentioned so often in the newspaper and on television. The love notes from the kidnapper weren't the worst side effect. The man had taken to snatching people from under Frank's very nose. People Frank knew and cared about.

Last week, Charlotte, a waitress from his favorite lunch spot, disappeared, and he feared his nemesis had taken her. She was a middle-aged divorcee who was an artist in her real life, as she used to say with a smile. Had two grown kids and a teenager at home. It was Charlotte's house that Frank had been staking out on that night. Perhaps she was still alive. He could hope.

Frank wasn't letting the kidnapper go. He'd catch him or have a heart attack trying, which, according to his wife, was a possibility waiting to happen. Peering around the tree, gun ready, Frank squinted his eyes looking for a target.

A blurry shape slithered around a shed—barely an outline—but it could have been a man. Another shot torpedoed through the snowflakes and Frank felt agony in his left shoulder.

Stifling a cry, the detective aimed at the shadowy blob and fired several times in succession, mentally counting the bullets spent so he'd have some left if he found himself facing the guy.

Screams of rage—something about a leg and fingers—pierced the night and the sound of something thudding to the ground was trailed by an eerie silence. Frank waited, breathing hard, the pain in his shoulder spreading like fire, praying he'd hit the kidnapper. That it was over.

After an eternity, Frank stumbled out in search of the body but didn't find one.

He returned to his car and checked on his backup. Bad weather had slowed it down, but it was coming. Soon the area was swarming with strobe-flashing squad cars, cops, and dancing flashlights. The falling snow morphed into icy daggers and the night slipped into a gray, wretched day, but other than a pool of blood in one spot on the ground, there was no blood trail, body, or corpse ever found. Just like the victims' bodies were never found. Alive or dead.

Days, weeks, months went by. No more phone calls or notes to the newspapers. No more people were taken, no more mud figurines were left as gifts on back porches, in mailboxes, or on windowsills. Eventually the investigation grew cold, the paper files dusty, and the computer file rarely opened. Frank's shoulder healed.

Frank wasn't worried. He was sure his bullets had hit the man and that he'd dragged himself away to nurse his wounds, which were either so severe they'd scared him out of the kidnapping business forever, or he'd dragged himself off to die. The kidnapper's death or the discovery of a dead body would have been better, more final, but Frank was relieved the kidnappings had stopped, as was the city of Chicago.

As the months turned into years, Frank convinced himself

that the man had either ended his crimes or was dead. He wouldn't have been able to let the case go otherwise. Though the media interest in the case faded more quickly, Frank didn't stop searching for the missing people for a long time afterward. But other cases just as heinous came along and filled his days. There were more murders to solve and criminals to arrest. Reports to fill out. Life to live.

Time passed.

Frank Lester lost his wife, Jolene, eight years later in a car accident.

His son, Kyle, went on to medical school in Chicago.

Frank took early retirement and, longing for a simpler existence, moved back to Spookie, his hometown, where he built a log cabin in the woods and settled down to enjoy life, find himself again, and write the mysteries he so loved to read. Bought a motorcycle and rode it often. Met an artist named Abigail Sutton and became close with her. Got his first novel published and fell into the easy rhythm of small-town life with childhood friends. Was happy.

And more time passed.

He'd all but forgotten the Mud People Killer he was so sure he'd mortally wounded that Chicago winter night.

But the killer hadn't forgotten him.

Chapter One

(The Present)

Abby Sutton learned of the missing girl on a rainy October morning as she was painting the mural on the back library wall. Turning to look over her shoulder at Samantha Westerly, editor of the *Weekly Journal* and also her friend, she had an uneasy feeling when Samantha mentioned the girl had disappeared three days ago and hadn't been heard from since.

"Shelly Lanstrom's missing? That scrawny little thing with the big brown eyes and long hair? The one who works after school as a cashier at the new IGA Supermarket? Can't be but sixteen or so?"

"Yeah," Samantha confirmed. "That's the one."

Abby shook her head. "That's awful." That girl treated everyone with respect, could count well, and never crushed people's bread. She had looked up to Abby because Abby was an artist. Abby was more alarmed than she was letting on. Shelly had been more than an acquaintance—she'd become a friend. Abby looked forward to seeing her when she did her shopping and couldn't bear to think that the girl was lost somewhere, hurt, or in danger. Or worse.

Sketching the mural on the wall, she was at that stage of

creation where she thought she'd never be able to pull it off. Too much wall, not enough talent. The library had commissioned her to paint something bookishly creative yet tasteful, preferably in subdued hues so it wouldn't distract readers too much. She'd decided on well-known authors chatting together at a summer café with flowers and foliage in muted colors as a backdrop. Or something like that.

The mural was a work in progress and she had two weeks to finish it and get paid before her bank account hit zero. That was the life of a freelance artist—either work or starve.

"Everyone's out looking for her," Samantha continued. "Family, friends, and the police. I hope to God they find her, Abby. Shelly is a good kid. Wants to go to college and has the grades for a scholarship. Has her priorities in a row, not like some others her age.

"I talked to her mother and she swore Shelly would never up and vanish like this unless something's happened to her. No one's heard from or seen her. She's missed her last three work shifts without calling in to explain, which isn't like her at all.

"The town's gonna be spooked if Shelly doesn't turn up soon. Lots of people have kids and this sort of thing just doesn't happen around here. Young girls up and missing, I mean . . ."

Samantha's smile was tight as she watched Abby drawing Mark Twain's face in pencil on the wall. Eyes were the hardest for her.

"What does Sheriff Mearl have to say?" Abby pressed, not expecting he'd say much. Sheriff Mearl Brewster was a typical laid-back small-town police officer and about as smart as a rock. He wisely tended to keep his mouth shut. Made him seem smarter than he actually was.

"He's the one who organized the search party that's out in the woods around Shelly's house right now. But," Samantha hesitated until Abby glanced over at her, "I have a bad feeling about this one. Call it a reporter's sixth sense. I've been nosing around all day and something's not right. It isn't merely a case of a teenage girl rebelling against her parents by running away, trying to scare them, or going off with a friend or a boyfriend. She's really *gone*. No one has seen her *anywhere*.

"Well, I'd better get out of your hair and let us both get back to work or you won't have bill money for next month and Spookie won't have a weekly paper. I'll keep you updated on the Shelly situation. Bye, Abby."

"Bye, Samantha." Abby returned to her work, listening to the rain music on the library roof, a sound that usually had the power to calm and mesmerize her. Not today. Sketching out the mural, she tried not to dwell on the missing girl. Which was impossible. Her disappearance brought back unwanted memories.

Three years before in another city, another life, Abby's husband Joel had walked out of their cramped apartment for cigarettes and had never returned. They'd been married a long time, had been deeply in love, and had been happy—she was sure of that. He wouldn't have just left her. She went through a nightmarish time. She raged, cried, called everyone they'd ever known, talked endlessly to the police and hired a Private Investigator, looking everywhere she could for two endless years.

Until Joel's body was found in his car deep in a thicket of woods—a fatal victim of a long ago robbery.

Finally she'd grieved. Since then, missing people had become an obsession to her. Couldn't help herself. She needed to help other people search for their missing loved ones.

If she hadn't needed the money from this job so badly, she would have joined the searchers looking for Shelly. But, as Samantha had said, they had more than enough people. Her walking out on her livelihood wouldn't help anything.

When the last of the daylight filtering through the windows had ebbed away, and her tired eyes told her it was time, Abby cleaned and packed up her art supplies in a duffel bag, climbed into her car and headed home.

It was a frosty fall evening, a preview of winter to come.

The rain had stopped but the air chilled a person's bones. Her house, on the edge of town, wasn't far, but now she was glad she hadn't walked that morning. If people were going missing, it might not be safe to stroll along the fringe of the woods alone.

She'd moved to Spookie—a quaint town so named because the first townspeople had thought it looked eerie with its thick mists and woodsy atmosphere—the year before and had bought a fixer-upper house and begun a new life. The kind of life she'd always wanted. For years she'd been a graphic artist knocking out mediocre ads at a city newspaper. Here in her new life she supported herself with free-lance artwork, painting watercolors or acrylics of people, their houses, their pets, or any commission she could get. She saved money by shopping at thrift stores, buying generic brands, and clipping double coupons.

The mural—a truly large commission—was an unexpected bonus, and if she did a quality job she could get more. She could charge three times as much for a mural as she did for other pictures. Which was good for her because these days she was barely making ends meet, still living partially on her savings and still doing without. But she was happier than she'd been in years. She already felt as if she'd spent her whole life in Spookie.

Abby made a stop at the IGA supermarket to pick up a few groceries and as she was going in, she ran into Frank Lester.

Frank was a retired big city homicide detective who'd returned to Spookie, his hometown, two years before. Now he filled his time writing crime novels, enjoying his log cabin out in the woods and gossiping at Stella's Diner. He was interested in what was happening around town and usually knew what was going on. That was the ex-cop in him.

"Fancy meeting you here, Abby," he said, smiling down at her on his way out, his arms full of bagged groceries. Frank didn't look his age, whatever it was. Possibly late forties. He backtracked and walked alongside of her as she snatched up a shopping basket and headed for the dairy aisle. She didn't like him seeing her sweaty, with paint-splattered face and clothes, weary from her day of work. She looked dreadful.

"What do you mean? Seems like I'm always here. Buying this or that. Today it's this." Abby shrugged as she picked up a gallon of milk, distracted by her errand and where she was.

A year ago the IGA had been Mason's General Store, more old-fashioned and with less merchandise. But the owner, John Mason, had been convicted of a triple murder and had been sent to prison. The store had been sold to the IGA supermarket chain and they'd remodeled to put in more shelf space and provide a larger meat department. The new store was bigger, but unlike its previous incarnation, had no local crafts and paintings, no bins of penny candy, and little of the quaint nostalgic charm.

Though Abby had lost a source of income because Mason had displayed and sold her artwork when the store had been his, she also appreciated the improvements. The IGA was larger and better stocked. It made it more convenient to do all her shopping in town now, instead of driving to Stanley or to the Wal-Mart in Chalmers, but she was having a hard time getting used to it. She still expected to run into Mason around every corner. His ghost haunted the aisles and he wasn't even dead. Not like the people—the Summers—he'd helped kill thirty years ago and bury in her backyard. But that was another story.

She grabbed a package of cheese. "I'm having toasted cheese and tomato soup for supper. But I needed milk for the soup. And cheese for the toast."

"Ah, and usually you're so organized," he teased. "Sounds appetizing, though a little skimpy for me. On the subject of food, I'm roasting a turkey in my new roaster oven tomorrow at the cabin. How about coming over around six o'clock and helping me eat it? I've got the last of those homegrown green beans out of my garden you like so much and sweet potatoes and marshmallows. Big salad?"

"Kind of early for Thanksgiving dinner, isn't it?"

"Roasted turkey is good anytime. Easy to make and there's always leftovers. Turkey sandwiches. Turkey and noodles. And so on. So I don't have to cook for a few days."

She met his amused blue eyes. Frank knew he had her. She couldn't turn down free food. Frank liked to cook and was expert at it, grew his own vegetables and baked from scratch. One of his many passions. "Okay, tomorrow night you have a guest for dinner. But I can't stay late. I started that mural today at the library and I have to be there early in the morning. On a deadline, you know."

Frank didn't say anything, he knew she needed the money and that was her real deadline. It was probably the reason he was always feeding her. Probably thought she was starving or something. Truth was, it was pretty close to that. She had to budget carefully. Watch every dime. These days she would have stood on her head and wiggled her toes for a thick juicy steak, but turkey sounded just as good. She wasn't picky—a leftover from her deprived childhood when there was never enough of anything, especially money or food.

"You heard about Shelly, who works here afternoons and who's gone missing?" Frank went right to the main course. Old cop menu.

"Samantha was at the library earlier and mentioned it. I hope they find her somewhere . . . at a friend's or a boyfriend's, and that her being missing isn't because someone has taken her. Samantha swore Shelly wasn't the type to run off, but maybe she and her mother had a fight or something. Shelly told me last week they were fussing a lot at each other." Abby offered up the information, her voice concerned.

"I don't think Shelly was actually fighting with her mother," Frank gave her his opinion. "They get along most of the time. Love each other. She and her family are very good people, are close knit and go to church every Sunday. That's what's so hard about this.

"They live a mile down the road from me. Shelly's the middle child, doesn't have a boyfriend—that anyone knows of—and she's as happy as a teenager can be. From what I know of her, family, schoolwork and her job fill her time."

"Sounds like you know a lot."

"I do. The first night Shelly went missing her mother phoned and asked if I'd help look for the girl. I've been searching for two days with the others and now even I'm getting worried. Shelly must be in trouble somewhere or she'd be home. We have to find her. Three days is a long time for a girl to be missing." Frank's face reflected a reality born of experience. "Chances of something being wrong rise with every day."

"Where was Shelly last seen?" Her curiosity was getting the better of her.

"At home. She left three mornings ago for school . . . through the woods on her bike. She rode it everywhere, liked being outside. Her teacher said she never got to class. No one's seen or heard from her since. No sign of the bike either.

"Anyway, tomorrow the search is fanning out into Chalmers, Stanley and nearby communities. They're bringing in helicopters and dogs. We've been making phone calls, knocking on doors, hanging flyers and combing hills and gullies. The rain hasn't helped. Covered all tracks. The sheriff has alerted police authorities statewide and the media smells blood. By tomorrow or the next day TV will have it and it'll go national. That's good. We need help. Molly wants to make a plea—to whoever took Shelly—asking for her back."

"You really believe there's foul play involved?" Abby was feeling heartsick for Shelly's parents, ready to sacrifice the mural painting and financial gain for the welfare of a lost child. She thought that tomorrow she might go help hunt for the girl with the others. Forget the bills.

"I'm afraid it looks like that, Abby. Wish I could say otherwise."

"You need more people for that search party?"

corns everywhere. There were parties and a parade down Main Street on Halloween eve. And they did just as much for the other holidays throughout the year.

Her kind of town all right.

At home she took a quick shower, made supper and fed her cat Snowball. Taking her bowl of tomato soup and sandwich outside, she sat on the porch swing bundled in a sweater, Snowball curled up beside her, enjoying the last of the light and the drizzling rain. The clouds were a mist of shadowed rose and mauve curling across the sky, the sun was winking on the horizon and the air had that mustardy sharp tang of fall. She couldn't breath deeply enough. She loved this time of day. Loved the sights and smells of the woods around her.

She thought over her first year there. Edna—the old woman who'd lived and died in her house—hadn't been able to take care of it toward the end and had let it fall into disrepair. Abby had bought it dirt cheap. She'd been scrubbing, painting and wallpapering ever since.

Now the place was truly hers. It looked and smelled like her. Felt like home. A small two-story house and a half frame structure, it had a large, sunny kitchen, a comfortable living room and a roomy hall in the back of the lower floor that she planned to turn into an art studio because its windows flooded it with light.

The second story was her loft bedroom. Fantastic wooded view out back.

Her gaze traveled the length of the front porch to the collection of hanging birdhouses, all colors and sizes, and beyond. The yard was large, crowded with towering shade trees that merged into the woods in the back. The place was private and quiet. Beautiful in the sunlight, the dark, the rain, and the snow. She cherished it.

Then real life snuck in and she brooded about Shelly and whether she was unharmed. If she were still alive. People went missing all the time, but as well she knew, it was different when it was someone you knew. Tragedy at a distance is not real—tragedy up close is.

Behind her the evening woods were silent as her mind called up a childish face with amber eyes and round cheeks. Shelly had this way of looking at a person and they could see the smile behind her eyes. See the intelligence. Her being missing was so sad.

Abby knew too well what Shelly's parents were going through. The endless waiting for the lost person to walk back in through the door and the disbelieving fear as the days went by—and they didn't go by fast enough. The promises made to the universe and God if he or she did return.

She'd made her share of such promises . . . for Joel . . . when he vanished into that black hole that so many people did every year. Hundreds of people, Frank had told her. One day they were by your side, laughing, loving and smiling, and the next they were gone. Just gone.

Abby went to bed that night feeling heartsick for Shelly's parents and unsettled over the memories Shelly's disappearance was resurrecting in her. She whispered a prayer that the girl would show up soon—and safe. Miracles did happen sometimes, or at least that's what she used to believe. And children, even more than grown-ups, she thought, deserved miracles.

Of course Frank didn't believe in miracles. It was the cop in him.

Chapter Two

Nora Gibbons, the day librarian, had given Abby a key to the back door, so she was at work on the mural by seven on Saturday morning. With a cloudless sky she'd wanted to walk but, because of Shelly's disappearance and since she was going to Frank's later, she took the car, stopping to pick up jelly donuts and coffee as a treat because she'd gotten up so early and she could eat as she worked. Besides, on Saturday mornings from six to eight the bakery donuts were half price.

As she painted she speculated if Shelly had been found yet, knowing that when she saw Frank later that day she'd get the answer.

It was after nine. The library was now open to the public and she looked up from her work to see people browsing among the bookshelves and a couple of kids reading at the tables. A young boy with flaxen hair, wearing worn jeans and a shirt many sizes too large, was clicking away at the library's computer in the corner.

Abby didn't know how long the girl had been watching her, or watching her bag of donuts. She'd bought extra because this wasn't the first time she'd seen the girl and boy. Today the girl was slouching in the chair at the table behind where Abby had left the pastries and the child's eyes hadn't left the white bag except to stare at what Abby was doing on the wall.

"You can sure draw good, lady. Did you go to college to learn how to do that?" the girl murmured when Abby took a break and a sip of cold coffee, her other hand rummaging in the bakery bag for another donut. The girl's voice hesitant as if she was unsure of speaking to a stranger.

"No. I mean I went to college, but they didn't teach me how to draw. Drawing was something I could just always do since I was a kid. I can look at something and draw it. I've been doing it ever since and people even pay me for it. They seem to like what I draw. Don't know why."

"Because you're a great artist. Your people look real." The girl glanced up at Abby with her copper colored eyes filling a thin fragile face. Someone had given her blond hair a bad home haircut and wisps of stray hair stuck out all over her head. Her clothes, ill fitting and frayed, could have come from Goodwill. She was one of the Brooks children. Seven of them plus their parents lived in the woods a few miles outside of town in a ramshackle house like a modern day version of the early television Waltons.

Their father, Emil Brooks, worked at one of the town's two gas stations—the one Abby filled her gas tank up at every week—and their mother, Rebecca, cleaned other peoples' houses, or used to. Town rumor was that she'd been sick lately. Emil never talked about his wife's illness, but often bragged about her being such a loving wife and mother and how smart his kids were. He'd shown Abby pictures of his children and she'd thought how hard it must be to raise seven kids nowadays on his and his wife's salaries. Minimum wage was paltry and she didn't think their jobs paid much more than that.

"You going to eat all those donuts yourself?" the girl asked when Abby's mouth was full.

Abby swallowed. "Help yourself." And shoved the bag toward the girl. She'd seen hunger before, experienced it herself as a child, and the girl was hungry, not normal hungry but starving hungry. It was that fever in her eyes, her waif thinness, and that sudden flush to her cheeks at the sight of food. "Want the rest? I've had my limit already for today." There were four donuts left in the bag. Abby had eaten two.

The girl thanked her, told her her name was Laura, and softly called over to the boy at the computer. "Nick, there's jelly donuts over here for you. Come and get 'em." People weren't supposed to eat in the library, but they snuck food in all the time and made sure Nora didn't catch them. As Abby had done.

The boy stayed long enough to gobble down the donuts, muttered thanks in her direction without looking at her and scooted back to reclaim the computer. Like his older sister, Nick wore hand-me-down clothes and a lost expression on his lean face, but he behaved politely. He'd wolfed down the donuts so fast it made Abby feel guilty she didn't have more to offer.

When every morsel of the pastries was gone the girl remained to scrutinize Abby's painting and bug her with questions. She didn't mind having an audience. It didn't slow her down any. She reminded Abby of herself as a kid.

"I'm going to be an artist someday, too, you know," Laura announced as Abby painted in Edgar Allen Poe's body.

Pleased with how the mural was progressing, ahead of schedule and coming along better than she'd hoped, Abby was in a magnanimous mood and felt herself drawn into a long and curious conversation with a child she'd just met.

At one point, Laura admitted, "My teacher, Mrs. Delaney, says I have a true artist's eye. I can draw anything. You want to see my sketchbook?"

"Sure." Abby took a few minutes and sat down to look at the girl's pictures. Laura's admiration and need touched her. She'd been her once long ago. Penniless little nobody who'd desperately wanted to be a somebody. Being able to draw had been her way of standing out from the crowd, of being special and gaining attention.

Her family hadn't been able to send her to college, but she'd earned an art scholarship with talent and high grades.

Unfortunately she hadn't finished her degree. Three years was all she got in. Life in the form of Dad getting sick, Mom never having worked, and Abby having to help pull up the slack had gotten in the way. She never went back to school. Had kept working and eventually got married. Life, as it always does, went on.

Laura's pictures were extremely accomplished. She was a natural artist. As good as Abby had been at that age, perhaps better. They were pencil drawings of her brothers, sisters, mother, father, and scenes from her life. They were well done and strikingly poignant. Children sprawled on a tattered sofa or playing on swings in the backyard. A weary faced woman standing behind a mop and a man—who had to be their father—smiling as he worked over the engine of a car. The girl's use of texture, light and shadow was exceptional and beyond her age. It was instantly obvious that Laura was a gifted artist, her sketches were that wonderful.

Abby's eyes went to Laura's face. She had this tiny scar in the middle of her forehead and her eyes tilted down on the ends. "How old are you?"

"Almost fifteen."

She didn't look it. She was scrawny for fourteen. Looked more like twelve.

"I know my pictures aren't very good . . . I'm sorry. They're not the best I can do. You're a real artist, I shouldn't have bothered you—" There was panic in Laura's voice as she grabbed the sketchbook out of Abby's hands.

"Laura, the pictures are exceptional." Abby laid a hand on her shoulder. "You'll make a great artist someday if that's what you want to be. You have talent."

The girl's smile changed her face and almost made her pretty. "You think so?"

"I do. Keep drawing." Abby gave her pointers on how to add life to eyes, how to create real looking leaves on trees. Laura asked if she drew more pictures if Abby would look at them as well.

"Sure. I'll be here during the day for at least another

week. Come by anytime." Noticing the girl's skinny arms and the way she emptied the donut bag to glean crumbs, Abby took Laura's sketchbook and flipped it open to a picture of a girl about eleven or so poised on a bike. The girl had a wistful expression on her face as if everything in the world was right when she was on her bicycle.

"I really like this one, Laura, could I buy it off you? How about five dollars?" Abby couldn't believe she'd said that, money being as tight as it was, but once the words were out she couldn't take them back. Yet she remembered what being a kid and being hungry was like. Cash was a treasure. It bought food.

Laura was stunned. "Why do you want to buy one of *my* drawings?"

"Because it's good. It's an investment. One day—when you're famous—I'll be able to say I knew you when you were just beginning. That I have something you drew. And," Abby grinned at her, "I like the picture. The girl in it reminds me of my younger sister." All those reasons were true, Abby thought, but the real reason she handed Laura the five-dollar bill was for the girl herself. She'd buy food with it. Share it with her brother. That's what Abby used to do when she'd been a hungry kid. She only wished she could have spared more.

Laura's hand enclosed the money tightly and she thanked Abby as she tore out the page and handed it over. Then both she and her brother were gone like summer breezes.

The rest of the day Abby worked on the mural and tried not to think about anything else except the delicious supper she would be having at Frank's house. Tried not to think of those seven Brooks kids living out there in the woods in a dilapidated and foodless house.

Tried hard not to think about Shelly. It made her feel uneasy.

By five o'clock her stomach was growling so she finished up early and headed out. The sun was setting as she drove up in front of Frank's cabin. The woods surrounding it were bathed in dwindling light and the night creatures had begun singing their symphony.

She liked going to Frank's. The woods were lovely and his cabin was like something out of a fancy house magazine. As she stepped up onto the porch the aroma of turkey beckoned. Frank's two German shepherds were romping in the yard and he called them in and moved them to the backyard. They liked to jump all over her.

Frank returned and the minute she saw the look on his face she knew something was wrong.

"That bad, huh?" she prompted and settled into another rocker beside him that had one of those tall backs and soft seat cushions that felt like sitting on a fat marshmallow.

Frank and she had become close since she'd moved into town last year. He cared for her, was perhaps beginning to love her, but he never pushed for what she wasn't ready to give. In some ways, she was still in love with her dead husband.

For her, Joel's death was barely a year old and had frozen time, but she couldn't grieve for him forever, she knew that. Joel had vanished, had actually died, three years ago. Even if she'd only discovered that he'd been dead the year before. Three years was a long time to be lonely. A long time to be unhappy. Abby wanted to move forward.

"Pretty bad." Frank's voice was strained. "Something weird happened today and it's thrown me. I'm sorry I'm not going to be better company."

"Spill it."

"I shouldn't be talking about it."

He was scaring her. His slumped shoulders and the dread in his voice weren't like Frank at all. Frank always had it together. Nothing scared him. So it followed that whatever was bothering him must be awful. "Frank, if it affects you in any way, you'd better tell me now. 'Cause it will eventually affect me."

"You're right. If what is happening is what I think it is . . . it will affect you. It'll affect the whole town." Releasing his breath, he said, "A small clay figurine was found in the Lanstroms' mailbox today."

If that was supposed to mean something to her, it didn't. "No ransom note?"

"No. Just an unbaked clay figure of a person . . . simple, crude really . . . probably meant to be Shelly. Had long hair and small frame."

"So?"

"I've seen that kind of thing before, Abby. Back in Chicago ten years ago while I was on the case of a serial kidnapper. One we never caught. He'd kidnapped a half dozen people—that we knew of—of different ages and backgrounds, which made his modus operandi hard to pin down. His pattern difficult to predict. My partner, Sam Cato, dubbed him the Mud People Killer because the clay figures, left in the victim's mailbox or around their house a few days afterward, reminded him of little mud people. The media picked the name up and ran with it. Whomever fashioned those mud things wasn't much of an artist, if you ask me. They sure were ugly.

"We never found any of the victims, nor their bodies, and never solved the cases. He must have worn latex gloves when he made the figurines 'cause there were never any fingerprints. Couldn't organize stakeouts because most of the time we didn't know the missing person was one of his victims until *after* we found the mud figure. Then it was too late. That was the biggest problem. By the time I saw the pattern the stakeout didn't turn out very well. But it seemed to stop him. No more kidnappings. Case and trail went cold.

"Anyway, Sam and I still keep in touch. He's still on the job, and there have never been any more similar disappearances in the Chicago area, or any more of the clay figurines seen since.

"Until now. Found here today in Spookie in Shelly's mailbox."

His words had unsettled her, but she hadn't soaked in their true meaning yet. "I see. What you're saying is . . . we might have a serial kidnapper/murderer in town—one you dealt with many years ago—and Shelly might be his first victim here?"

Frank's silence was his answer.

She had to ask, "How did you know the missing victims were murdered if you never found any bodies?"

The shadows of the fading day laced across his face and his voice was a sigh. "The killer told me so himself. Being the senior officer on the case, my name was used by the media a lot, and over the six weeks of the kidnappings the killer sent me messages. In rather unique ways. Never signed, but I knew who they were from.

"And he even called me . . . to taunt me and give me impossible riddles to solve on who he'd take next. Then he'd call the media and make fun of me when I didn't stop him. Couldn't figure him out. I was a cop, not a psychiatrist. Lord, I didn't know what the monster's motives were. Why he did what he did. Who he was going to take next. What goes on in their screwed up heads. Even an FBI profiler and a succession of psychics couldn't flush him out."

"You used psychics? Thought you didn't believe in them?"

"I don't . . . but a few of the families did. If it gave them comfort, I played along."

"Okay. Killers taunt cops all the time. So why is this one showing up a decade later to take up where he left off? Why here and why you?"

Frank creaked back in his rocker, his face tilted up. She could see his worry. "Told you I finally saw a pattern. Or lucked out. When someone *I* knew went missing I had a hunch it was his work. A long shot but I made a terrible mistake and did the stakeout myself. At that person's house about ten years ago I caught him in the act of leaving a clay figure, chased and cornered him. Never saw him clearly, it was snowy and dark. He fired shots. I fired back and assumed I'd wounded him, I thought mortally because I heard him screaming and carrying on so much. Sam got there as my backup and we tracked him, but, in the end never found him or his body. Then he just . . . disappeared.

"Months, years went by. No more notes or telephone calls. No more kidnappings. Case was closed. But I never forgot. Those clay figures, those six people taken and never accounted for, haunted me. Until today, I believed he had gone off and died somewhere. I wanted—had to—believe that." His fist gently pounded the arm of the rocker. "Now I know it wasn't true."

"So just because of that *thing* in the mailbox today you think it's the same guy, after all these years, and that he took Shelly? Where's he been all this time?"

"I don't know, but no two people could make those same ugly clay things. He's here now in our town, stalking more victims. The same guy.

"God, that figurine brought back bad memories. Those missing people . . . their families. I can't believe it's happening all over again. It's a nightmare. Wake me up."

"What do we do?" She was having a hard time taking in that a serial kidnapper out of Frank's past might be targeting their tiny, quiet, safe town. She wanted to get up, leave and come back; pretend their conversation had never been.

"Right now, Abby, not much. Lock our doors and put the word out. Alert the authorities and bring in help. Be very cautious. I've contacted Chicago police and let them know what's going on. They're digging out the records on the other cases, collecting evidence and sending copies to me. Sam's helping. We've been e-mailing each other like crazy all day. I can't believe this creep's returned from the dead and has followed me back home.

"Now Shelly's disappearance makes sense. A mile away. So close. The killer's mocking me, like before, by taking someone right out from under my nose."

"So Shelly's disappearance isn't innocent? She's been kidnapped?"

"Looks that way. As much as I hate thinking it, it's a possibility. No, it's more than that. That mud doll lets me know for sure. He *did* take her. Again I was too late. Too slow."

"She isn't dead, is she?"

Frank said nothing.

"And," it came to her, "Shelly won't be the last?" She could no longer see Frank's face. The country darkness had come, as it so often did, in a swift second.

"I'm afraid so. Let's not talk anymore about this right now. I need to think." He stood up and pulled her from her chair. "Let's go eat. For tonight let's have a nice meal. Normal conversation. I want to catch up on what you've been doing and what's going on in town."

The Frank she knew was back. "Abby, you're going to love the salad I made you. Got three kinds of cheese in it, bacon bits, tomatoes, and hard-boiled eggs. Chocolate cake for dessert. Hope you're hungry."

The meal was delicious, as all of Frank's meals were, but Frank's attention was somewhere in the past, he couldn't hide it. They ate and talked and after loading her up with doggie bags, he escorted her home in his truck to be sure she got there safely.

"Keep your doors locked from now on," he warned before he drove off into the night. "Be careful going out alone, especially after nightfall. Watch your back." And he meant it.

After giving Snowball leftover turkey, Abby went to bed. Early day tomorrow. The mural was coming along so well she wanted to get in a long full day. The sooner she finished the sooner she'd get the money.

During the night, in and out of sleep, she found herself listening for the sound of shoes crunching in the dead leaves outside. Listening for an intruder. She was being paranoid. Yet what Frank had told her about the serial kidnapper had frightened her. He went after people Frank knew and cared about. Frank knew and cared about her.

The autumn wind accompanied her prayers for Shelly and she also prayed that Frank wasn't right about what was happening in their town. Surely he'd made a mistake. There was no serial kidnapper stalking them. That happened to other people in other places.

Not to her and the people she knew. Not in Spookie.

The phone rang in the middle of the night and half-asleep she picked it up. "Hello? Hello?" No answer. There was someone on the other end, she could almost hear their breathing.

Blood pumping in her ears, she awakened quickly. "Who is this? Answer me!"

Her mind had a crazy thought: It was Joel somehow trying to reach her. What was he trying to tell her? Nah, that was crazy. Joel was dead. He couldn't call her or anyone else.

She hung up. Whispers beyond her home's walls uncannily echoing Joel's voice called to her as he used to do every evening when he came through the front door.

I'm home, honey. Laughter, his voice far away on the night air. Tired as she was, it took her a long time to recapture her sleep.

She kept expecting the phone to ring again and for Joel to tell her what he'd wanted.

Chapter Three

She dreamed of Joel again Sunday night, the way they used to go for late night walks together, the way his strong hand felt holding hers, and then, in the last second before awakening, she dreamed of Shelly. The teenager was crying, lost somewhere in an endless subdivision where all the houses were empty and all the people were either invisible or gone.

Then in her dream, Shelly turned into a mud person and crumpled into dust.

The sunlight was bright when Abby awoke but it was a relief to see morning. She took the car into town. After what Frank had revealed the night before she had no desire to walk anywhere by herself, even in bright daylight. Some stranger might come along, whisk her away and turn her into a hunk of mud.

Thinking of her younger friends and remembering that she'd read in the *Weekly Journal* that there was no school today because of teacher's meetings, on the way to the library she picked up two boxes of day-old discounted donuts at the bakery, some containers of coffee, and hot chocolate.

There weren't many people in the library, but Laura and her brother showed up a little after ten.

Frank had mentioned how sick Mrs. Brooks was and that

for the last few weeks she hadn't been able to work at all. Some progressive illness. Abby felt sorry for the kids. So she crammed most of the donuts into one of the boxes for them.

"I've drawn something special for you, Mrs. Sutton." Laura handed Abby a page from her sketchbook when she first came in. "It's a gift. You don't have to pay for it."

It was a sketch of Abby. Very flattering. Made her look prettier than she was and made her smile.

"Nonsense, I wouldn't think of not giving you something. It's a lovely drawing. We artists can't be giving our stuff away for nothing, you know. I don't. It takes money to live. And if you're going to be a real artist you'll need to make a living at it. So get used to charging for your work."

Laura didn't resist taking the cash this time the least bit. But her eyes kept going to the donut boxes. Next time, instead of donuts, Abby thought, seeing the bones sticking out from under the girl's thin skin, she should bring a big fat meat loaf.

Nick was moving up and down the aisles examining book spines and humming to himself. He was wearing the same clothes as Saturday. It struck Abby that no one was tending to these kids. She dug into her purse and came out with another five-dollar bill and gave it to Laura. The girl thanked her with lowered eyes.

"And these donuts are for you and your family," Abby said, pushing the box toward Laura. "They had a big sale at the bakery. Half price. Practically gave them away. I heard your mother's been sick so I thought donuts might help. I know they cheer me up when I'm not feeling well." Abby gave her the container of lukewarm hot chocolate and a handful of napkins and casually remarked, "You and Nick have some donuts and wash them down with this." She figured if she made too much fuss Laura would balk at the charity. Abby had had her pride as a poor child, too.

Abby worked on the mural as Laura and Nick ate. They observed her, stuffed jelly donuts into their mouths and kept an eye out for the librarian. Before they ran off with the remaining donuts Abby felt the need to tell them, "You two stay together and don't run around by yourselves, especially in the woods. Especially after dark. You hear me? It's not safe."

Laura flashed Abby an odd look, but nodded, as if she understood what she was talking about. "I'm always careful and I always watch out for Nick."

"Uh, huh. We don't want what happened to Shelly to happen to us," Nick piped up. "The boogeyman got her, our dad says. That's what happens when children go out alone into the woods. So we won't do that, that's for sure. We'll stick together like stamps."

Abby wasn't about to discredit their father, or scare them by telling them it was a human predator and not a mythical boogeyman who'd most likely taken Shelly, not that it made much of a difference. "It's better to be safe than sorry. Stay together." She wanted to say Shelly would turn up, but the memory of Frank's words stopped her.

Shelly probably wasn't coming home.

"We saw the boogeyman one night, didn't we?" Nick looked to his sister for corroboration. He wiped the powdered sugar smudged on his face with his sleeve. "Hiding among the trees behind our house. He was *big*. We told Mom and Dad but they didn't believe us. So I don't go out into the woods at night anymore. Neither do Laura or the other kids."

Abby's mouth was still open when the library doors closed and the two kids ran out into the sunlight. Had they really seen someone or had it been their imaginations? She didn't know but would have liked to have asked more questions. But they were already gone.

The hours passed. She'd skipped lunch, was hungry, and went to Stella's Diner for supper. If there was any place she could get the latest gossip and updates on Shelly's case, Stella's was the place. On Mondays the diner offered a blue plate special chicken dinner at $4.95 a plate. Couldn't beat the price and Abby thought she deserved a treat. The mural was over half done, she was ahead of schedule and she was happy with it. She'd put the authors' more famous books in their hands or on the café's tables. Thought it was a nice touch. Nora loved it.

Stella's was crowded on chicken night, as usual, and when she walked in there was her friend Martha Sikeston—the real estate woman who'd sold her her house—and Samantha, gesturing at her to join them. And so she did. She ordered dinner and then pumped Samantha, "Have they found Shelly Lanstrom yet?"

"No. Five days and counting. TV crews were at the Lanstrom house today. Cameras and reporters from all over the state. What a carnival. Molly and Carl are going to be on the national news tonight making a plea to Shelly's kidnappers to release her. I feel terrible for them. Molly cries a lot and jumps every time the phone rings. It breaks your heart. She's talking to a psychic for God's sake. Grabbing at straws, that's for sure.

"And Carl is in denial. He spends all day looking for his girl and making phone calls. Shelly is their only child and he adores her. This is killing him. I told you the other day I had a bad feeling about this one."

Martha's silver bracelets clinked as she stirred her coffee. "Molly's smart to consult with a clairvoyant. They might be able to help. A real psychic, that is." She was a petite brunet with a lot of class who wore a great deal of jewelry. All of it real. Her first husband had gotten her into selling real estate, though she had enough family money and a house as big as a castle not to have had to work at all, but she liked to keep busy. Her present boyfriend, Ryan, was a real estate agent in Chalmers. They made a cute couple, but Martha adored being single.

"I'll have to take a casserole or something over for them," Martha stated. "I don't imagine Molly's doing much cooking."

Everyone's face at the table was solemn and no one made eye contact.

"Do the police have any leads so far?" Martha asked Samantha.

"Well," Samantha acted miffed, "the sheriff and the FBI are keeping something back, I know it." She believed the people had the right to know everything, all the time, and that her newspaper had the right to print it. Samantha was definitely for freedom of speech.

Abby imagined that something might be the mud figure found in Shelly's mailbox, but Frank had asked her to keep quiet about it for now.

It's been five days since Shelly's disappeared.

Ten years ago the kidnapper had struck every seven days for six weeks. If Frank was correct about the Mud Killer connection and if the kidnapper was repeating his past MO, Shelly was victim number one. Someone else would be taken in another two days. Abby could hardly bear to think about it.

The three women got off onto other subjects and not a minute too soon. Abby was nervous Samantha would sense she was hiding something. The reporter was good at that.

Samantha caught them up on the rest of the local crime as the couple next to them argued over their bill. Old people on budgets. They counted every penny and took leftovers home wrapped in napkins or stuffed in to-go boxes. Made Abby smile. She did the same thing. Wasn't so different than them and she wasn't even old yet.

"The big story this week, of course," Samantha was saying, "is Shelly Lanstrom, but, besides that, we're having a bit of a crime spree. Someone's been breaking into houses. Through windows. Stealing stuff. Food, personal items. Little things mostly. Doesn't make sense. Who'd do such a thing in Spookie? Weird, if you ask me."

Abby was zoning out, daydreaming about what she had to do when she got home. Wash a load of clothes. Take a chicken out of the freezer for tomorrow's supper and stick it in the crock pot in the morning with veggies so by evening the meal would be done. That would work. Clean out the tub. Boy was it scummy.

"Oh, and talking about crime, don't forget Myrtle's stalker." Martha's pink lips were curving up in a smirk as she spoke, while Samantha was trying not to follow suit.

Myrtle Schmitt was an elderly eccentric who wandered about town dragging a wagon full of junk behind her. Her treasures, she called them. Objects she'd drag out of other peoples' trash or out of their backyards. The thing was, Myrtle wasn't nuts or destitute. She lived in a trailer at the edge of town, had a fat bank account and a healthy financial portfolio. The old woman, people gossiped, was actually wealthy.

Bizarre behavior ran naturally in the Schmitt family. Myrtle's younger sister, Evelyn, lived behind Abby in a run-down house along with numerous cats and dogs—fifty or more. A person could hear howling or caterwauling at any hour of the day or night through the trees. Like a zoo in her backyard.

Old Myrtle, as peculiar as she was, was also a friend of Abby's. But Myrtle and Martha, opposites as rags and silk, had never gotten along. Myrtle was a whimsical storyteller who liked to embellish and Martha was a realist. If it wasn't black or white, Martha couldn't see it, while Myrtle saw rainbows.

Maybe that was why Abby had so much affection for Myrtle. As an artist Abby saw rainbows, too.

Abby looked at Martha. "What's this about Myrtle having a stalker?"

"Old lady knocked at my door yesterday morning at sunup—I'm not kidding, it was that early—mumbling about how some man was stalking her. Tailed her every time she left home, she said. She was pretty shaken up. I didn't know what to do. I didn't see anyone and you know how Myrtle is

with that wild imagination of hers. Always thinking someone's chasing her, trying to rob her or something.

"Who'd want to anyway? Old mooch never carries money.
She badgered me to call the police. Put in the report. I played
along and pretended to 'cause she refused to leave until I
did. She wouldn't go to the station. Too afraid the stalker
would see her, she said. Didn't want to talk to anybody. Then
off she went, happy as a looney bird I'd called it in."

Myrtle's wild imagination. Nice way of putting it. On top
of everything, Martha believed Myrtle was a sandwich short
of a picnic but Abby knew better. Myrtle had . . . intuitions
or premonitions, whatever a person wanted to call them that
sometimes turned out to be remarkably close to the truth.

So Abby listened when Myrtle talked. She was about the
only one that did. On the way home she'd take a side trip and
pay Myrtle a visit. With the knowledge she had of Frank's
suspicions, that it was an old adversary of his, she had a few
questions of her own.

She sat there eating chicken and thinking about Myrtle's
stalker as her two friends chattered on about this person and
that person. Town gossip. Nothing she hadn't heard before.

Gray twilight filled the diner's window and Abby had the
urge to scurry home and hide. It was an old urge and one that
she'd once lived by before she'd moved to Spookie and had
forced herself to break. But tonight the nagging concern of
being safe behind locked doors had more to do with Frank's
mud doll than any antisocial behavior. She nibbled at a piece
of chocolate cake that would inevitably go straight to her
middle and then she said goodnight to everyone. She wanted
to drive by Myrtle's and see if she could catch her at home.

The woods were already gloomy where the fog had
drifted in to meet the trees circling Myrtle's trailer. No porch
light, no lights around at all. There was a strange eeriness to
the location that didn't escape Abby. All whispering shadows and chilly winds. Made her shiver. No wonder the old
woman got scared, she thought. Living out here would scare
her, too. At least Abby's house had lights around it.

With dented siding and rusted skirting, the old lady's trailer was in sorry shape. If Myrtle had money she sure wasn't putting it into her property. Abby left her headlights on so she wouldn't trip and fall on her bottom in the dark and went up and knocked on the front door.

She wasn't surprised when Myrtle answered. The old woman didn't like traveling around at night, she'd told Abby often enough, *because that's when the ghosts were out and they would get you.*

"Abigail, I was expecting you," Myrtle croaked, opening the door barely wide enough so Abby could slide in. "A premonition told me." She was dressed in a ratty tweed winter coat that was buttoned up to her neck. Tiny and bony, she was all coat and very little woman.

"What else did your premonition say?" Abby sat down on a couch that looked as if Myrtle had dragged it home from the trash dump and tried not to gawk at the disarray around her.

Myrtle wasn't much of a housekeeper, her eyesight being too poor. There were cardboard boxes and clothes piles everywhere. Dust an inch thick. Abby had never been in Myrtle's home before and looking around at the mess made her feel sad for the old lady.

It must be hard when a person could no longer take care of themselves or their home anymore. The place needed a good scrubbing. Abby could offer to help, but Myrtle had her pride and wouldn't allow it.

A sly expression slid across Myrtle's wrinkled face. She plopped down beside Abby on the sofa and her bird hands fluttered into her lap. "My premonition also hinted that somebody else is going to come up missing here real soon. Besides Shelly."

Shocked, Abby stared at her. "I hope your premonition is wrong."

Myrtle was picking invisible lint off her coat. "They're never wrong. You should remember that, girlie, from last year." Last year when Myrtle had helped Abby solve the Summers' murders.

Not knowing what else to say, Abby got to the reason she was there because her headlights wouldn't stay on forever, they'd run down the battery. "Heard someone's been skulking around your trailer, Myrtle. Did you get a clear look at the person?"

"Nah, not too good a look. It was dusk. I'd been out in the woods picking flowers. I like flowers. Pretties up a place. Best wild lilies out by Gage's, about three miles back in these woods. Got to be careful of Gage's Bog, though." Her head cocked to the side and her eyes shone like round mirrors. "If you make a wrong step, it'll suck you up and pull you down worse than a pool of quicksand.

"But I know where to step and where not. Grew up in those woods. I know them well."

"The stalker?" Abby reminded her.

"Oh, yeah. Yesterday I was coming home because it was getting dark, and I suspected someone was tailing me, hiding behind the trees so I wouldn't see them. Only got one glance, 'cause I had a case of the heebie-jeebies by then and had started running. As fast as my old pair of scrawny legs could take me anyway.

"It was a tall person is all I can say . . . real tall . . . limping along like Frankenstein. I didn't look back again. Just got my skinny old body home and locked all the doors. I think he's been watching me a lot last few days. I feel eyes on me all the time. Maybe I'm the next victim to disappear." She bobbed her head.

"And, Abigail, you'd be best off if you kept your eyes open too. He's out there waiting to take another unwary person. Lock your doors and windows."

He? Abby didn't want to discount what Myrtle was telling her, not with what Frank had said. Didn't want Myrtle to think she didn't believe her so she said she'd be careful. She asked Myrtle another question or two, which the old woman answered in as few words as possible.

Abby had come over out of curiosity to listen to Myrtle's story, but now after being with the old woman for a while she wasn't sure if she could believe it. Myrtle was behaving more strangely than usual, if that was possible.

She kept asking Abby the same things over and over. If she'd driven to her house, if she'd seen anyone suspicious on the way and if the ghosts were out yet. Myrtle brought up three times that she'd had a frozen salisbury steak dinner for supper. Told Abby at least five time that she'd lost her diamond ring and couldn't find it anywhere. Scary thing was, each time she told Abby something she acted as if it was the first time. Age must be catching up with her.

Myrtle insisted that Abby stay for a real visit. She turned on her feeble porch light and Abby ran out to her car to switch off the headlights. Myrtle gave her a bowl of chicken soup and proceeded to ply her with town gossip as she bustled around the trailer fiddling with one thing or another.

No longer disoriented, Myrtle had settled down and was almost making sense. Still in her coat, though Abby thought the trailer was too warm, she told Abby what Samantha had already said, that some of her neighbors' houses had been broken into.

Myrtle rambled on about that and other things until Abby excused herself by saying she was exhausted. "Been painting the library mural all day and I need to go home and get some rest." But it was more than that. She'd heard too much, knew too much, and was worried too much. That's the real reason she was tired.

"Sure, you youngsters need your sleep. Enjoy it while you can. Wait until you're my age." Myrtle chuckled, escorting Abby to the door. "I never sleep anymore. Never tired. Time for sleep when I'm dead and in the ground."

"Not me." Abby's hand on the door. "I like to sleep. Nothing better than snuggling up under the covers in a soft bed and drifting off when you're weary. Makes me feel safe. As if nothing can get to me then."

"Then get on home and be safe." Myrtle winked at her.

She left Myrtle's place unsure what to believe. As fond as Abby was of Myrtle, truth was, this time the stalker might be in the old woman's mind. After all, someone was missing and the whole town was in uproar over it and Myrtle, susceptible as she was, was sure acting crazier than usual.

But Abby was cautious going home anyway. Getting out of the car she made sure she was alone and no one was lurking on the side of the porch or behind the trees around the house. The wind had picked up and the scent of coming rain was a promise in the chilly air. She let herself in and locked the door behind her. Glad to be home.

Before she went to bed she phoned Frank and filled him in on what Samantha had said about the series of break-ins around town and what Myrtle had said about a stalker.

"From what I could make out the suspect I chased that snowy night in Chicago was tall," Frank's voice was flat. "Very tall. Over six-foot-six or something. I might have shot one of his legs. He was screaming about his leg being hit. That could make him limp, I suppose."

"It could. If you believe Myrtle's tale. She was really weird tonight. I couldn't tell if she was telling the truth or making it all up." Holding the wireless phone in one hand Abby bent down to stroke Snowball. Annoyed at her for being gone so long, she gently bit her ankle and ran off hissing and meowing. What an attitude. Abby loved the cat anyway. As a kitten, Snowball had shown up wet and starving at her front door one stormy night a year ago and she hadn't been able get rid of her since.

"Doesn't matter if she made the stalker up or not," reasoned Frank. "In a few days we'll know what we need to know. I'm holding my breath until then." He sounded tired. Searching for Shelly the last five days, discovering the mud doll and all that it meant had worn him out.

They exchanged a couple more words and hung up. Abby watched television and went to bed. Outside the rain began. Made her feel cut off from the world, isolated, hidden and safe.

The doors and windows were locked and a piece of two-by-four was propped against her side of the bed. Her homemade defense weapon—a wooden club. She kept one downstairs and one up. If someone tried to break in she'd be ready. Give them a big bump on the head or a broken face. Nobody was surprising her.

Her late husband had taught her that trick because she hated guns and she'd never have one in the house. Years ago Joel had taught her to shoot because of a neighborhood crime spree, but shortly afterward her brother, Michael, had accidentally been shot by a friend in a hunting accident. Michael had died.

She'd loved her brother, and afterward couldn't stand to look at a gun, much less touch or shoot one. To this day guns still reminded her of losing him. Reminded her of the pain and so she didn't like to talk about it. It hurt her to remember.

That night the phone didn't wake her up and she had no dreams. For the first time in days she got a good night's sleep. Probably because her waking hours were becoming scary enough.

Chapter Four

The next three days were quiet as Abby kept busy on the mural. At the rate she was working, she would be done by the coming weekend. The hardest part was over. Everything was laid out and drawn in. All she had to do were the finishing touches—the easy part. Relief and excitement washed over her. Things were going so well.

The weather was perfect—sixties during the day and fifties at night. The leaves on the trees were autumn colors and the town was in second gear for Halloween. The merchants had strung tiny orange and black lights along their storefronts and the courthouse had put its traditional life-size witch-on-a-broom out in front. Sure sign that Halloween was close.

The diner was serving holiday brownies for dessert and the Tattered Corners bookstore's window was filled with vampire and ghost novels.

The police were still searching for Shelly. No sign of her anywhere. She had never come home and there was no note of any kind. Just the clay figure left in the mailbox. Abby tried not to think about how seven days had now passed.

She hadn't seen Laura or Nick at the library for days and by Thursday afternoon she was wondering where they were. They went to school, but school started at nine and let out at four and she was at the library most days from seven A.M. to six P.M. or longer. Where were they?

Finishing early for the day, she drove home. The night before she'd made a pot of chili and decided to take a generous bowl of it over to the Brooks' house. Should be enough for all of them. As sick as everyone said Mrs. Brooks had been lately, Abby thought dinner might be appreciated. And she'd be able to check up on Laura and Nick and meet the rest of the family.

She had trouble finding their ramshackle dwelling, though Frank had given her directions. Like most people in town, Frank knew the Brooks well. Their ranch house was concealed by the trees far back from the road and its driveway, patches of loose rock peeking through the weeds.

Abby parked as close as she could and walked to the door. At three-thirty the sun was a pale ball balanced on the horizon. The night came early in October and she wanted to be home when darkness fell. She'd hate to be out there in the middle of nowhere without any streetlights at night. Like Myrtle's place, the Brooks' house, being on the outskirts of town where the woods crept in, was frightening these days.

A girl about seven years old opened the door, said her name was Penny, and let Abby into the house after she'd introduced herself and explained why she was there.

Her mother was in bed, Penny mouthed in a mousy voice, but she'd go tell her Abby was there and that she'd brought dinner. The girl seemed excited about the food.

Abby waited in the front room on the couch, hugging the container of chili and a bag of crackers, surrounded by shabby furniture and frayed carpets. There was a funny smell in the air. Mildew or ancient dust, she couldn't tell which. A bony dog scurried past and a cat's paw swatted at her from under the sofa. She heard coughing and children squabbling over something in another room and realized that some of the kids were in the kitchen scrounging for food. It was supper time, but she didn't smell anything cooking.

This was what it was like to be poor. She remembered.

Laura appeared out of the dim hallway. "Mrs. Sutton, you

brought us food?" A look of grateful confusion warred with hunger. "What is it?"

"Homemade chili. I made too much. Here." Abby put the bowl and the crackers in Laura's hands. "Go ahead and take it into the kitchen and you kids eat. It needs to be reheated, though. How's your mom doing?"

"Mom knows you're here and wants to meet you. I've talked about you so much. Go on back. Last room, end of the hall. I'll be there in a minute with a bowl of chili for her." Laura took the container and went into the kitchen.

Abby heard chattering voices and the sound of the oven door opening and closing as she headed down the hallway. She guessed they were heating the chili up. She'd brought it in an ovenproof bowl just for that reason. She hadn't been sure the Brooks had a microwave.

The room at the end of the hallway was sparsely furnished with a scratched up dresser, a large bed in one corner, and a chair. That was all. A frail woman was standing by the bed tying a robe around her waist. She turned to greet her visitor, swayed, and Abby reached out to steady her before she collapsed. Her ashen, streaked hair was gathered into a loose ponytail and her face, gaunt and haunted, was the face of a sick woman.

"Don't get up for me. You need to be in bed, Mrs. Brooks. I can visit while you rest." Abby pushed a chair to the edge of the bed and sat down. "Laura's bringing you a bowl of the chili I brought over. With you being sick I thought you and the kids might like some homemade chili. The kids are in the kitchen eating now."

She asked Abby to call her Rebecca. "That was kind of you, Mrs. Sutton. They love chili." She spoke slowly as if she had to think about her words before speaking.

"I've been under the weather lately. I haven't done much cooking. Laura and Charlene, my two eldest girls, have been filling in for me. Canned or frozen stuff mostly. They do the best they can when their daddy's not here.

"That's who I thought you were when I heard someone in

the living room—Emil, my husband. He never came home this morning after his work shift at the gas station in town. You know the Clark? He works nights there, but he's usually home by eight A.M. Now it's supper time. Hasn't called. That's not like him. Not like him at all."

There was this distant look in the woman's eyes that Abby had seen before . . . in her own father's dying eyes. She wasn't suffering from a minor illness. The woman was really sick and the family didn't have medical insurance. Which meant Rebecca probably hadn't seen a doctor regularly, if at all.

Then Rebecca's last words soaked in.

"Your husband hasn't come home and he's ten hours late? Have you called the sheriff?"

"No. I trust my husband. There's a reason he hasn't called. I'll give him a little more time. But it was kind of you to come by to check up on the kids and me. Bring that chili. Laura's told me so much about you. She admires you. Wants to be an artist like you."

Abby smiled. "Someday she may be better than me, Rebecca." The woman had to be around her age, but she looked older. "Laura's talented. She has the potential to be a good artist. If she keeps her grades up and continues to work on her drawing skills, I bet she could get an art scholarship to college."

Laura's mother nodded. "It's all she talks about since you put the idea in her head. But she's only a freshman in high school and has a long way to go till college. Has always made top grades, though. Now she won't settle for anything less than an A. She's driven. Has to get that scholarship, she says. I'm proud of her. So is Emil. Thank you."

They spent a while conversing. Mostly about the kids and how difficult it was raising seven of them. "It was my idea to have so many," Rebecca spoke in her weak voice. "I was an orphan and craved a big family so I'd never be alone again.

"I didn't count on getting sick," she confided. And then added softly, "I have MS. Have had it for a long time now.

The children don't know. But it's been getting worse the last year. Everyone's been so good about taking care of me . . . taking care of everything. We have no medical, so I don't go to the doctors much. Can't afford the medicine some months. Do those doctors know how expensive that stuff is? I don't think so."

"How about Medicaid? With your income you should be eligible for it."

"Emil tried, but he makes too much. Imagine that? Eight dollars an hour and it's too much." She shook her head. "My husband hates charity and says that Medicaid is charity anyway. But for my sake, he'd swallow his pride and beg. He's a stubborn, but loving man. I don't know why he hasn't called me. Not like him," she repeated.

Rebecca stopped speaking when Laura brought in her supper.

Abby sat there in the dim room with them making small talk as Rebecca ate her chili. She tried not to think about what had been on her mind since Rebecca had disclosed that her husband hadn't come home. Abby wasn't going to give the woman any more worry than she already had so she said nothing. Besides, Rebecca's husband was only late, not missing.

Not yet.

But it was Thursday. Eight days since Shelly had disappeared. One week and a day.

Abby left the Brooks' house before nightfall and hightailed it to Frank's. Caught him working on his novel. He came to the door dressed in a sweat suit and sneakers with that look of distraction she'd come to recognize as his writing face. He wrote most days from eight to six, but because of the search for Shelly he'd been writing in the evenings. She knew that.

"Sorry to disturb you," she apologized. "It's important."

"I can take a short break." He waved her in. "You look as if you have something on your mind."

Once inside, she blurted out, "Emil Brooks didn't come home from work this morning and he hasn't called his wife. Which, as his wife said, isn't like him at all. She's not well, as you know, and they have seven kids. He always comes home right after work. Doesn't that sound suspicious?"

Frank didn't hesitate, he grabbed his jacket, his car keys and wallet, and practically shoved her back out the door. "Take your own car so you can go home afterward, but follow me to the Clark station. Stay close." He got into his truck, drove off, leaving her in the dust. She had to drive like crazy to keep up with him, but she did.

When she arrived, Frank was there with the manager, Norman, who was stocking shelves with candy bars. Three Musketeers. Snickers. Paydays. Some generic brands she'd never heard of. He was grousing under his breath to himself at the small size of the bars.

Reverting to his cop demeanor, Frank was questioning Norman when Abby came in. "So Emil wasn't here at the end of his shift when you came in this morning?"

"No. At first I was mad and then got to thinking. That isn't like Emil. He's dependable. In all the years he's worked for me he's always been here when I come in. Doesn't leave the station without telling me. Doesn't leave the money unguarded in the cash register, that's for darn sure.

"He's due here in forty-five minutes for tonight's shift and I just called his house again. Got one of the kids who says he's not there either and that he never came home today at all. They hoped he was here doing a double shift. That's when I went out back and saw his old Ford parked where it usually is. Locked. Empty. No sign of Emil.

"Now I'm stumped. Where would he go without his car? Emil's not a drinker, a gambler, or a womanizer that I know of. Doesn't do drugs. So where the heck is he?"

Where indeed, Abby thought. "He's supposed to start his shift in less than an hour?" She met Frank's glance. Things were beginning to bother her and she could see Frank was bothered, too.

"Supposed to." Norman's attention was distracted by something outside the window.

A woman had pulled up to the pumps in a vintage cherry

red Cadillac and was sliding out of the car showing a lot of bare thigh. She was about thirty, a pretty blond wearing a tight skirt. Nice legs. Abby didn't recognize her and thought she must be from out of town. Poised before the pumps, the woman seemed to be having a problem and was gesturing over her shoulder for Norman to come out and help her. Norman was a middle-aged man with a paunch, a wife, and two kids, but he liked to flirt.

In a second he was out the door, saying as he went, "I've called in another guy to work tonight. Can't take the chance Emil won't show. If he doesn't work he doesn't get paid. Hate to do that. I know his family needs the money. Either one of you see Emil tell him to call me. Pronto. If he wants to keep his job."

"We will." Frank watched Norman barrel out the door and rush to the woman's aid. The station's manager pumped gas for the customer as she giggled and chatted with him. "That Norman. One of these days his wife's gonna catch him at that and she'll clobber him. I know his wife."

"Serves him right. But women like that don't fool me. She can pump her own gas, for heaven's sake. She's just lazy."

"Spoken like a true feminist." Frank was looking around but for what, Abby had no idea.

She gave him an exasperated look. "So . . . what are you thinking?"

"Did Emil Brooks work here his whole shift? Why is his car still here? And where is he?" Frank mused aloud as they left the gas station. He ushered her into her car and spoke through the open window. "You go home, Abby. It's getting late. I think I'll stick around for a bit and see if Emil shows up at seven for work."

"If he does, call me at home." Abby kept seeing those hungry kids and their sick mother. What would they do if Emil never came home? She didn't want to dwell on that. Poor Rebecca. Poor kids.

"Sure, I'll call you either way. Go on home. And don't stop for any reason."

"I'll be careful. Won't pick up any hitchhikers."

Frank didn't think that was funny and frowned. "Be sure you don't."

Hours later as she was getting ready for bed, Frank phoned.

"Emil Brooks didn't show up for work tonight," he announced somberly. "And more interesting news, Martha stopped by the gas station when I was there and told me something else. On her way home last night from her boyfriend's house, around two A.M. or so, she stopped for gas at Clark's and Emil wasn't there then. No one was. Gas station was open but empty. She pumped her own gas and left the money on the counter and dropped by the station tonight to complain to Norman."

"Emil Brooks left sometime during his shift?" Abby divulged the obvious.

"Maybe. Or something happened to him."

Wednesday, her thoughts repeated. *Emil disappeared on Wednesday.* Exactly a week after Shelly. But she didn't have to say that to Frank. She was sure he was thinking the same thing.

"Abby, never got to tell you, I got my advance check today for my novel, so how about having an early breakfast with me tomorrow at Stella's—my treat? We can discuss the situation and decide what we should do next about it."

She liked that he said *what we should do next about it.* Made her feel needed. "But if Emil's really missing, that's a problem for the police, isn't it? What can *we* do about it? Go after the kidnapper ourselves?"

"If I have to."

Recalling Frank's history with the kidnapper, she understood. "All right. I'll see you at eight tomorrow. We'll have breakfast and then I'll head off to the library. As close to finishing the mural as I am, I need to work as many hours on it the next few days as I can."

"It's a date." And Frank hung up.

The next day was a perfect fall day, sunny but cool. Stella's Diner had the usual breakfast crowd munching on bacon and eggs or spooning oatmeal. Retired people meeting their friends, talking or playing checkers or cards over coffee and biscuits and gravy. Business people gulping down decaffeinated coffee with their shredded wheat before they went in to the office. People living their lives. Thinking they were safe.

"Emil still hasn't come home," Frank confessed the minute Abby sat down across the table from him. "Hasn't been seen anywhere by anyone. I phoned Rebecca Brooks before I came here and she hasn't heard anything from him, either. Not a telephone call or message of any kind. She's frantic. I advised her it's time to call the police."

The bright light shining through Stella's windows highlighted Frank's handsome face and his longish pepper-gray hair neatly combed back. Today his eyes were that feverish tint of blue they got when he was worrying a problem.

Frank was eating Cream of Wheat and fresh fruit with his coffee. Decaf nowadays because he was on this health kick and diet, along with daily walks. His doctor warned him to get his weight down and get more exercise or he'd be a candidate for a heart attack. Any minute. Scared him enough with his last check up results that Frank had actually stopped smoking. He was having a harder time with that than anything else.

Abby couldn't get used to seeing Frank without a cigarette in his hand, but she was proud of him for quitting. She'd quit two years ago herself and still craved a cigarette every time she got stressed. She wanted one now real bad.

"You think Emil Brooks is victim number two?" She spoke what was on their minds.

"He could be." Frank sighed. "If so Rebecca will be getting a special delivery in her mailbox sometime in the next few days. Then we'll know for sure."

Stella brought more coffee as Frank was finishing his meal and Abby ordered pancakes. Dressed in a pink pantsuit with a flowered apron over it, Stella's ivory hair had been chopped off short as a boy's and she'd changed her shade of lipstick from her customary red to hot pink.

When Stella brought the pancakes, she grilled Frank, "I hear Emil Brooks is missing now, too. Know anything about that?" News traveled fast in a small town, Abby thought, not surprised. Like Myrtle, Stella always seemed to know what was going on in Spookie. Sooner or later everybody wound up in Stella's gossiping.

"Not much more than you, Stella, I imagine. He didn't return home yesterday after his shift at the gas station and hasn't been seen since. When was the last time you saw him?"

Stella chewed on the end of her pencil, thinking. "Wednesday evening before his shift he was in here for a cup of coffee and a piece of cherry pie. He loves my cherry pie. And, let's see . . . he was with Opal Colter. Some rumor has it that she's his girlfriend." Stella's eyes glinted and her pink lips curved into a dismissing grin.

"Emil has a girlfriend?" Abby hoped it wasn't true. She'd met his kids, his wife. She took another bite of pancake, though her appetite suddenly wasn't what it had been before.

"Well, hearsay says she is. You know how that is. Maybe yes, maybe no. All I know is she and Emil meet in here a few evenings a week for coffee before he starts working. They talk. Laugh some.

"But to be fair, I never saw him do more than touch her hand or smile at her. I think they're only friends. Went to school together, I believe. I mean, Emil's wife has been sick a long time and if anyone ever needed a friend, he does. He works so hard and has so much on his back with all those kids, sick wife and all."

Stella lifted her bony shoulders and dropped them. "Go ask Opal where Emil is. Maybe she knows what's happened to him. She lives behind the bookstore in a tiny off-white house with turquoise shutters. Can't miss it. Got her name on the mailbox."

After Stella sashayed off to take someone else's order,

Frank raised an eyebrow at Abby. "Aha. Perhaps Emil ran off with Opal and he's not missing at all. Perhaps he's had enough of kids, ailing wife, and no money and took off. Happens all the time. Lousy as it is, it's possible."

A husband accused of running off when he'd done no such thing was a sensitive area with Abby and Frank knew it. When Abby's husband disappeared three years ago people also believed he'd left her for some other woman or for some other reason just as hurtful; not that something terrible had happened to him. No woman wants to think her husband loves her so little that he'd run off leaving behind unanswered questions and tremendous pain.

"No. Not Emil Brooks. He didn't run off. With or without another woman. I met his wife and kids, saw the way they cared about him, saw his home. I won't believe it. By everything I've seen and been told he loves his family. He's a good husband and father."

Sitting there in silence they finished their meals and Frank then announced, "Well, I'm going to see Opal Colter and ask her what she knows. If she's home, I mean." The words weren't out of Frank's mouth and he was standing up, putting money for their bill down on the table. "You go on and get to work, Abby, and I'll let you know later what I find out."

"No way. I can take a few minutes out of my work schedule to tag along, Frank. Besides, I owe it to those kids and Rebecca to find out the truth. I hope Emil hasn't run away with Opal and left that family to fend for itself. I have to find out for myself now or I'll go nuts fretting about it. Let's go."

On the other hand, running off with a girlfriend would be better than being kidnapped and dead, Abby was thinking as they left the diner and strolled down the street.

Opal Colter's house was a block away and Frank wanted to walk it, saying they both could use the exercise. He could speak for himself.

"You think it's too early for visiting?" She was peeking in Opal's windows as Frank knocked for the second time. House looked nice inside. Lots of knickknacks and shiny furniture. Pretty color on the walls. Fat chairs and big screen television. Comfy.

Frank checked his watch. "It's after nine." And knocked again as they waited. No answer. Frank glanced at the yard. There were newspapers lying in the grass. A few of them. The mailbox was empty. There was no car in the driveway or the garage.

"Looks like she isn't home. You go on to work, Abby. I'll be in town this afternoon on an errand I have to run and I'll swing back later and see if I can catch Opal at home."

She agreed and they walked back to her car. Frank listed a couple other things he wanted to look into concerning their little mystery, as he called it. He promised to stay in touch if anything developed and then they went their separate ways.

Watching him walk away, Abby had a really bad feeling about things. Guess Samantha was rubbing off on her.

The rest of the day as Abby was in the library painting the mural, she couldn't stop thinking about the Brooks family. What would they do if Emil didn't come back? It depressed her to think about it. She told herself she'd work until three o'clock and then take a ride out to see how they were doing. Take some bread and milk.

Maybe by then Emil might have come home.

Chapter Five

Snowball didn't want Abby to leave and jumped in the brown paper bag she was filling with canned goods for the Brooks. She'd cleaned out cabinets and used her last couple of dollars to buy milk, bread, and lunch meat for the kids. As tight a budget as she was on, she wanted to help them. Hungry children did that to her. Made her want to feed them.

After pulling the cat out of the bag, she locked up the house and drove over to the Brooks' place with the sun still high and bright in the sky. Again, wanting to be back before nightfall, she was rushing.

Emil hadn't returned home. Hadn't called. No one at the Clark station or around town had seen him. His car was still there, locked and untouched. She ached for Rebecca and the kids.

Rebecca met her at the door in a worn robe, unsteady on her feet. But at least the woman was out of bed and moving around. They sat at the kitchen table and drank hot tea while Laura took the groceries Abby had brought and made bologna sandwiches for the other kids. Putting lots of mustard and pickles on each one. Rebecca thanked her for the food with a grateful smile.

"I can't afford to say no to a helping hand anymore," Rebecca said as she poured another cup of tea. "With Emil gone and no money in the house, all I can say is thank you. I was wondering what I was going to give them for supper. The food you brought will fill my kids' stomachs. There's nothing left in the cabinets or the fridge. Emil got paid on Wednesday. He disappeared on Wednesday night, so the check's gone with him.

"Sick or not, I'm going to have to go back to work if Emil doesn't come home soon. Somebody's gotta bring in some money. Emil and me don't believe in taking welfare. We've always taken care of our family ourselves. Always. But that could change."

Abby looked at her but made no comment. Rebecca was too sick to be cleaning other people's houses, she could see that. How were they going to make it? If the townspeople knew what was going on, they might help with donations for what the family needed. It'd be tricky convincing Rebecca to accept that much help, but she could try.

Abby didn't stay long. Visited with the kids and helped clean up the kitchen before she drove home as the night was coming in.

Laura was troubled over her father's absence and had been calling relatives the last two days to see if he was with one of them. He wasn't. Abby wished she could have said or done something to comfort the child, but couldn't think of what.

She surely couldn't tell them Frank's fears that a serial kidnapper might have taken her father. It would scare the children more than they already were. Abby remembered when Joel had disappeared, nothing anyone had said had helped her. They'd been just words. They never stopped the sorrow. A person worries in their own way, carries it on their shoulders alone, and sometimes no one else can share it.

First thing Abby saw when she got home was Snowball crouching in attack mode in the grass on the side of the porch. There was an awful racket in the trees above. A blue jay was screeching and diving at the cat furiously. Abby ran over and snatched up the baby bird quivering in the grass beneath Snowball's jaws and waited for the angry mother to swoop out of the skies at her. The bird didn't. The trees grew silent.

It was as if Abby could feel a hundred bird eyes on her, waiting to see what she was going to do. To them she was surely a monster.

"No, no, Snowball, mustn't hurt the birds," she chided the cat gently, as she cradled the frightened blue jay baby in her hands. It looked too young to fly. There was down in its feathers. Looking up into the tree above her in the twilight, she located the nest. Holding the bird carefully and walking around the house, she got a ladder from the shed in the back and propped it against the tree trunk. Climbing the steps slowly so she wouldn't fall and break her neck, she replaced the baby bird in its nest. Her good deed for the day.

"Now, stay there, ya hear?" she whispered to the tiny creature. "I don't want to have to do this again." The bird, a cute little thing probably terrified out of its mind, stared at her with blank eyes. Cats with razor sharp teeth and people picking it up were too much for it. Abby hadn't seen blood so she hoped it would live.

Having done the best she could, now it was up to fate.

As she was putting the ladder away she saw the mama blue jay fly to the nest. Good. Abby went inside, happy to be home.

She was eating supper in her kitchen, feeling bad for the Brooks family and trying not to obsess about what was going to happen next, when the doorbell rang. Snowball scooted off to hide under the sofa and once Abby looked out the peek hole she answered the door.

It was Frank. Didn't look happy, either. She almost didn't open the door, but knew he wouldn't go away so she let him in.

"Well, Opal Colter finally came home," he said right off. "She's been at her sister's for the last two days. Says she hasn't got a clue where Emil might be and was upset when she learned he'd come up missing. So much for that lead."

Bad news, just as Abby had feared.

"And, by the way, because I know you're curious, Opal and Emil are not fooling around. Opal says they're good friends and have been since they went to high school here together. That's all. Have a lot in common. He often needs a shoulder to unload on and Opal's been a widow for a while so she also needs a friend. Opal says they're like brother and sister. Would never do anything to hurt Emil's family.

"And I believe her. Martha and I have the same kind of friendship."

"So . . . Emil wasn't fooling around," Abby summed up. "That's a relief. Rebecca and the kids will have enough to deal with if Emil never comes back. A scandal on top of that wouldn't help. You know how gossip is. I was over there before I came home. Brought them some food, and they haven't heard from Emil, either. That leaves us where we started. Emil's missing."

"Yes, he seems to be. Rebecca's already reported it to the sheriff. The search has begun."

"He's the second victim, isn't he?" Abby got Frank a cup of coffee after he'd politely turned down a turkey sandwich she'd offered to make him. Leftovers from his dinner the week before.

"Could be. Tomorrow will be the third day he's been gone. Think I'll pull an all-nighter outside the Brooks' house tonight. Hidden, of course. See if there's any special deliveries."

He meant the clay figurines. "Has anyone heard anything about Shelly, yet?" knowing the answer before he opened his mouth again.

"No new developments," Frank admitted, looking heartsick. "They've searched everywhere. Made appeals on the news. Nothing. She's vanished.

"This is like ten years ago all over again." He hung his head in his hands and Abby laid a hand comfortingly on his shoulder.

"This isn't your fault, Frank," she spoke softly. She felt

awful for him and changed the subject to inquire about his writing progress.

He lifted his head and gave her a melancholy smile. He knew what she was doing. "I saw my mystery novel in our local bookstore this afternoon for the first time. Claudia has copies." Claudia owned and ran Tattered Corners. "I just stood there like a chump grinning at my books. With my name on the cover. Made me so happy I could have cried. I worked so hard for what I have now. So hard. My life was so good. Now . . . this.

"Isn't it funny how life is? It gives you one thing to be really happy about and then it gives you something crappy all at the same time so you can't completely enjoy your happiness. Why does it do that?"

Strange thing for Frank, of all people, to ask her, she thought, but she knew what he meant. They were in the same boat. She had her new life. She was happy. But there was always the memory of Joel and the torment she'd gone through for two years haunting that happiness. Yet for Frank these disappearances were worse.

Sitting on the couch beside him, she shrugged her shoulders. "That's life, I'm afraid. Highs and lows. The good and the bad all rolled into one."

"I never thought anything could make me feel better than solving a case, Abby. But seeing that book on that shelf is a close second. Makes me want to rush home and get back to work on my new one. I'm nearly done with it." Frank laughed softly. "Now I have something keeping me from writing. How can I write in the middle of this nightmare? When people I care about are in danger and when that monster is out there somewhere?"

"You do the best you can. That's all any of us can do."

Abby proposed starting a collection for the Brooks family and Frank thought it was a good idea.

"They need everything, Frank. There's no food in that house. No money coming in now. We have to help them. All those kids. I feel so sorry for them."

"I'll spread the word. The town will rally around and help, I know it will. It always does. All we have to do is ask."

Abby knew he was right. She'd always thought it was a myth that neighbors helped one another in times of need until she moved to Spookie. In Spookie it was true. People took care of one another, consoled one another; were there for one another.

They said goodnight and Frank left. He didn't want to miss catching anyone attempting to leave something in the Brooks' mailbox.

Abby locked the door behind him and watched through the window as he got into his truck and drove away.

As she was eating her turkey sandwich, settled down in front of the television ignoring the news, Myrtle phoned. Didn't say who she was, never did, but Abby identified her scratchy voice immediately.

"You know, thought I'd tell you that I was over at Constance's house today—she's that widow I groused about the other night, remember?"

Abby recalled their discussion the other night. "Yes." Constance was the helpless widow whose husband had died a few months ago and who had been pestering Myrtle to death needing this and that. The one who didn't drive and had never balanced a checkbook or sent a bill out in her life. Myrtle had her hands full with that one.

"Well," Myrtle went on, "Constance said someone tried to break into her house last night. Broke a window and everything. She turned all the lights on, called the sheriff and started yelling her head off. Chased whoever it was plum away. Or so she said. Thought you might like to know since you and Frank are on those missing person cases now. It might tie in some way."

"Who told you we were on any cases?" Abby huffed. How did these things get around, she wondered, and not for the first time.

"Town grapevine. Everyone knows you and Frank are on the Shelly Lanstrom case. Asking questions and poking around. Like you two did before when you found those scraps of paper at your house and wanted to find out what happened to those two kids and their mother who used to live in it."

Abby remembered. Thirty years before three people, Emily Summers and her two twin children, had disappeared from Abby's house and she, Frank, and the town had solved the mystery together. Discovered what had befallen the three—they'd been murdered—and why. Now the town thought they were some kind of crime solving duo. It was almost funny.

"Now," Myrtle said. "I hear another person's gone missing—Emil Brooks. We have faith in you two. Know you'll find those missing people. Frank being an ex-cop and you just being good at those kinds of things. Digging up clues and all. Putting the pieces together."

Abby moaned into the phone, but didn't try to deny anything. Wouldn't do any good, not with Myrtle anyway. "Frank's on the case, can't help himself, but I'm staying out of it, Myrtle. I'm just an artist, not a detective."

And serial criminals scared the hell out of her. It was one thing poking into a thirty-year-old mystery and another getting involved with a serial kidnapper, killer, or whatever he was.

Abby would never understand why people hurt or killed other people. Her theory was that they were insane or evil. Best to stay as far away from them as she could. She was no fool.

But Abby promised Myrtle she'd tell Frank about the break-in after she'd asked what had been stolen. She couldn't help herself. And finding out it was mainly food, blankets and clothes that had been stolen, she hung up. Myrtle was a sweet old lady, but as interfering as they came. Had to be in the middle of everything that went on in the town. Nosy as could be.

Speculating if the break-in had anything to do with the

disappearances, Abby went to bed. Samantha had said there'd been a lot of petty break-ins lately, too. Same kind of stuff stolen. Food. Necessities. Supplies. Hmm.

Snowball was behaving peculiarly, scurrying around her bedroom like she was on speed or something. She'd run across Abby's bed and then lunge at the window; peer outside into the dark for a while and start the circuit all over again.

Abby looked outside, but couldn't see anything or anyone. Sometimes Snowball acted peculiar—she was a nervous animal—so Abby chalked it up to that. Finally she had to chase the cat out and close her door or she'd never get any sleep.

The phone rang in the middle of the night and, yanking herself from a dream where she was working at the newspaper again and was having trouble remembering how to turn the computer on and keep her clothes from falling off, at first Abby couldn't speak. When she found her voice, again, no one answered.

Irritated, she slammed down the receiver. The desperate hope, no matter how crazy or fleeting, that her dead husband was on the other end of the line, as usual, made her stomach queasy. And feeling the way she was, she knew she wasn't going to get back to sleep easily. She missed Joel sometimes so much and hated the way it made her feel. Alone.

Her good sense told her the phone call was almost certainly some wrong number or a prankster who thought it was funny waking people up in the middle of the night. Some joke.

Though her heart wished it had been Joel. Trying to tell her where he'd been the last three years and begging for her forgiveness for putting her through hell. Only he'd had no words.

It was after four o'clock and dawn would come at five-thirty, so she got up to make a pot of coffee. She liked this time of morning, so her anger at being awakened faded as the new day's light seeped into the house.

Another day, another chance. Start fresh and count her blessings. As the sun came up she was on the front porch swing, cuddled in her jacket, listening to the blue jays, baby and mother, squawking. All was well.

Abby fell asleep sitting up in the swing and only awoke as Frank's truck pulled into the driveway. Darn, she hadn't even brushed her teeth or washed her face yet.

What could be so important that he was here this early? She got off the swing, gestured for him to follow her inside as he stepped out of his truck and went to get another cup of coffee. Hers was cold. Maybe she'd sneak into the bathroom and brush her teeth, wash her face real quick.

She'd need to be awake for whatever Frank had to tell her. She knew that cloudy look on his face and it wasn't good.

Chapter Six

Frank had guarded the Brooks house all night. No one had come or gone, he explained to Abby. The house had remained silent and lightless once everyone had gone to bed. Every so often he'd walked the perimeter of the yard and moved in closer around the house to be sure no one had snuck in.

When the sun rose Frank was still there and, to be sure, he checked the mailbox, a dented black barrel that held only emptiness. He was so relieved that there was nothing there that every muscle in his body released the exhaustion and helplessness he'd been experiencing for days.

He was exhausted and could barely keep his eyes open.

Yet Shelly Lanstrom was still officially missing and it was because of him. The kidnapper was here because of him. Frank didn't need Emil on his conscience, as well.

He'd had the truck in gear and his foot leaning on the gas pedal when a girl tapped on the window beside his head. She had the blond hair and brown eyes of a Brooks child. He put the vehicle in PARK and rolled down the glass.

"You've been out here all night, mister. I saw you. My mom says she knows you and to come in for a cup of coffee. She has something for you."

Frank followed the girl into the house. He knew the

61

Brooks from around town, had talked to Rebecca Brooks at the grocery store in better times and had been waited on at the gas station by Mr. Brooks. It broke his heart to think of the Brooks kids without a father.

Rebecca was sitting at the kitchen table, her face pallid and lined with time. "Well, Frank Lester, as I live and die. What are you doing staking out my house all night?" She knew who Frank was. Everyone in town knew who Frank was.

Frank laid out most of the truth as gently as he could. It didn't make sense to lie. He told Rebecca about the case ten years ago and the clay figures appearing after someone had been kidnapped. That he feared this pattern might be repeating and that Emil might be the second victim. Her face seemed to age instantly and her eyes saddened as he spoke.

Frank realized that something was wrong. Rebecca was more afraid than before.

"What you were waiting for is already here, Frank. Nick found this on the outside of his windowsill yesterday afternoon." She reached behind her, took something from a cabinet shelf, and handed Frank the clay figure her son had found. "None of us knew what it was, thought it was left by some kid as a prank, but I kept it."

Frank, fighting to keep in his anguish, took the thing into his large hands and stared at it. It seemed to be a man, close enough to represent Emil. How in heaven did the kidnapper get it on that windowsill yesterday afternoon in broad daylight without being seen? And the kidnapper was changing his modus operandi by delivering it in the day and not at night. What other aspects of his routine would the kidnapper be changing?

There was no doubt that Emil was the second victim and that Frank's fears had become reality. The Mud People Killer hadn't died ten years ago. Frank's bullets must have only wounded him and he'd returned for payback.

All the memories, the dread, and frustration of ten years ago washed over Frank like icy water. The nightmare was beginning all over again—or someone was copying the killer's style. Another criminal who knew Frank's history and wanted revenge for something else.

The possibilities and uncertainties boggled Frank's mind.

He went outside and searched the area around the window, took an attentive walk around the house and found nothing else out of the ordinary. When he was satisfied that there was nothing else that'd been left, he went back inside and shared a cup of coffee with Rebecca. Tried to answer her questions. He pressed her for more details about Emil's life and the hours before he left for work that last evening, hoping that there was something he could use.

He asked the kids if there had been anyone unusual hanging around the house last week. Had anything out of the ordinary happened?

The boy, Nick, whose windowsill the clay person had turned up on, gave him his story. "I'm sure it wasn't there yesterday morning when I got up. Would have seen it," the boy reported. "It was there when I got home from school yesterday. Sitting on the windowsill. Yucky, isn't it? Looks like a little kid made it. Look how big the head is. Laura could do much better. She's an artist." And he hadn't seen anything or anyone hanging around.

Thinking about that monster traipsing around the house and staring in on the sleeping children enraged Frank. He'd ask the sheriff to keep an eye on the Brooks kids, especially now. Nick or one of the others could be the next victim. Though that would be out of character for his guy. In the past, the kidnapper hadn't taken more than one victim from a family. But Frank knew that could change, too. He couldn't count on anything anymore.

After all, the kidnapper had taken a ten-year break. He could have other surprises for them.

Frank snuck a fifty-dollar bill under the sugar bowl before he left. He'd seen for himself how little the family had and wanted to help.

The clay figure tucked in a brown paper bag Mrs. Brooks had given him lying beside him on the truck seat, Frank had driven to the sheriff's office. He'd let Sheriff Mearl know another mud person had been found so the sheriff could let the State and Feds know.

It was time to warn the town what they were up against. Time to step fully back into the old nightmare.

At the police station, while he waited for the sheriff to arrive from home, Frank called his former partner, Sam, in Chicago and brought him up to date. "We're going to need help down here. I don't know if Sheriff Mearl will ask for it or not, but we're going to need it. See if you can pull any strings and get us some. We should expand the search for both victims. Now. Time's running out. I'll get back to you after I see the sheriff."

Considering his previous involvement, Frank knew that though he was retired he'd possibly be asked to coordinate with local authorities in the hunt. He didn't want to be part of it, but as he saw it he'd have no choice. No one—except Sam Cato—knew more about the Mud Killer than him. It was *his* fault the kidnapper was in Spookie.

And most importantly, Frank wanted to catch him so badly.

His meeting with the sheriff had been long and frustrating. When the first clay figure had been found Frank had explained to him the history. But not everything. Now he told the sheriff about his own earlier involvement and how he'd shot at the kidnapper years ago and that Frank thought he'd been dead all these years.

"You really pissed him off, if he's come for people you care about ten years later. Trying to make some sort of a point, is he?" Sheriff Mearl grunted. "Where's he been?"

"Don't have a clue and don't want to know," Frank had replied calmly. "But he seems to have this twisted bond with me. Wants to torment me. Again. Because he enjoys it or because I hurt him, or both."

"This second kidnapping will really upset everyone around here," concluded the sheriff. "One girl missing is bad enough, but two people, those freakish mud things, and the link to a serial killer that's been in hiding for a decade is going to turn the press into a hungry beast. We're in for a wild ride. Thanks a lot, pal."

The town sheriff was a local boy, short, pudgy, and seemingly slow-witted, which was deceiving because he wasn't as slow as he acted. His father, Cal Brewster, had been sheriff before him and Mearl had inherited the job. The man wasn't a bad sheriff, merely lazy. The town's usual peacefulness had made him that way. No wonder he didn't like what Frank had laid on his plate. It would mean more work for him.

"Sorry, never meant to bring Chicago back with me, Mearl. You're a cop, you know how it is. It was my job to track and catch him. Stop him. Serial criminals don't follow our rules. I thought the guy was dead and gone. That it was over."

"Well, you were wrong. He's here and we're going to have to deal with him." The sheriff had been at his desk across from Frank scribbling something on a pad of paper. He and Mearl had never seen eye-to-eye on police matters. Mearl was a by-the-book cop and Frank believed you did what you had to do to solve the crime and catch the criminal.

And since Abby had moved into town, there were other things they didn't see eye-to-eye on as well. Like who should court Abby. Everyone knew that Mearl had an affection for Abby. She was courteous to him but wouldn't date him. It was easier for Frank to steer clear of the sheriff than to argue with the man. It'd be awkward if Frank had to punch him out, Mearl being the sheriff and all.

"Maybe it wouldn't be so bad if the press got wind of this whole situation, Sheriff. It'd bring us support and might help flush the killer out. If nothing else, I think the people need to know he's out there stalking them so they can protect themselves. There are going to be more victims if we don't stop him."

The sheriff hadn't looked up. "I know," he muttered. "Let

us handle this from here on in. That's my job now, not yours. We'll keep in touch, Frank. If we need anything more, I mean.

"All I can tell you, Frank, is to take care. If the kidnapper gets tired of torturing you he might just decide to come after you."

"I almost wish he would—to end this. I'd take my chances if it meant having a crack at catching him again." *Or trying to get rid of him again*, was what Frank had been thinking. Whatever it took to get the man.

Frank should have gone home to bed, but first stopped at a fast food place for a bag of sausage biscuits and then headed to Abby's. He'd found her curled up on her front porch swing in her jacket, cat in lap and sleeping. Not for long.

By the time he hit the porch, she was rubbing her eyes, brushing her tangled hair back from her face and heading inside. When she'd moved to Spookie, her hair, a golden shade of caramel, had been long. A few months ago she'd had it cut shorter and layered. Looked good with her oval face and her green eyes. Frank liked it. He also liked seeing her in the morning. She didn't need make up. She was pretty no matter what.

He followed her into the house and into the kitchen. The cat attacked his feet every step of the way, wanting to play. Frank scooped Snowball up and cuddled her before letting her go and she ran out of the room. Frank could see her bouncing around in the living room like a crazy ball. He wished he had half the energy.

"So spill it," Abby demanded.

Chapter Seven

"Hi to you, too, Abby. Sorry I woke you up. You looked so peaceful out there . . . curled up in your jacket. I should be home sleeping, too, but I needed to talk to someone. Remind myself there are good people in the world and good things worth waking up for." Frank was rattling on and he only did that when he was stressed. "It's such a lovely day I thought I'd enjoy a little of it and make a stop to have breakfast with you."

He held up the white bag as if it were an offering. "I brought sausage and biscuits from our local Hardee's. Enough for two or more. You have coffee?"

"Sure do. Fresh and hot. Help yourself. I'll be right back." Abby escaped to the bathroom to wash her face and brush her teeth. Slipping out of her jacket, she put on a robe hanging on the bathroom door and returned to the kitchen.

"The delivery was made." Frank sipped his coffee and ate his biscuit as if he were starving. It was his way of covering his emotions, Abby thought. He cleaned the crumbs up with his fingers meticulously as they fell and behaved as if nothing was wrong, when everything was. "A clay figure was left on a windowsill at the Brooks house. As we feared, Emil is victim number two. Father of seven and husband to Rebecca. A hardworking, good man who's never hurt anyone and is a friend to everyone. And I'm to blame . . . because I didn't catch the kidnapper, didn't stop him ten years ago . . . and I don't know how I can go through this again."

"I'm so sorry, Frank." Seeing his despair, Abby laid her hand over his. His skin was cold. "But you already suspected he was here and had taken Shelly, didn't you?"

"In a way, I *knew*—with that first mud person. I didn't want to accept it, though." He shook his head. "But I suspected it before finding that clay figure. I'd had this awful feeling in the pit of my stomach when Shelly had gone missing. Evil has a feeling of its own. After years of watching, chasing, and catching them, I can almost sense when a criminal is around. My skin shivers.

"And ten years ago this guy made me feel like a snowman. He's a bad one. A man without a conscience or a soul. I believed he was insane. Or that's what I told myself. It's the only way I can understand how a person can do what he does. Taking people away from their lives and their families. Hurting so many people.

"I've spoken to the sheriff and divulged everything I could recall about the kidnapper. Gave Mearl the second clay figure and strongly suggested he release all the information to Samantha at the *Journal* and the other news media. People need to know that a kidnapper is among us. That he'll strike again soon."

Frank handed her a sausage biscuit, but with what he'd been telling her she had little appetite. Fright did that to her. *Someone was taking people.*

"I can't get the kidnapper or that clay thing out of my mind." Frank rubbed his eyes, his body trembling with exhaustion or rage, she wasn't sure which. She'd never seen him so shaken. "I *have to stop him* before he hurts anyone else."

"I hate to ask this but . . . what *does* he do to his victims?" Abby was staring out the windows at a russet-leaved tree swaying in the yard and a beautiful cerulean blue sky filled with a warm yellow sun. So deceptively normal.

"From the beginning we feared he killed them. He had *said* he killed them, but we had no proof and no way of knowing because bodies were never found. We had and still have no idea how he disposes of them.

"We don't even know how he kills them. I've prayed that he at least kills them quickly. It's maddening to dwell on it. I try not to. Don't you, either.

"My only thought is to catch him."

"What do we do now?" Abby tried to take Frank's advice. Not think about the victims or their fate. Emil had seven kids and a sick wife. Shelly had her whole life ahead of her.

It didn't work. She couldn't stop thinking about them and the distress they'd left behind. She of all people knew what it was like to lose someone suddenly and not know what had become of them. It was an ache that never went away.

"Abby, we have to be alert. The whole town does. We shouldn't take our safety for granted and we should keep our doors locked.

"Let me give you one of my guns to protect yourself with."

"Keep it. I don't like guns."

"Abby, please, this isn't a game. This guy means business. In four days, if we don't stop him, he's going to take another person. He's waited ten years to get revenge on me and he has something special in store. I'm afraid it's only the beginning.

"And you and I, well, we're . . . close. That makes you a target."

Abby shook her head firmly. "No gun. But I'll keep my wooden club close. Take it everywhere I go. Promise. I'll run from car to house. From house to car. Look around and behind every bush before I take a step in any direction."

"A gun would keep you safer than a club. With a gun you don't have to get near an assailant to bring him down."

"I hate guns, I told you."

Frank gave up on the gun angle. "Until this guy is caught I should stay away from you then. I shouldn't have come over this morning. But it's hard getting used to being paranoid again. I thought I'd left that all behind in Chicago when I handed in my badge."

He stood up to leave. "The kidnapper could be tailing me and watching us now. Though I'm sure no one tailed me from the Brooks house. I was careful. No one was behind me or anywhere around me."

There was nothing Abby could say because he could be right. The kidnapper could be following him. Could have followed him there. For a moment she was panicky and then it passed. If Frank said no one had followed him, then no one had. She trusted Frank.

"I should stay away from the people I care about for a while." He was beside her and leaned over to whisper with a gentleness she couldn't mistake, "And I couldn't bear it if something happened to you, Abby.

"So I'm going home now."

She walked him to the door and he drove away. Frank Lester was falling in love with her. She'd known it for a long time. Didn't know how she felt about it yet. Too soon. She was flattered. She was unsure. Most of all she was afraid of hurting him.

Because for Abby her husband's death was fresh. In her heart she still sometimes felt married. Still thought of Joel as her love. But Joel was never coming back. Never. And she had to go on with her life. It wasn't a betrayal, but a necessity.

Was she ready to fall in love again with anyone else? With Frank? She didn't know. But she did know he already loved her and he was everything she admired in a man. She put the thoughts out of her head. She had a lot more to be uneasy about than if she was ever going to find love. There might be a madman stalking their town and right now that was what they had to concentrate on. No time for daydreaming. No time for love.

Frank phoned half an hour later. She was drinking coffee and eating the sausage biscuits he had left. Snowball was rolling around on the floor like a kitten. Her antics made Abby smile. How could there be anything as evil as a serial killer out in the world when there were such good people like Frank and loving creatures like Snowball. But then there were a lot of things she didn't understand.

"There was a note with my name printed on the front waiting on my screen door when I got back," Frank's voice spoke in an eerily calm tone. "It said,"

Two down, four to go. Missed you, Frank. See you soon.

"No signature. Even after ten years I recognize the hand-writing." Frank's anger coated every word. "I'm taking the note to the sheriff. Get it dusted for prints and analyzed. Not that it'll uncover anything. I've been here before. He's too smart to leave prints or clues.

"Abby, he was here in my yard, on my front porch. I can't believe his gall. He's playing with me. I've got to stop him somehow."

There was such weary hopelessness in his voice her heart hurt for him.

"Good thing is, Frank, if he was at your house, he wasn't following you. Didn't follow you here." She couldn't let Frank know how horrified she was at the situation. The monster from Frank's past was becoming too real for her.

Frank was quiet for a second. "You look at the good in everything."

"I find it helps me get through the day. Call the sheriff, Frank, and let him come by and get the note. Then you lock up tight and get some sleep. You sound awful. Call me to-night after you get some rest."

"Now that's an excellent idea—the sheriff can come to me. I am tired."

"Good night, Frank."

"Good night, Abby."

Chapter Eight

The bakery was packed as Abby stood in line and eavesdropped on other people's conversations. The topic of the hour, as it had been for days, was the disappearances. They'd been in all the papers and on the news, along with their connection to the Chicago Mud People Killer from a decade past. Everyone was scared and jumpy. The townspeople crowded into the shops early in the day and by dark the streets were deserted.

It'd put quite a crimp in the Halloween planning festivities. Who needed make-believe spooks and frights when you were living the real thing.

Frank's warnings were heeded by everyone. Abby scrutinized everyone and everything around her wherever she went. She was as paranoid as a fly in a fly-swatter factory and detested feeling that way.

She missed Frank. Never thought she'd miss anyone again, but she missed him. His telephone calls, his dropping by with fast food or for coffee, and his friendship. She found herself reaching for the phone to call him, but stopping. The kidnapper was after him, Frank said, no telling how closely he was watching and listening and the guy had tapped phones before. Frank didn't want to take any chances. Better to be safe than sorry was one of his favorite sayings and in this instance was also the most appropriate one.

The town had been overrun with reporters and FBI agents in suits asking questions—a horde descending on them like intrusive locusts. The *Journal*'s front pages, as well as every other newspaper in the state, were filled with stories about the crimes and the serial killer. They speculated on why he kidnapped and killed and what he did with the unfortunates he took. Where he'd been and why he'd come back after ten long years. The connection between Frank and the killer was made and their history told. The story was driving the news media crazy and the feeding frenzy had begun.

Her box of pumpkin cookies tucked under her arm, Abby was leaving the bakery when Myrtle caught up to her. A skinny clawlike hand clamped around her arm.

"The killer tried to grab me! Wasn't content with just stalking this time, he tried to get me. I swear it!" Myrtle's breathing was ragged, as if she'd been running. Wrinkled face flushed a russet red and her hair was sticking up straight around her head like Sputnik.

"When? Where?" Abby led her to a bench beneath a tree and gently sat her down. The woman was beside herself, sweating and panic-eyed. Myrtle was one of the most fearless old ladies Abby had ever known. It got to her that she was so frightened. "Tell me."

"This morning at my place I was outside, ready to go on my rounds when I heard someone moving in the woods behind me. This huge brute—dressed shabbily—was coming at me. Only thing that saved me was I heard him before I saw him. My ears are as sharp as a twenty-year-old's, even if I don't see so well. Well, I took off running like the devil was after me. I got away because the guy limped and stumbled a few times. Surprised him, I think, that I could move so fast for an old broad. Anyway, I took a shortcut through the woods and hid behind trees whenever I heard him behind me.

"Exercise," she exhaled, leaning against the bench. "That's the key. I power walk all the time all over the place. Looking for my treasures, you know. Keeps me quick." Her breathing eased and the fright in her eyes dimmed, but she still looked like she was going to faint.

The day was a cloudy taste of autumn. Two weeks before Halloween, the weather had steadily become cooler. Temperatures in the fifties during the day and forties at night. Golden and purple leaves crunched beneath the old woman's shoes as her restless feet moved back and forth.

Abby put her arms around her. "It's all right, Myrtle. You're safe now. Soon as you've caught your breath we'll get you to the sheriff's office. I'll drive. And you can tell your story to Sheriff Mearl."

Hopefully, they'd believe Myrtle this time. She had a reputation for making stories up and everyone knew it. "Maybe you can help them come up with a sketch of the guy."

Myrtle's eyes fell on the bakery box. "If I go to the sheriff's can I have some of whatever you've got in there?"

Abby smiled. If Myrtle was thinking about food she was fine. "Sure." She opened the box and handed her friend one of the orange iced cookies. Best sugar cookies Abby had ever had—she was addicted to them. Didn't help her diet any, though. "You can have as many cookies as you want."

Abby helped the old lady to her feet as the wind whipped around them and a chill, more than just the wind, slivered up her back. Myrtle was shivering in one of her skimpy housedresses so Abby gave her her sweater. "And I bet Sheriff Mearl will have a fresh pot of coffee on to go with these cookies when we get there."

Abby got Myrtle to the sheriff's office and stayed as her friend gave her report of the incident to one of the sheriff's officers, Deputy Stevens. The sheriff wasn't in the office that morning and wouldn't be until later that day. Officer Stevens was a new hire, young and eager and annoying as a puppy. At first he didn't seem to take Myrtle seriously until Abby stood up for her, saying she believed her and so should he.

He called in a police sketch artist and they spent time getting a face and a description.

The problem was, as Abby saw it and remained silent about it, Myrtle's eyesight wasn't all that good. She had the sneaking suspicion Myrtle was making up some of the suspect's features. The deputy, as green as he was, must have had the same suspicion. Abby could sense his skepticism by the end of the session, but he didn't question anything Myrtle said. Instead, he offered compassion for what she'd gone through and was impressed she'd gotten away.

"You're a resourceful woman, Myrtle," he told her. "And a lucky one."

"Yep, I know it. God was watching over me, I imagine." The interview and the ordeal had worn Myrtle out. Her shoulders began slumping and her eyes kept closing. She looked like an elderly rag doll propped up in a chair.

"Mrs. Schmitt, I wouldn't go home or be alone for a while," the deputy counseled. "He saw you. He might come after you again."

"Can she get protection?" Abby would feel better if the old lady had a guard for a bit.

The deputy looked at her. "We can't spare anyone right now, Mrs. Sutton. Everyone's out looking for the Lanstrom girl and now Mr. Brooks. And their kidnapper."

Abby stared at the officer. "So what's she supposed to do? Fend for herself? One old lady apparently doesn't matter much?" She was being too harsh but she couldn't help herself.

The deputy relented. "I can swing by and keep an eye on her—as much as I can. Can't promise twenty-four-hour protection, but I'll see what I can do."

"That's better than nothing, I guess." But it wasn't enough and Abby had an idea.

She turned to Myrtle. "Come and stay with me for a while. Your stalker won't know where you've gone. Won't be able to find you. You'll be safe and we'll have a visit." It was much more secure than that trailer Myrtle lived in. A kid could break into that thing. And Deputy Stevens could patrol or sit out front at Abby's place as well as Myrtle's.

"I have to put the finishing touches on the library mural," Abby said, "but it won't take long. I'll lock the house up when I leave you there. No one will be able to get in and I'll be back real quick. What do you say?"

It was no surprise when she took Abby up on the offer. Free food cooked by someone else and someone to talk to, Abby was sure she was thinking. Myrtle reminded her of her grandma and since the day they'd met, there had been a bond between them. It would ease Abby's mind to have her over for a few days. Besides, Abby could use the company.

Abby took Myrtle home with her, fed her cheese sandwiches and a bowl of soup. When the old woman said she was tired and went off for a nap, Abby locked the doors behind her, left the house and went into town to work on the mural. Nearly done, she was impatient to finish.

Before she left, Abby phoned Frank. He should know about Myrtle's little run-in with her stalker. Frank wasn't home so she left a message on his machine.

The library was nearly empty as she worked on the mural. Yet she felt as if someone was observing every move she made and it gave her the willies. Her work at the library was almost done except for one or two last details. She liked walking away, letting her art sit for a few days, and then adding those final touches.

Nora, on the other hand, was already satisfied and wanted to pay her in full. Abby didn't argue. She'd return in a couple of days and add to it if she thought it needed touching up.

After Nora paid her, she handed Abby an envelope to take along to the Brooks house. "The workers and some of the library's patrons took up a collection for the family and since you mentioned you were going out there today, could you give it to them? It's money to help. For food and bills."

"I'll give it to them. Rebecca won't like taking it, but, for the kids she will. It was good-hearted of you and the others to collect it."

"I feel sorry for that family. A lot of people do. They're taking collections all over town. Tell Rebecca there'll be more. Wish we could do something like that for the Lanstroms, but they have plenty of money. Money won't do it for them. Hear Molly is having a breakdown and Carl has holed himself up in the house—when he isn't out looking for the girl."

"According to the newspapers," Nora commented, "Emil Brooks is the second victim. Rebecca could be a widow already. It's terrible. Who'll be next?"

"No one else, we hope."

Abby told Nora about Myrtle's adventure and that she was staying with her for a few days.

"You think it was the kidnapper chasing her?"

"Myrtle thinks it was. And Frank believes it could be him because he limped."

"Can't be safe anywhere anymore," Nora mumbled, scared like the rest of them.

Heading home, Abby would have done anything to swing past Frank's place for a visit to see what was going on, but she didn't.

Instead she drove over to the Brooks house to drop off the money. They needed it. Rebecca was in bed, looking paler than anytime she'd ever seen her. She took the cash without hesitation, too weak and grief-stricken to resist. She'd listened to what Frank and the police had to say, she'd seen the news on television and read the newspapers. She knew that her husband was the kidnapper's second victim and might not be coming home.

Abby stayed long enough to help Laura and Charlene prepare supper for the family and then she tried calling Frank again, but only the answering machine picked up.

She went home. Didn't want Myrtle to be left alone for too long. The old woman might burn her house down. But mostly, night was coming on and she didn't want to be out on the roads when it arrived. The kidnapper was out there somewhere trolling for another potential victim and she didn't want to be it.

She wasn't happy until she got behind her own walls with the doors locked.

Night came and with it a cold rain as she and Myrtle—now awake—sat down to supper then watched some television. Myrtle couldn't stop talking. Lonely old woman. No matter how she protested, Abby could see she liked being there and having someone to talk to. She ate three helpings of noodles and rice and a big bowl of chocolate pudding.

Spent half the time peering out the windows, waiting for her stalker to find her and then fell asleep in the chair as the television flickered across the darkened room. Abby put the old woman to bed on the sofa and, after making sure all the doors were locked, went up to bed herself.

She'd left a wooden club by the sofa just in case. Better safe than sorry.

Chapter Nine

He saw her in town coming out of the library. Recognized her as the woman that his enemy—the cop—had been having breakfast with in the diner the week before. She was someone special to the cop. A friend, perhaps, or more. He followed her back to a modest yellow house on the edge of town, wary that the woman or the cop sitting out in the squad car might see him. He wasn't going to make the same mistake as with that old lady in the small trailer.

With the old lady he'd been sloppy. Letting her see him like that. Not that he'd planned on taking that crazy old woman. Oh, he'd been watching her, but his inner voices, those whispers in his head whose advice and directions he had to follow, hadn't told him to take her.

So the old woman wasn't the next one he was supposed to steal, yet she'd seen him and he'd impulsively taken after her through the woods. The voices didn't tell him to do that. That was his own bad idea. The old crone had somehow slipped away and because the voices hadn't actually ordered him to capture her, in the end, he let her escape. Well, she'd gotten away on her own. She'd been fast for an elderly person.

Truth was, and he'd never say it aloud or let his voices hear him say it, but he really didn't enjoy taking people so he was glad she'd escaped.

Now his voices were telling him this woman who lives in the yellow house could be the next one he must take. But he wasn't sure. The voices were muted. He could hardly hear them. Lately it had been like that and it confused him.

He wished they'd just go away and leave him alone. Why wouldn't they?

He loitered outside the yellow house, out of sight from the young cop, waiting for the voices to tell him what to do next. Maybe, if he were lucky, they never would.

The night was raw and the rain dripped down his car windows blurring his view of the house. He waited. He did a lot of that. While his voices remained silent, as they had for almost ten years after his . . . *accident*.

That's what he'd called it. That time in Chicago when the cop had caught him on an icy night putting his gift in that mailbox and shot him. *Shot him.* Well, he'd been shooting at the cop, too. Wished he still had that gun but his mother had found it and gotten rid of it. She'd said guns were dangerous and shouldn't be allowed in the house. Said she didn't want him to get another one and he hadn't. She'd been right about guns being dangerous.

'Cause Lord, those bullets had hurt. One of them had taken off three fingers on his left hand—clean as a whistle—and one of them had hit him in the left leg. He still limped. He'd been afraid to go to the hospital—they would have asked too many questions—so he'd taken the bullets out on his own and doctored himself as best he could. He'd nearly died. Was in a deep sleep for days.

When he awoke, his voices had disappeared. They were gone for a long, long time. Without them to tell him what to do, he'd stopped taking people. It'd been a relief. He'd been sick from the gunshot wounds for a very long time, but he'd gone on with his life. Took care of his mother after she had her stroke and worked a string of mindless jobs. Almost felt normal.

He'd liked it.

Then a few months ago the voices had begun again and he hadn't been happy about it. But they were so much smarter than him and he couldn't get rid of them. The more he tried the louder they became. If he didn't listen and obey they drove him crazy.

Nothing specifically precipitated their return after ten years. It had happened at about the time he had gotten fired from his last job. The voices started out as indistinct whispers and grew clearer and more adamant each day.

Between the voices and those strange see-through people that were always hounding him, sometimes he thought he was crazy.

And, as the times before, he changed. He once more started having blackouts and found himself places he didn't remember going to. Once he woke up coming out of someone's house with an armful of canned goods and blankets. Stealing. Mother wouldn't have liked that.

First thing the voices told him to do was take care of her—once and for all. He loved his mother but she'd been so sick for a long time, she no longer looked, acted, or talked like his mother. The voices ordered him to get rid of her and expressed surprise he hadn't thought of it before. Lying up in her bed all day not knowing who or where she was or who he was couldn't be much fun. Not much of a life.

He'd done her a favor in ending it, the voices had reassured him.

It'd almost felt good to take action again. For years he'd drifted aimlessly, his hand and leg hurting, his mind asleep. He didn't make his clay people anymore. Without his voices, his muse, he couldn't fashion them. Made him sad. He'd become good at his clay people. How could he be such a great artist and no one see it?

One time this woman, some art director at some fancy art gallery had laughed at his creations. Called them "ugly primitive." Said he had no talent. What had she known?

After his mother was gone, the voices remained and told

him what to do. And, as before, he gave up trying to fight them. They were stronger, smarter, and louder than he was.

Close up the house. Take your freedom. Take what money you have from working and go. Track down the cop that hurt you. Make him pay. Change his life as he has changed yours by picking up where you left off before. Make him sorry he ever tried to stop you. Show him and the world you're smarter than any of them.

If he thought it was odd, the voices being gone so long and returning out of the blue, he didn't dwell on it. His whole life had been strange. Never knew his father. Lived with his mother all his life . . . all forty-some years of it. Couldn't recall what he'd done yesterday sometimes. Followed voices in his head that had him do the most bizarre things.

Even he accepted they were bizarre, but he couldn't stop doing them. He kept breaking into houses and stealing things: food, personal items he had no use for, small appliances. Mail. Sometimes he'd sneak in and out, take or not take things, without leaving a clue and sometimes he smashed up anything in his path.

He didn't know why he did those things. The voices made him do them.

And there were those people he took. He couldn't remember what he'd done with them. They were just gone. Gone forever. But he left his clay people in place of the ones he'd taken. The voices directed him to do that. *A trade.*

Running his good hand along his chin and through his long greasy hair, he thought it was time to take a bath. Had it been two weeks or three? He couldn't remember, but he smelled. That would call unwanted attention to him. Which wouldn't be good.

He sat outside the woman's house and listened to the night and to the rain that had turned into a full-fledged storm with lightning and thunder. He listened for his voices and they finally told him what to do next.

He put on gloves and his black sock cap to keep his hair out of his face, got out of the car and made his way through the gloom and the downpour, lying low. Hidden. Sure of himself. The voices had explained how he should do what he had to do.

Balled in his gloved right hand was the cloth he soaked in the liquid that put people to sleep. His voices told him to sneak up on the cop outside and make sure he didn't wake.

Leave the cloth on long enough to put the cop to sleep for a while, but not forever as the others. Leave the body.

Get the woman in the yellow house. Number three right on time.

He snuck up to the back window and with the rain and thunder hiding the noise, he broke the glass and let himself in. No alarms went off. The house had no burglar system and the woman lived alone. He knew that.

She was sleeping in the upstairs bedroom. He'd seen the light come on and go off earlier. Making his way up the stairs in the dark, the second wet cloth was snuggled in his good hand. It was easy. His eyes adjusted to the lack of light enough for him to see outlines.

He was holding the cloth over her face as she struggled when the phone by her bed began to ring. Startled him enough that he hesitated and the woman pulled away and slithered to the floor. He grabbed at her, scooped her up in his arms, placing the cloth back over her face.

That's when something hard hit him on the back of the head. Good thing he was wearing a wool sock cap. Couldn't get DNA off a sock cap. But, whew, it hurt.

He dropped the woman like a sack of rocks and put his hands up to his head. Pain.

A jagged bolt of lightning lit up the room for a moment. Pivoting around, covering his face with one hand, he peeked out and saw it was the old woman from the trailer. Dressed in a fluffy pink robe, her hair sticking up all over the place, and her face contorted, tiny and angry, she swung at him again with a big stick of wood.

"Take that, you overgrown Frankenstein!" And the stick hit him in the leg. More pain flew up through his kneecap and exploded in his thigh.

Darn that old woman.

His voices had abandoned him. They always did when he got in trouble. So he reacted out of the instinct to survive. Thinking his thick coat would protect him from the breaking glass, he spun around and jumped through the window and fell the two stories to the ground. Hitting the mud hard, he rolled and scrambled up and limped away into the woods back to his car. Crawled in and drove away as quickly as he could.

Beyond the agony in his head and leg he experienced disappointment that number three had slipped through his hands. He'd been scared away too easily. Why had he run off because an old woman had lit into him? It had been the surprise of it, he thought. Confused him.

His voices would be angry with him for being a coward. Ha, maybe they'd leave him again and maybe that wouldn't be so bad.

He had to get away and take care of his leg before he passed out. The same leg that the cop had shot years ago. He was in excruciating pain, his head bleeding, and it was all he could think about. He had to doctor himself because he didn't dare go to the hospital.

Oh, he'd been here before.

He drove to the cheap motel he'd found in the next town, fighting dizziness the entire way. The motel was a rattrap, but his room was tucked in the rear and no one seemed to care what he did as long as he paid each morning. For now, it was his sanctuary.

His head hurt. His kneecap hurt. *Darn that old woman.*

Chapter Ten

"You saved me, Myrtle," Abby mumbled when she came to. "Saved my life." She was fuzzy from whatever the intruder had put over her nose. It was as if she was in some kind of wacky nightmare. She wanted to giggle or sleep. Sleep was winning. She had to fight to stay awake.

Myrtle exclaimed, "It was the same creep who stalked me through the woods, I'm pretty sure. He broke in downstairs, snuck upstairs and tried to snatch you. I knocked him silly with that club of yours."

"I was meant to be the next victim," Abby gasped in shock, giggling from the lingering fumes, battling to stay conscious. Myrtle had saved her and she was still there. Still alive, she thought, though her brain was like cotton and she couldn't appreciate the full ramifications of it all yet. "How . . . can . . . I ever . . . thank you?"

"Fix me a snack and we're even. I'm hungry." Myrtle was beaming, chin cocked up, eyes glittering in the room's overhead light. "And don't thank just me. Thankfully the phone woke me up or I wouldn't have heard the scuffle up here. Wouldn't have been able to come to your rescue. Good thing you showed me where you put that wooden stick of yours. It worked real well. Gave him a headache, I bet. Not to mention the whack I gave his kneecap," she snickered.

"The phone?" In the back of Abby's mind she heard the echo of its ringing, yet as the rest of the night's experience her thoughts weren't clear enough to make sense of it. The nightstand clock displayed 2:07 in the morning.

Outside the storm was a shadow of itself, the lightning a tamed light show across the windows. "Who was on the phone in the middle of the night?"

"Beats me. It stopped right after I came awake. Lucky thing, though, cause it woke me up enough to hear what was going on up here. Then I was too busy saving your butt to think about it."

Abby shook her head. The only phone calls she got in the middle of the night were wrong numbers or dead space . . . the ones she fancied were from Joel. And that was too spooky to contemplate.

Myrtle helped Abby downstairs and waited on her for once. Got out the cookies and the milk and phoned Frank. Abby was in no condition yet to make sense. She kept drifting in and out. Muttering nonsense about her dead husband.

"It's the middle of the night but it's an emergency," Myrtle declared. "Frank would want to know."

And anyway, Abby mulled it over as the delayed fear settled in soft waves, the secret was out. If the person who had broken in and tried to take her was Frank's long-lost kidnapper, he hadn't targeted her because she lived in a yellow house. He'd made the connection between Frank and her. That they were friends. Had to. Only thing that made sense. And if he'd been after Myrtle, he would have tried to take Myrtle. Wouldn't he?

Instead the intruder had tried to abduct her.

Frank arrived in less than fifteen minutes. He'd been running down a lead on the disappearances that evening and hadn't gotten Abby's earlier messages about Myrtle's troubles until it was too late to return her call.

"Thank God you're all right," was the first thing he said to Abby after Myrtle let him in. He pulled Abby out of her chair and hugged her so hard she couldn't breathe.

"Frank," she murmured, her head finally clearing. "Did you try to call me about an hour ago?"

Frank gave her a funny look, shook his head. "No. I was asleep an hour ago. Myrtle's call woke me up. I got your other messages, about Myrtle's mishap, but was going to call you in the morning. Why?"

"Oh, nothing." Abby waved the matter away. He'd find out about the phone call soon enough. Myrtle would probably say something.

The old woman began rattling on about what had happened and how she'd saved Abby, all the time stuffing home-made chocolate chip cookies into her mouth and washing them down with milk. She was so proud of herself.

Frank released Abby and met her eyes and saw the fear in them. "There's no one outside anymore. I searched. He's long gone. I rang the police on my way over on the cell phone and checked Deputy Stevens out in the squad car on my way in. He's okay but out cold. Been chloroformed. Tipoff was the strong ether odor around him. They're sending someone to see to him. Must have used chloroform on you, too.

"You were lucky, Abby. In all the time this man has been taking people, I've never known him to fail. An angel must have been watching over you. Both of you."

Myrtle returned Abby's smile. The drug was wearing off and Abby understood fully what had almost befallen her.

She began to tremble and Frank rocked her in his arms.

"It's all right," he soothed. "He didn't get you. You're safe now. But he's not going to give up." Frank sent a stern look at both women.

"Abby, Myrtle . . . you're both packing up your things— after you speak to the sheriff—and are coming to stay at my place. Snowball, too. No back talk. It's final. You're coming home with me *tonight*. You can stay as long as you need to. Until this man is caught or I think it's safe. I have extra rooms, lots of blankets, and plenty of food."

"Oh, goodie," Myrtle muttered, "a pajama party. I didn't

mind staying a night with you Abby, but I sure don't want to camp out at some man's house for days or weeks. People would talk. Not to mention I have business to attend to and work to do at my place. Can't stay away too long. I think I'll just go on back home."

"*No* you won't. Not unless you want to disappear forever." Frank was blunt. "I know this guy. He doesn't like to be made a fool of. Myrtle, the smacks you gave him with the stick might slow him down—had to have hurt him—but it won't stop him. He'll be back. For you . . . or for Abby."

Frank gazed into Abby's face. "I think either you or Myrtle were meant to be his third victim. Since he actually tried to take you, Abby, I'd say you were first on his list."

As awful as it was, Abby feared it was true. And she didn't want to think about it. Better to think of practical things. "What about the broken windows? There's one in the kitchen and one upstairs in my bedroom where he jumped out. Can't leave them open to the weather and all. It's supposed to rain more tomorrow."

Frank assessed the damage and when he returned, he said, "I'll get someone to come out and board up the broken windows tomorrow. Luke at the hardware store makes house calls for his friends. Won't charge you much, either. I'll get you a special deal because he owes me for a favor I once did for him."

Abby was glad she'd finished the library's mural and had the money in the bank. She decided to take Frank up on his offer. She couldn't hide away at Frank's forever, but for a while she could. She'd think of it as a vacation. A protective custody vacation.

Being attacked in her own home had terrified her.

The sheriff showed up and spewed the usual questions, but seemed peeved that Frank was taking charge and whisking them away to his cabin. Abby was sure Mearl would have preferred to put her under his protective custody. He'd been flirting with her since she'd moved to town. Fat chance.

As pigheaded as the sheriff was, even he could see the growing bond between Frank and her.

Then Frank took the sheriff aside to speak with him privately.

When the sheriff had the information he needed, Frank piled Abby and Myrtle into his truck and drove them back to the cabin.

Tucked into a strange bed in someone else's house an hour later, her cat snoring beside her, didn't bother her. Knowing Frank would protect them, Abby felt safe and sleep claimed her quickly. The kidnapper would be an idiot if he tried to get to them there. Frank had two huge well-trained attack dogs and a lot of guns. Abby knew that because he'd showed her where he kept every one of them.

The next morning soft sunlight woke Abby from her nightmares. At first disoriented by her surroundings she soon remembered where she was and why. A sick feeling crept under her skin and spread. She'd been lucky last night. Thanks to Myrtle and the telephone.

Getting out of bed and slipping on a robe, she went in search of a bathroom with Snowball prancing along beside her. After freshening up, she and the cat chased the food smells to the kitchen downstairs. Snowball wasn't happy to be away from home, but as long as she was with Abby she coped. When things got to be too much for her she hid under furniture.

Snowball disliked the dogs but Frank, amiable host that he was, promised to keep them outside during their visit and exiled them to the backyard.

The old woman and the ex-detective were in the kitchen. Myrtle was wolfing down pancakes and yakking about her mutual funds and how they'd been in the toilet lately. That she thought the stock market would fall to at least seven thousand before it got better, no matter what the financial wizards were saying about a recovery.

Myrtle had on the same clothes as the day before, but had

had a bath, she gleefully told Abby with a grin on her face, had combed her hair and scrubbed her face. "Sweetie," she purred, "you look like you just escaped from the spook house, but don't look bad for an almost dead woman." As usual Myrtle blurted out exactly what she was thinking. Somehow old people could get away with it.

"Thanks, old lady." Abby grinned at her, grateful to be there in Frank's sunny kitchen. She couldn't linger on what might have happened if Myrtle hadn't interrupted her kidnap attempt the night before. Out cold as she'd been, a fly could have defended itself better. Where would she have awakened? Would she have awakened? She was lucky to be alive and that almost outweighed the leftover horror at what might have happened.

"Pancakes?" Frank stood with a spatula in his hand, the flapjacks bubbling on the grill. Wearing a cook's apron, he seemed comfortable in his kitchen. He liked to cook and was enjoying them being there even despite the circumstances. Perhaps because of the circumstances. Frank was happy Abby and Myrtle were alive.

"Not right this minute, thanks. Maybe later. Coffee is what I need for now." Abby helped herself to a cup and settled down to watch Myrtle eat. Three helpings. Being stalked by a kidnapper hadn't affected her appetite.

"What now?" Abby pressed Frank as he dribbled syrup over his pancakes. His appearance was ragged, as if he hadn't slept. There were bags under his eyes and a day's growth of beard shading his face. She knew he was in on the investigation because of his past relationship with the kidnapper, yet she had no idea if they were any closer to catching him—the man who'd taken two people, scared the life out of Myrtle and had tried to grab her.

She wanted to ask, but was afraid she already knew the answer. Frank was disgruntled that the killer hadn't left blood or prints behind in her bedroom. He must have been wearing gloves. Frank didn't offer up any updates, which must mean the police weren't any closer to finding the man.

"Now?" Frank stopped eating and his eyes went to the

woods outside the window behind the cabin. There was a blue jay sitting on the windowsill. Abby wondered if it was her blue jay that had followed her from home. "Now we catch that monster and put him away before he hurts anyone else. I'm not sure how to do it. Either he's very clever . . . or very lucky.

"And worse, I still don't have a clue as to *why* he's taking these people here, other than I know them. But that's not why he started kidnapping. He was doing that before I came into the picture. There's no gender or age pattern to his method. Doesn't make any sense.

"Ten years ago we had a profiler take a crack at him before he started targeting my friends, and the profiler couldn't put a full face on the guy. He determined that the kidnapper was abducting his victims out of some need to have control, to feel special, important; that he was cunning, middle-aged, probably ashamed of his looks, and a loner with no close ties. Your standard kidnapper profile. Me? I think he's insane. Plain and simple. Needs to be stopped. That profiler thought the kidnapper wouldn't deviate from his usual MO Well, I think he might. Already has in some ways and I wouldn't put anything past him now.

"It's a decade later and a whole new ball game.

"So I have to be sure both of you are protected. After what happened with the deputy in front of your house, I've asked my ex-partner, Sam, to come down and help. Sam's a shade smarter than the local boys and he's had more experience with serial criminals. With this one in particular. He's taking some time off and should be here real soon." Frank's lips curved up. "Let's say he owes me. And I'm not leaving you two women alone until he gets here."

Myrtle finished eating, announced she'd eaten too much, and was going to her room for a nap. Real story was she liked the guest room and its big soft bed. The fancy bedspread and matching curtains and the pretty furnishings. Frank had decorated each guest room with care.

"That old woman saved my life, Frank," Abby said after

Myrtle was gone. "Anything she wants from now on, I'll try to give her."

Frank chuckled. "A fortune in donuts, pie slices and free food, you mean?"

"Something like that."

"I'm dreading the telephone calls," Frank let out suddenly. "I know those are next. Sooner or later the kidnapper's going to start bugging me. It's going to be so hard . . . hearing that repulsive voice of his again." His face showed a heartbreaking resignation Abby had never seen before. His shoulders drooped.

"Maybe he won't call you this time?"

"I wouldn't mind that, though anything at all that could tip his hand would help us." Frank got up and refilled their coffee cups. "His voice was always inhuman, cold, as he'd described taking his victims . . . as if they weren't human beings. Merely objects he'd disposed of. It was like talking to a machine. Made me sick.

"I used to have this dream that the victims weren't dead. That he didn't kill them. They were all alive somewhere imprisoned and if I could just *say the right words, do the right thing,* he'd let them go free. As if it were all some cruel game and the kidnapper knew the rules and I didn't. I hadn't had that dream in years until last night after I brought you and Myrtle here."

He looked at her with troubled eyes. "I could have been having nightmares about you."

Abby laid a hand over Frank's. "I'm okay, Frank. I'm here. I'm alive. He didn't get me or Myrtle." She responded with a brave smile. "That's something. Means he's not infallible. If he messed up twice, possibly he will again."

"And I have to be there next time when he does. Because him being here—terrorizing my town—is my fault."

"Listen," Abby spoke softly, "you're not to blame for this. This maniac would be taking people somewhere else with or without the revenge motive and the tie to you."

"Yeah, I wish he were taking people from someplace

else . . . like Mars. But who he's taking is strictly personal, Abby. He's paying *me* back. For trying to catch him. Thwarting him. Shooting him. I must have really hurt him for him to come after me after all these years."

She could feel Frank's frustration hanging over their heads. After what she'd gone through the night before it was more gloom than she could handle. She wanted things to be normal for a while, even if they weren't.

"Frank, did I tell you that you make the best pancakes I've ever eaten?"

"Better than Stella's?" He threw her a teasing grin as if he didn't believe a word; the old Frank was back.

"Yes, better than Stella's. You're so good you could get a job there as their next cook."

"Thanks, I'll keep that in mind if I ever need to make some quick money.

"Oh, by the way, I rang up Luke at the hardware store and he's going to fix your windows by the end of today. Give you that triple-paned glass that's harder to break and won't charge you except for materials. Gonna put some stronger locks on the doors, too, without charge. He's relieved to hear you and Myrtle are okay. He sends his regards."

The windows were being fixed which was one less thing for Abby to fret about. Left her room to fret about the bigger things like almost being abducted and disappearing forever. "Thanks Frank. I'll phone Luke after breakfast and thank him myself."

Two hours later Sam Cato arrived. Over the years she'd heard about Sam from Frank, and all about their Chicago escapades, yet had never met him. About as tall as her, in his forties, Sam was skinny with short black hair and almond shaped eyes that hinted at some Japanese blood. Dressed in a suit and tie, a delicate gold watch on his wrist, he couldn't have been more different from Frank and his straggly hair, blue jeans, and T-shirts.

But Sam was a working cop, Frank wasn't. Married twenty years to Jenny, his childhood sweetheart, Sam had three kids he adored. His sixteen-year-old daughter Michelle was a musical prodigy and on her way to becoming a concert pianist. His older boy Alex, twelve, had a genius IQ and wanted to be a physicist. His youngest child, seven, was named after Frank and, as his father, was nuts about baseball.

Frank introduced Sam and Abby liked him immediately. The man had a winning smile, laughing eyes, and a sharp wit. Traits he hid the moment he became serious.

Myrtle wandered down for a snack and after she'd met Sam wandered into the living room and plopped in front of the television to watch court dramas. The events of the day before had finally caught up with her and she was pooped, she said.

"So you're going to be my bodyguard?" Abby queried Sam.

"One of them. I'll also be helping Frank, coordinating with the police here and in Chicago, following up on leads. Chicago wants this guy as much as Frank does. I never forgot what he did ten years ago, either. I thought he was dead, too. Believe me, this has been a shock." He sent a knowing look Frank's way.

Abby could tell by the sharpness in Sam's eyes and the intuitive questions he posed about the case so far that he was a capable detective. And she could tell that Frank was pleased Sam was there. Frank needed a friend and seemed more at ease since Sam had arrived.

After bringing Sam up to speed, Frank left the cabin and drove into town to see the sheriff, who'd called him to come in for a reason Abby couldn't pry out of him. Sam Cato would stay behind, guard them, and check in with Chicago on the status of the investigation.

Last night's storm had morphed into a crisp sunny day. The breezes rustled in the leaves around Frank's cabin and misty horse clouds galloped across the sky. Too beautiful a day to stay inside. Myrtle was glued to *Judge Mathis* on television so Sam and Abby went out on the front porch to sit in the rockers, coffee cups in hands.

Abby wanted to know more about Frank's other life in the

big city and Sam obliged her. They ended up discussing many things, including Frank's dead wife, Jolene.

"Jolene was Frank's treasure. After her death in that car accident he wasn't the same. Loved his boy, Kyle, and stayed in the city until the kid graduated from high school. That was the only reason he stayed. Frank's a country boy through and through; never liked the big city. Too big. Too noisy.

"So when Kyle went off to medical school, I wasn't surprised when Frank took early retirement and moved back here. He loves this town and used to tell me stories of his having grown up here, about his friends, and how close the people are to one another. A real Mayberry, he called it and says it hasn't changed much. And this place he's built is lovely, isn't it? Peaceful and serene."

Abby nodded as the cop's gaze admiringly took in the porch and the yard beyond.

"Real shame a criminal's trying to ruin all this for him."

He questioned Abby about the abduction attempt the night before and she recalled what she could. She was sure Frank had told him all about it, but Sam wanted to hear it from her.

"Didn't see his face, I'm sorry. Just a big fuzzy blob along with the terror before I passed out."

Sam asked her a couple more things about the attack and then, at her urging, told her stories of when he and Frank were working together. Abby nearly forgot why she was staying at Frank's. She found herself laughing at Sam's jokes and his memories of a younger Frank.

A person could only be scared for so long and Abby ached for life to be simple again. She wanted to laugh and forget she was in danger, and easily slipped back into normalcy.

She and Sam chatted like old friends as they watched the day from the porch.

When Frank drove up and settled his lanky body in the rocker beside Abby, she put her good mood away. His somber face reminded her of why she and Myrtle were there.

"Drove by your house, Abby," he said. "Luke's almost done. Says hi. Says he'll wait for the money. No problem."

"I called and found out my home insurance will cover everything," Abby interjected.

"That's good. I figured it would. Luke said his wife wanted to bring over a casserole for you, but I said you and Myrtle were staying here for a while. I got it covered. I don't want to offer any more targets to our kidnapper. I'm not sure he has my cabin staked out." Frank released a long sigh and shifted his frame in the chair. "Luke didn't stay long after I explained what had happened last night. He's worried. Got five kids of his own and he's keeping them all inside except for school. His wife is taking them and picking them up every day."

Abby didn't say anything. She knew how desperately Frank wanted to catch the kidnapper and push him off a mountain. He'd told her so the night before. He hated being afraid all the time for the people he cared about. It wasn't the way he wanted to live. He hated the kidnapper for making it so.

That evening Abby fried chicken and Frank made the potatoes and fresh garden salad. Sam set the table and whipped up his specialty, butterscotch pudding with whipped cream, for dessert. Myrtle, fickle old woman that she was, allowed them to wait on her and was delighted with the gathering. The night before she'd almost had to be dragged to Frank's cabin, but now had decided she liked it. Liked staying in a clean, lovely room and being fussed over. She'd begun to look on her stay as an extended holiday and tonight was a party.

After supper Frank released the dogs as protection from intruders and everyone lounged on the porch and debated what they'd do next. But they didn't talk about how long Abby and Myrtle would stay or about the botched abduction. Abby thought it was because Frank was afraid to admit how close she'd come to being taken.

The moon wasn't out and without a porch light nothing broke the darkness around them. Frank had switched off some of the lights in the living room so the light was faint. No sense in broadcasting too loudly their being there to anyone more than they had to. Though he was sure the dogs would let them know if someone came onto the property, he was determined not to be a prisoner in his own home.

Myrtle, who'd insisted on going outside with all of them, was sleeping and snoring in the chair next to Abby, wrapped in one of Abby's heavy sweaters.

Snowball was curled up in Abby's lap, asleep. Frank and Sam would rather have been working with the authorities trying to catch the kidnapper, but Frank thought she and Myrtle were still in danger and wasn't letting them out of his sight.

"We can't assume anything," Frank pointed out, keeping his voice low so it wouldn't carry on through the air. "The kidnapper is unpredictable."

"Before I left the city," Sam spoke softly, "I caught the newscast with the police sketch Myrtle gave them of the suspect. The media hounds have the scent and they've got their teeth into this and I don't think they'll let go. We're getting more coverage every day. It should help. They've even revived the name I gave him a decade ago: The Mud People Killer."

Frank's voice was a contemptuous whisper. "From now on reporters will be swarming all over us, snapping pictures and wanting titillating details of what happened last night to the ladies. It'll be just like ten years ago in Chicago. We'll be in the spotlight. No privacy. And this creep thrives on publicity. It'll just egg him on."

"Much as you despise the media, Frank," Sam objected back in another whisper, "getting the word out will help track him down. It'll generate leads."

Later in the day Sam had changed into slacks and a sweater. A cigarette hung from his lips and smoke swirled around him. A habit, unlike Frank, he'd been unable to break.

"Those cigarettes will kill you before any criminal will," Frank nagged his friend.

"You sound like my wife. I've been trying to quit these disgusting things for years. Can't. I'm hooked. I've stopped so many times and then a nasty case comes along and I go right back to them. In my defense, this is the first pack I've smoked in two years," Sam shrugged. "Sorry."

Frank backtracked to the previous conversation. "As I see it, good thing is that for the first time we have a composite of our kidnapper. If it is our kidnapper and I believe it is. First time anyone's seen him and is still around to talk about it. Hope it helps. Maybe someone who knows him or has seen him will step forward and say something. It's got to help. Can't hurt. 'Cause right now, other than that, we have nothing."

Abby didn't have much faith in Myrtle's composite, but she didn't have the heart to tell Frank and Sam that.

As the two men made plans in low tones, Abby stared out into the night, thinking. *Is the kidnapper out there in the town now or is he closer? What's he done with those people he took? Are they still alive?* She was quivering beneath her jacket and felt like weeping, but tears wouldn't come. Frank's arm went around her shoulders and he squeezed gently as if he knew what she was thinking.

He was such a good man, she thought. Such a good man.

"We're going to catch him, Abby," Frank promised. "He's going to slip up and we'll be there to put the cuffs on. Now go on and get some sleep and Sam and I will bring Myrtle along behind you." Next to them, Myrtle was talking in her sleep, fending off a dream attacker.

Snowball jumped from Abby's lap and scurried off the porch into the night shadows. Frank would let her in when he went up to bed and she'd be cuddled on Abby's pillow by the time Abby fell asleep. Snowball learned quickly. Frank's house was home for now.

Abby said her good-nights to Frank and Sam and went up to bed, but didn't sleep well. She dreamed of Myrtle and those ghosts that Myrtle said prowled around at night in the dark. They all seemed to be in her nightmares—giants without faces who limped and stole people. The panic was so real it woke her up. She snuggled with Snowball and worried about the missing people and what tomorrow would bring.

She wanted things to go back to normal, but she knew that wasn't going to happen anytime soon. She fell back asleep and dreamed of Joel. Of when they'd been young and the future was but a lovely dream to come. They were building their dream house and Abby was so happy.

When she awoke again she didn't know what was real, the dream she'd left or the dream she'd awakened into.

Both made her sad.

Chapter Eleven

It was early, not yet seven A.M., and the sidewalks and streets were empty. When he'd slowly driven through town he'd seen her. Since he'd missed the woman in the yellow house, gotten a beating to boot—a bump on the back of his head and a swollen knee—his voices had continued to plague him because he'd fumbled taking the next person. They wouldn't leave him alone, but wouldn't tell him how to fix things, either, so he thought that if he found another one to take—on his own—they'd leave him alone.

He went out looking for someone else.

And there she was . . . number three. Walking down the empty street alone. He could take her and get back on schedule. He'd act on his own and make the voices proud of him. Make them stop harassing him. That's what he'd do.

He was taking a risk coming out in the open like this in the daylight, but the opportunity was there. All he had to do was drive up, roll down the window, gesture to her, slip out of the car and take her. It would be easy.

Slowing his car enough to match the woman's pace, he pulled up beside her.

"I'm lost. Can you tell me where Lauren Street is?" he asked her, keeping most of his face and head in the shadows of the car interior. His head and leg didn't hurt as much as those bullets had all those years ago, but the pain was still a dull thudding ache.

The woman hesitated and he caught the flicker of uneasiness in her trusting eyes. Eyes the same shade of blue as his mother's eyes had been. Cold, selfish blue.

He tried not to be distracted by the man in the backseat, which was hard to do because the man wouldn't stop talking nonsense to him . . . and he stank. Must be his ratty clothes. They were tattered and filthy and caked in mud. The man had eyes like a dead mouse. Looked like someone he'd once taken and that thought nagged at him along with the worry about what the mud the man was leaving on his backseat.

Mustn't pay the bum any attention. Mustn't listen to the dribble coming out of its slack mouth. Mustn't. Like the others sent to torment him, he mustn't pay them any attention. They were nothing but ghosts.

The man driving the car laughed and made a joke. "I'm always getting lost," he said to the woman out in the sunlight, ignoring the thing in the rear seat. "I could get lost in a parking lot. My mom says I have as much sense of direction as a cow." The joke broke the ice and the woman warmed up to him the minute he made her laugh. "Lauren Street—left or right?"

The woman giggled.

It worked. She moved toward the car and leaned down to peer in. He moved back a scoot so she couldn't see his face clearly. Wouldn't do if that happened. She began to explain how to get to Lauren Street, the cloth clutched in his left hand, he was ready to leap from the car and grab her, pull her in.

He was pretending not to understand, had the map lying on the seat beside him to cover the hand holding the cloth, and also so she could show him exactly where he had to go. He started opening the car door when the voices hissed at him not to take her. *Number three has gotten away. This creature with eyes like your mother's can't be number three. You have to take the one in the yellow house. Yellow's the right color, not blue.*

He was stunned for a heartbeat. Didn't know what to do. Squinting at the woman, he tried to recollect the last thing she'd said but couldn't. Everything had fled from his mind. She was still talking, but her face now registered alarm as she backed away from the car.

He'd missed his chance.

Mumbling something—a thank you—he told her he'd find it on his own or something like that. It helped to be polite, too, if a person didn't want to be suspicious. They were apt to think a person was trustworthy if one kept their tone mild and courteous.

He drove off as quickly as he could, furious at his voices for not allowing him to do what he'd wanted. She could have been—should have been—number three. Now he was behind schedule and his mother would be so piqued at him for being late. She never tolerated tardiness, either.

Not knowing what to do next, he drove around aimlessly muttering to himself, ignoring the dirty man in the backseat, his thoughts flying every which way until he found himself at the motel.

The man stuck to him like a burr and limped behind him into his room. He yelled at him and, with an eerie smirk, he slunk away into the shadows he'd come from.

He needed to rest and think. Lying down on the lumpy bed in the dim room he took pleasure in the silence. The voices left him alone. There was only the noise from the TV in the adjoining room. Sleep came and wasted the rest of the day. When he awoke, the sun was lowering into the horizon and the filthy man had returned, glaring at him with vacant eyes from a chair in a gloomy corner.

He threw a shoe at the shadow but missed it and hit the wall instead.

He left the room and drove around to buy a bag of hamburgers and a soda from a fast food place, then continued to the woods where he liked to be, roaming through the swamp that hid deep between the trees. There were minefields of deep chasms in the earth, quicksand and water thick with mud. He had to be careful where he walked.

He stayed until the sun began to dip below the tree line, taking its light from the earth. Then he left. In the darkness he'd never find his way out and he couldn't stay the night.

Night was when the mud people spied on him from behind the trees and from the shadows. He'd been free of them for years . . . until the voices had returned. And so had the mud people. Dripping wet or covered in grime, they stalked him wherever he went these days. The night woods were the worst. They were everywhere.

He had to run to get away.

He didn't know who these people were. They never spoke, only stared and pointed at him. His voices refused to speak of them, pretending they didn't exist. But he knew they did.

Sometimes, like the bum, the mud people rode with him in the car or walked through his motel room. If he made a big enough racket they'd sometimes leave. He avoided the thought that some of them sometimes looked like people he'd met or might have known long ago, or else might know in the future, which was ridiculous because he didn't know any people besides his mother, except the ones he'd taken. Never really had friends. Didn't have friends now. His voices had always kept him from having friends. They wouldn't allow it.

He was so lonely sometimes.

After he left the woods he drove past the yellow house. All the lights were off and it looked empty.

She was over at that cop's house hiding from him. That's where she was, he knew it. What was he going to do about that?

Go get her? Not tonight. Too soon. They'd be waiting for him. Expecting him to try to take her again.

You have to wait, his voices badgered him as he drove

through the night. *Be patient. Abigail Sutton's number three and you have to get her.*

No way out of it. Right now he was going back to his room to write his enemy—the cop—another letter. Going to tell him he'd won this time. That the woman in the yellow house had gotten away and he was moving on to his next one.

He chuckled. They would be lies, of course, to throw the cop and the woman off. Now that was a smart idea. They'd let their guard down and he'd grab the woman.

He was thinking of sending a letter to the newspapers as well. He'd seen the sketch on the television that was supposed to be him. He found it funny—it didn't look anything like him.

Looked more like this guy that used to live next door to him or someone he once met in the street coming home from the store. His mother always needed something or other from the store. Sometimes she'd send him three times a day when he wasn't sitting in some doctor's office waiting for her. His mother was a hypochondriac. Always sick or thinking she was.

Anyhow, he'd never tell the cops the drawing didn't look like him. In fact, he'd pretend that it did. Pretend he was scared that they were closing in on him. Yeah, that's what he'd do.

When he was done with the letters he'd treat himself to a late movie over in Chalmers. An adventure or an animal story because those were the kinds of movies he liked.

His motel room was overcrowded with gawking, mud-covered beings. The first thing he had to do was chase them out. He was really getting tired of them following him everywhere. Wished he could find some way to get rid of them, but they were hanging around waiting for number three.

Sometimes they came with him when he took someone new and hovered around to glare at him with their creepy eyes. Never spoke. Never let him know what they wanted.

All he knew was that lately the mud people had grown in number and were pestering him even more.

He wished they'd leave him alone. Wished the voices would go away, too. He was sick of all of them.

What had he ever done to deserve this?

Chapter Twelve

It was weird being at Frank's. But Abby liked living in a rustic cabin out in the woods, being treated like a queen, and served tasty meals. Who wouldn't? It was like she was staying at a fancy bed and breakfast at no charge.

Frank went overboard cooking and baking for them and was a gracious host. If she hadn't been there for the reason she was, she'd be having a fine time.

"I feel as if I'm in heaven and I've decided to adopt Frank. Could stay here forever," Myrtle said after the first day, gleefully rubbing her wrinkled hands together. And to think, at first the old woman hadn't wanted to come.

Frank had laughed, yet Abby got the impression he wouldn't have minded if they'd stayed indefinitely. And aside from being worried sick over the two missing people and what to do next, Frank was relieved that he could keep both of them close by. He said it gave him peace of mind.

"Halloween's only a week and a half away and the town's canceling festivities because that maniac is out there somewhere taking people. Everyone's scared to death. Won't let their kids out to play or go anywhere alone. Main Street is empty by dark," Martha told Abby on the phone, "and Stella's diner has been closing every night at six because her business is down so much."

The next evening, Frank's guests lingered on the porch munching on warm homemade brownies. His dogs were running around and through the yard. He'd received another letter from the killer that morning, tossed onto his porch, and it had thrown him into a rage. It'd taken Abby a while to calm Frank down. "How in the world did he get anywhere near the house without one of us seeing or hearing him?"

The note had mentioned Abby and, oddly enough, said she'd nothing more to worry about. The kidnapper was going on to his next victim. She was too hard to get at now because she was at Frank's cabin. She was too protected.

Frank didn't believe a word of it. Abby wanted to in the worst way. It would make things so much easier if she could resume her life knowing she was safe from abduction. Frank and she talked about it and in the end she'd listened to his advice and agreed to stay under his protection temporarily. She couldn't promise how long. She needed to make a living and had a life. At least she had one before the attempted kidnapping. She couldn't hide away forever. Even if they never caught the guy, what would she do? Hide at Frank's forever?

I haven't forgotten you, Frank, and what you did to me, the killer had written. *Composite looks a lot like me, but you and the police are never going to catch me. I'm smarter than you. Go ahead and try.*

The letter really upset Frank.

"Like old times," he groused. "He takes people, taunts me and I chase. He plays this sadistic game with everyone. Ridicules me in his letters. I wound him and he tries to hurt me any way he can. Doesn't care how. Coming after you is one way. But how did he know I cared so much about you?" Frank wanted to know.

"Maybe he doesn't know that you do. Maybe I was just someone he saw you with?"

"Maybe."

There were no leads on Shelly or Emil's disappearance and the investigation was at a standstill. Everything that needed to be done was being done. All the clues and leads were being followed up. The FBI and local authorities had grilled Abby and Myrtle on what had happened to them. Wouldn't be long now, they said. Abby hoped they weren't lying though Frank was sure they were. The police and the FBI, as usual, were saving face. Yet so far, with all their manpower and technology, the FBI seemed to have no more of an idea about how to catch the kidnapper than Frank and Sam did.

The night skies were clear and the stars were sparkling like glitter. A chilly night but they had coats on as the four of them ate brownies and kept most of their troubled thoughts to themselves.

Sam was an avid card player and the four of them had been inside playing pinochle most of the evening. Abby had lousy luck at cards and hadn't won one hand.

They'd been outside only a short while when Martha drove up.

"No one followed you here, did they?" Frank asked right away.

"Not that I know of. Didn't see anyone. Drove all the way over with my lights off."

"You're kidding?" Frank's voice was mildly amused.

"Yes . . . I'm kidding," she teased back as she settled on the top step of the porch. "You're having a party and didn't invite me?" She was bundled up in pants and a heavy jacket and shivered in the cool air. Abby couldn't see her face.

"Yeah, some party," Abby remarked sarcastically. "Sitting out here in the dark. We're all incognito. Hiding out like criminals at Frank's place. Can't go anywhere, can't do anything. Scared of unknown noises and shadows. We've been having a ball. Want to play pinochle? I'm getting really good at it. I'll warn you, though, Sam Cato here will win. He always wins. Should have been a professional gambler instead of a cop."

"No, thanks," Martha answered. "Checkers is my game. I usually take the red."

Then she got serious. "Abby, you scared me with your close call the other night. I had to come over and make sure you were really okay. Frank told me to wait a day to give you a chance to recuperate or I would have been by yesterday."

"I'm fine, Martha. I'm alive. Thanks to Myrtle. She knocked the stuffing out of the guy." Abby gave Martha the encapsulated story. She was astounded they'd gotten away, but grateful they had.

"You shouldn't be out alone, Martha," Frank said. "Especially after dark. Not with the kidnapper out there. Abby and Myrtle were extremely lucky the other night. You might not be so lucky. I'm telling everyone to stay away from here. I should have called you today to say just that. Can't believe I forgot." He told her about the letter he'd received that morning.

"I'm not afraid." Martha opened her purse and produced a small caliber handgun that shone in the faint light seeping through the cabin windows. "And yes, Frank, I have a permit to carry it. It's legal."

"I won't ask you how you got that permit," he bantered back. "I believe you. But having a gun and using a gun are two different things. Are you prepared to shoot someone if you're attacked? Or what if he surprises you and you can't get to the gun quickly enough?"

Martha's voice was firm. "He won't surprise me. I'm vigilant. Keep my eyes wide open all the time," she clucked at Frank and zeroed in on Sam. "And, Frank, who is this handsome man sharing the porch with you?" As if she could see him in the feeble light.

"This handsome man is Sam Cato, who used to work with me in Chicago. Remember? My old partner? I've talked about him enough. Sorry, Martha, he's happily married to a lovely woman named Jenny and they have three gifted kids."

"Okay. I get the message. He's unavailable. But, no matter, I'm happy with Ryan. Nice to finally meet you, Sam." She reached up and shook Sam's hand. "Frank has spoken often of you and the old days. The way he puts it you were Watson and he was Holmes. So you're down here to help us, huh?"

"Backup," Sam replied dryly.

"Any help is appreciated." Martha cocked her head toward Frank. "They think your boy approached another potential victim about seven in the morning. Connie Tucker. He approached her in a car. For some reason, she got nervous—he looked and acted squirrelly—and she backed away. Slipped into the bakery where she works and he drove off. She reported the incident to the police who, in turn, told Samantha at the newspaper, who in turn gossiped it to me. The funny thing is the police aren't sure it's the same guy who attacked Myrtle . . . the description Connie gave was very different than Myrtle's."

Abby knew she should say something. Myrtle was dozing in a chair so she leaned over and quietly confessed to Frank the old woman's problem eyesight and her opinion that the composite Myrtle had given the police earlier that week might not be accurate.

"I'll go have a word about it with the sheriff tomorrow." Frank sighed, unhappy at the revelation. "Connie say what kind of car he was driving?"

"A big car, that's all she said. Connie doesn't know a Ford from a tractor."

"What color?"

"Who knows? Dark she thinks," Martha replied. "Connie's totally color blind."

"Great. How lucky can we get? I just hope they obtain a more accurate composite of the man from Miss Tucker. I'd be interested in seeing what she comes up with."

Wouldn't they all. The kidnapper's shadow was a shroud that had fallen across their evening, not that it had left them for long the last few weeks. They sat there in silence with their own morose thoughts as the crickets sang behind them.

"Well, enough of this gloom and doom," Martha piped up. "On another subject. I've decided to fly in the face of fear and throw a huge Halloween shindig on Saturday. One of the reasons I came by was to invite all of you and anybody else you want to bring. Rug rats included. Most of the celebrations in town, even the parade, have been cancelled. Nobody wants to go out after dusk without a bodyguard.

"So I'm giving a costume party no matter what the circumstances. I'll lock my place up like a fortress if it'll make you feel safer. Lock the front and back gate and turn on the electric fence." Martha was big on security systems.

"But as much as I love costumes . . . *no masks* this year, unless they're drawn on. If we know everyone then the kidnapper can't slip in." She scooted up a step and grabbed one of the brownies off the plate. "Can I count on you all to attend? Sam, too, if you're still here."

Sam responded first. "I haven't been to a Halloween party since I was in college. Free food and treats. Good company. Maybe we can get a card game going. Count me in."

Frank and Abby exchanged looks. "Don't see how a party can do any harm," he shrugged. "Might do some good. We all need a break. Martha, you want us to bring food?" Usually everyone made something special and the result was a smorgasbord of treats. Though with Martha there was never any sense in it. She made mounds of food, liked to cook as much as Frank, or she brought in catered delicacies. To Martha money was for spending.

"Sure, you can bring food if you want, but you don't need to. I'll provide the main meal, drinks, Halloween treats, and ambience. I'm turning the manor into a haunted castle. Gonna have hanging skeletons, vampires in coffins, lights, and spooky sound effects. Saw it in a magazine. It's gonna knock your socks off."

"Sounds like fun. Who else is invited?" Abby wanted to know.

"The whole town. Anyone who wants to show up, except that creepy kidnapper, of course." No one laughed and Martha went on chatting about the get-together.

As Martha gushed on about her party the blackness moved and swirled at the end of the yard. Abby's imagination turned the pulsating patterns into objects and a skulking person. Was the kidnapper out there now watching and waiting with twitching fingers to take one of them?

She remembered an old movie she'd seen when she'd been a child. *Ten Little Indians*, or something like that. About ten people holed up in a house who were being slowly picked off and killed, one by one. And no one could stop it.

Sitting there she felt like one of those characters. Felt like she had a big target painted on her head. But she also had some hope now. . . . Maybe Frank was wrong and the kidnapper was looking for another victim, not her. She was protected and unattainable. She was safe. He wasn't out there in the bushes after all. She could hope, couldn't she?

She felt guilty for thinking such things. If victim number three wasn't her then it would be someone else. And that would be awful, too.

"By the way, Abby," Martha nudged her from her reverie. "Samantha wants you to meet her for breakfast tomorrow morning at Stella's. Wants to get your story of what happened the other night straight from the horse's mouth so she can print it on Wednesday. Front page. Breakfast her treat if you show up. Inquiring minds want to know. And it'll help to warn other people. They'll believe it if it comes from you. I'll come out and pick you up. Tag along. Play bodyguard. Safety in numbers. I'll bring my gun."

Martha glanced at Frank. "That is if your jailer will let you out."

"She can go anywhere she wants," Frank huffed, mockingly indignant. "As long as it's daylight and she has me or Sam with her. No offense to your bodyguarding prowess, Martha, but I don't trust the kidnapper. He could still be after Abby. Just trying to throw us off so we let our guards down. She needs police protection."

"I'll escort her," Sam volunteered. "You can stay with Myrtle and take care of those chores you mentioned. I've got to go into town for some personal items anyway and it'll give me a chance to scope out the place. Meet people. Ask questions. Never know, might even stumble onto some clues you missed."

"Spoken like a detective." Martha patted Sam's leg. Sam seemed surprised but didn't move. In the dark Abby thought he was smiling. No doubt Frank had told him how big a flirt Martha was. All harmless. She was devoted to Ryan. "I'll see both of you about ten tomorrow morning?" she confirmed with Abby.

"Sounds good to me." Abby glanced over at Sam, who gestured an okay. "We'll be ready. It'll be nice to get out."

"And Martha? On the way back I'd like to stop at the Brooks' place. I want to see how Rebecca and the kids are doing." Abby knew that Frank had asked the sheriff to send a patrol out past the Brooks' house as often as he could—make sure they were all okay.

"No problem. Actually, Samantha's holding money that's been sent to the newspaper for them. A lot of caring people in this town. We can drop it off at the same time. I've heard Rebecca's taken a turn for the worse. That poor woman and those poor kids. No husband, no money, and no one to fall back on. Their relatives, a couple aunts and uncles, all live out of state and none of them have much of anything themselves. I'm bringing a basket of food along for them. I feel the need to help."

"They'd like steaks, I bet." Abby tried to sway her. Bet those kids hadn't had steaks in a long time, if ever. "And a couple of large roasts."

"Ah, steaks and roasts with all the trimmings—vegetables and potatoes—right?" Martha had a generous heart and a deep purse. "Maybe desserts and goodies for the kids?"

"I'm sure they'd appreciate that, too."

The five of them huddled on the porch as the night turned colder. It *smelled* like Halloween and Abby's mind filled with nostalgic memories of childhood and the years with Joel. When she and Joel were married they went to costume parties every year, they'd decorate and celebrate the holiday as if they were children. She'd make candy apples and popcorn balls and they would both dress up and give them out to the trick-or-treaters at the door. Because out of all her memories, the Halloween ones had always been special to her. She was glad Martha was having the party. It'd been years since she'd attended one. She couldn't wait.

Martha said good-night after getting everyone's promise to come to the bash on Saturday, and drove off.

That night Abby dreamed of a past Halloween with Joel. They were on their front porch cutting out jack-o'-lanterns and putting candles in them. Her pumpkin was small and she was carving a scary face with teeth and angry eyes. Joel's pumpkin, as usual, was a huge pumpkin and a happy one with a big grin on it.

It'd been twilight on Halloween eve and there was a sprinkle of cold rain. She could hear the trick-or-treaters coming down the sidewalk their way. Could still hear them. Inside the front door was a heaping bowl of candy. She'd made caramel apples dipped in pecans, along with fancy little sandwiches and a Halloween punch with ice cream. She and Joel were hugging and kissing in between telling each other about their days.

Joel had been a carpenter and she had been working as an ad artist at the local newspaper. At that time she liked her job. Had friends and a fair boss. Those were the happy days. It wasn't until the paper changed hands and her boss left, the workload tripled, and most of her friends had moved on that it became intolerable.

They finished their pumpkins, lit them and went to put on costumes because friends were coming for a party. Abby knew she was dreaming, but she reveled in the good memories; didn't want the dream to end and woke up with tears in her eyes, the taste of caramel in her mouth, and the giggles of the Halloween children in her ears.

Abby lay in bed in a guest room at Frank's house and thought about the years after Joel and before she'd come to Spookie. She'd been so lonely and had spent so many years frozen, not really living. She couldn't go back to those lonely years and she hated that kidnapping monster who was destroying her new life there. In Spookie, she'd actually been happy. Until now.

Martha was coming by at ten so Abby had coffee with Frank and Sam in the kitchen around nine-thirty. Myrtle was upstairs sulking. She'd wanted to go into town with Abby and Martha, but Martha had made it clear the night before she hadn't been invited.

At Stella's Diner Samantha and Sam Cato were introduced. They made a joke of their names being similar, then got to business. Abby provided Samantha with an account of what happened to her and Myrtle two nights before. She convinced Samantha to slant the article toward the heroism of the old woman. The least she could do for Myrtle.

Samantha scribbled the details down as they had pancakes and sausages, said she'd go out later that day and talk to Myrtle as well, then started interrogating Sam about Chicago ten years ago and the Mud People Killer.

"Why didn't the Chicago Police Department catch him ten years ago, Sam?"

"Oh, we tried. Put every man we could on it but the guy was too clever. Always a step ahead. But as Frank put it, the real problem was knowing which missing people were *his* victims. A lot of people go missing in Chicago. It's a big city. We never knew if it was our guy until the mud doll was delivered and by then it was too late for a stakeout. Made it near impossible to get a break in the cases."

"How's it going to be different here?" Samantha wanted to know.

The cop's eyebrow shot up. "One, we've figured out more pieces of the puzzle. The perp likes to take people Frank knows. Two, this isn't Chicago. Someone goes missing here and everyone knows it. That's our prime advantage. Maybe we can get one step ahead of him this time."

"Everybody's waiting for this guy to strike again,"

Samantha told Sam, her eyes flicking to Abby and Martha. "They're living in fear. I knew Shelly and Emil and can't believe they're gone. When I go to the IGA I expect Shelly to be there. I drive by the Clark station and still look for Emil to fill my tank. I jump at noises and find myself glaring at every stranger in and around town. My fingers on my cell phone ready to call the police.

"I don't trust anyone and I despise living like this. I've run stories on the kidnappings and I'm getting calls from the bigger newspapers wanting more information. Television crews from across the country have been flooding into town since the Lanstroms went on-screen to plead for their daughter's return."

"How about the other victim's wife—Rebecca Brooks?" Sam questioned Samantha. Abby thought he was asking as many questions as the reporter but hadn't written a thing down. Must have a good memory. "Has she gone on TV, too?"

"No. They've been trying to get her on camera. She refused at first and now she's too sick. It's heart-wrenching. Not that she knows anything. She doesn't. I've spoken to her. Emil went to work last Wednesday and never came home. No one's seen him since.

"I can give you a copy of my notes from my interviews with the victims' families, Mr. Cato. Anything I can do to help. Keep you informed on what I learn from any of my sources."

"I'd appreciate that, Samantha. Frank wanted me to ask you for your notes anyway. And anything else relating to the two abductions here."

"You got it," the reporter responded.

"Abby?" Samantha asked as she ate the last biscuit in the basket, "I've had inquiries about whether you'd be interested in going on TV and telling the story of your foiled kidnapping. Myrtle, too. They've even mentioned money."

Abby put her hands up in a stop gesture. "No way am I going on TV. Might as well tie me out in the town square tonight as live bait. I don't need my fifteen minutes of fame that bad. I'm laying low and protecting my butt. Sorry."

"Knowing you, Abby, I relayed that exact message to every TV reporter who requested an interview. But that won't stop them from bugging you, you know that. How about Myrtle?"

"Well, she's a little spacey most of the time. Heaven knows what she'd do or say on television in a blinding spotlight. But you'd have to ask her in person. When you see her at Frank's, you can ask her."

"I will." Samantha nodded.

They'd been friends since the first week Abby had moved into town. Samantha was the best reporter/editor Abby had ever known and also the most human. She never put a story above a person. A rare thing. Working at newspapers so many years had given Abby first-hand knowledge of reporter types, so she should know.

Samantha handed Abby a fat white envelope. "Money for the Brooks family. A lot of money. People have been sending cash in all week since the story went out."

"We'll deliver it to them before the end of the day," Abby promised.

They ate, drank coffee, and introduced Sam Cato to everyone who wandered in. Turned out Sam liked to talk as much as Frank and soon it felt as if he were one of them. When people found out he was a detective friend of Frank's, they warmed up to him like an old friend.

In between shoving pieces of pancake into her mouth, Martha turned to Abby. "While I have you here in front of me, could I ask you about doing another painting for me?" Martha looked tired today. There were scratches on her hands and arms, proof that she'd been gardening again. It's what she did to relax, besides redecorate her house and spend money.

"I've redone my garden," she said when she saw Abby looking at her hands. "Ordered special stone benches and trellises. A new gazebo that's so breathtaking it's out of this world. I'm so happy the new landscaping will be ready for the party Saturday.

"And sitting in the garden this morning, it came to me that in its fall glory with the mums blooming, beautiful lemon yellows, warm oranges, and the greens of the leaves, it'd make a stunning picture. About three-by-four feet in size, I'm figuring." Martha moved her hands as far apart as she could. "It'd look lovely in my dining room above the fireplace.

"Do you have time to do it for me, Abby? Ask any price. It's yours. I saw the finished library mural and it looks amazing. The colors and the detail. I thought I'd better get your work while you're still unknown and fairly inexpensive. A couple more murals like that and you'll be out of my price range. What do you say?"

Abby blushed, she was flattered. "Of course I'll do it. I love painting landscapes, woods and gardens, you know that. And I'm in between work. Good timing." It also meant she wouldn't have to go out looking for more work and she'd have money for next month's bills. Martha was her best customer. She'd done two other commissions for her already and Martha paid on time and her checks never bounced.

"Excellent. Come early on Friday and we'll take photos from any viewpoint you like . . . and then you can help me get ready for the party."

Abby agreed. Martha continued inviting everybody she saw to her party and for a short time, thinking about her new commission and Saturday's party, Abby nearly forgot about the bad stuff.

Then the explosion came, rattling the glass in the diner and startling everyone.

"What the heck was that?" Stella's red lips expressed the question on everyone's mind. She hurried to the door and stuck her head out. Coming back to their table she said, "Smoke's coming down the street past the bookstore. Something's on fire, I reckon. Something big."

Samantha flew from her chair, taking her camera, which

was always strapped over her shoulder along with her purse, and ran out the door. Being nosy, the rest of them followed and didn't have far to go.

Five doors down, set off by itself and circled in trees, a house was burning. Smoke hid most of it and trailed into the sky, billows of angry gray contrasting against the bright blue sky. The pungent odor of burning wood filled the streets.

"Selena Tucker's house blew up." Abby heard someone say as they edged as close as they could to the raging fireball. Flames licked at the structure and a series of smaller explosions kept the crowd far enough away. The police and a fire truck stuffed with volunteer firefighters arrived on the scene and herded the crowd farther back, saying there might be more fireworks. With mouths open and eyes glued to the spectacle everyone complied.

Sam went off to chat with the sheriff, never completely letting Abby out of sight. When he returned he told her, "Sheriff claims it was either a gas pipe explosion or someone blew up the house on purpose. Said he was no expert, but that was his take on it. When the firemen and arson investigators are done we'll know more."

"My bet would be on the second option— *on purpose*," Abby told Sam. "That was Selena Tucker's house. Selena is Connie Tucker's mother. Connie is the woman who gave the police the composite of our possible kidnapper. She and her mother, Selena, both live here. Or did. Was anyone inside at the time of the fire?"

"They don't know that yet, either." Sam was studying the flames when he wasn't observing the crowd around them. Abby didn't need to make the association between the woman who lived there with her mother, the burning house, and the kidnapper. Sam was a smart cop and he'd worked it out, too.

Martha exchanged words with one of Selena's neighbors and Samantha took photographs for the next issue of the *Journal*.

And Abby was feeling worse than an hour ago when she'd

been sitting in Stella's eating pancakes. The explosion wasn't an accident. She looked around. The kidnapper could be hiding behind a tree or a house gawking at them now. Made her feel sick.

"If you're ready, Abby, let's get back to Frank's. He'll want to know about the explosion. Get a look at the scene while the clues are still fresh."

"I'm ready." Firemen were scurrying around and everywhere there was smoldering debris and water puddles. It was a mess. "But, remember, Martha and I have to make a stop along the way at Rebecca Brooks' house. Martha has food and I have the money collected by the newspaper. They need both."

"We can do that." Sam's eyes reflected the dying flames. The fire had devastated the dull yellow-framed building and it was collapsing. The firefighters had given up and were standing around to witness its death throes. If anyone was inside, they had become cinders like the house. Abby was relieved to leave the scene before anyone was brought out of it.

Abby, Sam and Martha said good-bye to Samantha, who was busy talking to the firemen anyway, and drove out to the Brooks' place.

Lying in her bed, her skin pale and her breathing labored, Rebecca Brooks appeared weaker than the last time Abby had seen her. Her husband's continued absence and the hardship of trying to care for seven kids without money was making her condition worse.

Abby brooded that any woman could be a Rebecca under the right unfortunate circumstances. Sick, penniless, and now husbandless. There but for the grace of God goes anyone. Abby, husbandless herself, felt sorry for the woman and wanted to help.

Martha and Sam lugged in two large baskets of supplies stuffed with wrapped meat—steaks, roasts, hamburger, and more—as well as canned goods, fresh fruit, and cake. Had to be a couple hundred dollars' worth of groceries and Abby was awed by Martha's generosity.

They showed the food to Rebecca and gave her the newspaper money. She actually cried she was so grateful. "This will help so much. I appreciate it, Martha."

And to Abby, "Thank you, too. Thank Samantha and ask her to express my gratitude in the paper to the people who contributed. People have been very kind since Emil . . . disappeared. Church people, too. Don't know what I would have done without you all. Bringing us food and money to live. Caring for the children. I'll never be able to repay everyone."

"You don't have to," Abby stated. "The whole town is behind me when I say, if you need anything, don't hesitate to ask. Everyone wants to help. And you can call me anytime at Frank's. Even if you just need to talk, Rebecca. Please."

"I will," Rebecca assured her with a brave smile. Abby could tell she was in pain and wished there were something more she could do for her. If she'd been a nurse, perhaps, but she wasn't. She could help in other ways.

Abby, Sam, and Martha prepared supper for the kids and made up a tray for Rebecca in her room. Grilled steaks, baked potatoes, and canned green beans. Each child had as much steak as they wanted. Chocolate cake and milk for dessert. It was good to see them smiling as they spooned in the food, though the kids were skinnier than the first time Abby had visited and their eyes more haunted. They missed their father. No amount of food or kindness would change that.

After supper, Laura showed Abby new pictures that she'd drawn and Sam seemed to have formed a bond with Nicholas. The kids hated to see them leave.

The three adults returned to Frank's to find the house empty. No Frank. No Myrtle. Before they could show their surprise, Frank burst through the front door right behind them.

"*Myrtle's gone!* Don't know where she went. I left her alone for just a little while. Got a call about that house explosion and had to have a look for myself.

"I *told* her to stay in the house and I locked all the doors. Wasn't gone long. I was outside searching the area around the house when you guys drove up.

"There doesn't seem to be any sign of forced entry. Or any sign of Myrtle. She's not around here *anywhere*." Frank was frantic. Sweating, though it was fifty degrees outside. "That old lady is a royal pain. When I get a hold of her—"

"Do you think she's been taken?" Martha was peeking out the window. No matter how she complained about Myrtle, Abby knew Martha would feel bad if the old woman disappeared under suspicious circumstances. Underneath it all Martha had a soft heart and wouldn't wish harm on anyone. Except the kidnapper.

"Not sure," Frank's voice cracked. "How would he have gotten into the house with all the doors and windows locked? Nothing's broken or has been tampered with that I can see—unless she let him in. No . . . she's not that daffy."

Abby thought about Myrtle's bad eyesight, her stubbornness, and it made her head hurt. Would the old lady have let a stranger in under these circumstances? No telling. He could have fooled her. Pretended to be someone else. A cop or a cable guy. Anyone. Myrtle was gullible.

"Or—" Frank continued, obviously unsettled. "She went home. On her own. She was complaining all morning again about being trapped here like a bug under a bowl. She's so fickle. One minute liking being waited on and the next indignant about it. Said she had bills to pay, animals to feed and floors to clean. Junk—er, treasures—to collect. She could take care of herself, she said. I let it go in one ear and out the other. I should have paid more attention."

"And maybe she went in one door and out the other?" Abby chimed in, trying to make a joke. No one laughed.

"Let's check her trailer." Martha was already out the door, Frank behind her and Abby behind Frank.

Sam proclaimed he'd wait until they found out if Myrtle went home or not before calling in the hounds and he'd stay behind in case Myrtle showed up back at the cabin. "While I'm waiting I'll make a pot of stew so you'll all have something hot to eat when you get home."

"He loves to cook, what can I say," Frank quipped as they

climbed in his truck. "When we get back he'll have the meal on the table. Sam makes the best homemade biscuits. As good as Stella's." He focused on food because he was concerned about Myrtle.

If they didn't find her at the trailer or in between, they had a problem on their hands.

"You think the house explosion was a distraction so the kidnapper could go after Myrtle again?" Abby asked Frank in the truck.

"Could have been. Among other things. We don't know yet if she was taken or merely ran off," he reminded her.

No one was at the trailer.

They searched the woods around it and knocked on the door until their knuckles were bruised. No answer. No Myrtle. Frank suggested they stop by a few other places. They drove by the diner, the grocery store, the bank, Myrtle's sister's house, and any other place they could think of looking for her. No Myrtle. They searched until the sun went down.

Back at Frank's, he alerted the sheriff and put in a missing person's report. He asked Sam to hold off calling the FBI for a while longer.

Then they all helped Sam serve supper and sat around eating stew and biscuits with long faces. Even Martha, who'd been invited to stay, had little to say.

Abby knew she was feeling guilty about not letting Myrtle come with them that morning. She had wanted to. Frank blamed himself for leaving Myrtle alone. With every hour since they'd discovered her missing their mood had grown darker.

Abby worried too, and didn't have much to say either. The meal was a silent one.

Later, as they sat on the porch after supper, Frank was the first one to break the silence. "You know they found two bodies in that house explosion. Sheriff informed me."

It was warmer tonight than the last and the moon was a crescent of glowing ivory with far-reaching fingers of faint light. The shadows whispered secrets along the edge of the yard but they wouldn't tell her what had happened to Myrtle. Abby could see Frank's face in the moonlight. Martha had gone home and Sam was inside talking to his wife on the phone. She could hear his deep voice through the open door behind her.

"They were Selena and Connie Tucker's bodies. Connie's the one who gave the police the last composite of the kidnapper. The firemen suspect the explosion was arson. It takes special knowledge and training to blow up a house like that. I think our guy did it. Abby, the kidnapper's not following his old MO. This fire . . . these killings aren't his style. He's evolving."

"You're saying he killed those two women because Connie saw his face." Abby told Frank what he already knew. "You think he took Myrtle for the same reason? Cause he thinks she could identify him?"

"It's possible. But her description was different than Connie's. One of them is right and the other's not. Unless Myrtle's composite was the real thing, I can't believe it would serve him any purpose to get rid of the old lady. And if so, why did he burn the Tuckers' house down? Not that he needs a reason to do anything he does. Never has before."

"Get rid of *what* old lady?" A familiar scratchy voice came out of the darkness beyond the porch and Myrtle, pulling her wooden wagon, trundled up to them.

Abby was so happy to see her she jumped off the porch and ran over to hug the old woman. So did Frank. It was a Kodak moment.

Frank yelled for Sam and he came running out. "Myrtle, where the hell were you? Why didn't you tell someone you were leaving? We tore the town apart looking for you. We thought the kidnapper got ya."

Sheepishly, she answered, "I know. Stella at the diner told me. But I'm fine, as you can see. He didn't get me like he did Connie and her ma. I never thought you'd all be so worried. I had to stop by the trailer and take care of some things.

Birds had to be fed. Got some more clothes. I didn't stay there long, though. I left you a note, Frank."

Myrtle squatted on a porch chair, having left the wagon at the bottom of the steps. Even in the moonlight Abby could see she was filthy. Covered head to toe in dirt and grass. "Said I'd be back later. Always keep my word."

"There was," Frank's voice was stern, "no note, Myrtle."

"Oh, yeah," she muttered, hanging her head. "That's right. Maybe I forgot to write it. I was going to. Must have forgot." She peered up at them with weary eyes and a sly grin. "Sorry. But I'm back—got any supper left? I'm starving."

They escorted Myrtle into the house where they gave her a plate of food and the three of them, Sam having finished his telephone calls, hovered over her. Frank was angry with her for the stunt, but Abby was just glad to have the old woman back. They'd have to keep a closer eye on her.

"You know," Myrtle confessed as she sat down to her stew. "I saw the kidnapper out in the woods earlier. Out past Gage's Bog. I was taking a shortcut to my trailer and I heard this car motor. I hid behind a tree and along comes this big purple junk heap. The man got out of the car and took off into the woods. Same creep that attacked Abby, I'm sure. I reckoned he was going to be gone for a while and thought I'd look through his car and see what I could find. Maybe a dead body or something. I tried to get in but it was locked. He came back too soon and so I hid under the car. I was as close to him as I am now to you—except he didn't see me. He was covered in soot. Stunk like burning wood, too. Bet *he* blew up Connie and Selena's house."

Astonished at their good luck, Frank probed further, "What kind of car?"

"I don't know. Don't know one car from another. All look alike to me. Big purple monstrosity of some kind. Had four wheels and bumpers. Windows. Any old car. But it was big, ugly looking cause the paint was worn, and it was real purple. That red purple, you know?"

"Burgundy," Sam offered.

"Yep. Burgundy. Older car. Had a light broken in the rear, too."

"You didn't get the license number, did you?" Frank held his breath.

"Nah, sorry. I didn't have time to look before he came back and I dove under the car. Noticed the guy was limping more than the last time I saw him. Sounded sick, too, huffing, puffing and panting. Coughing like he had a cow in his throat. Oh—" She wiped her mouth off with a dirty hand. "Something else. I peeked out as he was getting in and one of his hands was in front of my eyes. He's missing a couple fingers on his left hand."

"Now those are the kind of details we can use," Frank exclaimed, showing excitement for the first time. "Thanks, Myrtle, you've really helped." He was no longer angry at her.

"Where's Gage's Bog?" Abby questioned Frank, having heard of it before but not knowing much about it.

"It's a section of swampy land a few miles behind Myrtle's place that's pockmarked with muddy ponds, pools and quicksand, not to mention lots of Copperheads and water spiders big as your hand. The locals stay away from it. People have wandered in and not come out."

"Then that's one place I'm not wandering into." Abby grinned and lowered her voice. "This is good, isn't it? Myrtle seeing his car? Broken taillight. His missing fingers? We know more than we did before. That should help."

"Everything helps. I'm going to call the sheriff back. Tell him we found Myrtle and relay the new information. Suggest he search every inch of the woods behind Myrtle's place. Maybe the kidnapper left something behind."

Frank and Sam went into the other room and Abby heard Frank talking on the phone while she sat in the kitchen and kept Myrtle company. Suddenly, listening to the old woman carry on about her close call, she was exhausted.

At least she would be able to sleep that night. If Myrtle hadn't come back it would have been impossible. She was glad Myrtle was all right but irritated she'd made them all worry.

Abby called Martha and let her know Myrtle was okay. Then she excused herself and went to bed because it'd been a long day. And sleep always helped.

Chapter Thirteen

The voices woke him as he lay in bed at the motel and told him to blow up the house so the woman who worked at the bakery wouldn't identify him.

She saw your face. Turn on the TV.

There he was all over the twenty-five-inch screen— another possible version of what the police believed he looked like from the new witness. This time his stomach churned. The drawing did kind of look like him. Misshapen and heavy jowled face with tiny round eyes and combed back greasy ebony hair. Low forehead. *Whoa.* How did she see him well enough to get such an accurate description? He'd been so careful.

This is not good, he thought, dragging himself out of bed and heading for the door. His voices were chastising him for having been stupid, accosting that woman in full daylight and worse, letting her get away. They were giving him a headache. A really bad one.

You need to fix this mess. You have to get rid of that woman. Get rid of her. For good. Find her house and blow it up. You know how. You've done it before.

Can't I just take her? He'd pleaded with them.

No, she's not your next victim, you know that. Do what we tell you to do. Now.

But it's still dark, he'd protested.

Go. Now. Take care of it. It will take time.

How? he requested.

And his voices had told him.

He knew where the woman lived. Last night he'd been in town after nightfall and had seen her leaving the bakery at closing. He'd followed her to a yellow house and seen her go in.

Yellow houses weren't lucky for him.

It was that gray twilight right before dawn. The house was cloaked in misty gloom, surrounded by trees, and the brisk wind was knocking branches together noisily, which would cover most noises. Parking the car a block down the street, he took a bag of objects he would need from the trunk and trudged to the house.

It was simple to slip through one of the back windows. He used his toxic cloth to put them to sleep. He opened up the gas line enough to slowly fill the house, then left. It would take awhile for the result he wanted. He'd have to wait.

He limped to his car and, after taking a short nap, was soon awakened by the explosion. He drove by the burning house to watch the flames, getting caught in the fog of smoke that poured from it. No one had gotten out. Mission accomplished. His voices were pleased with him for once and told him to go get some of those breakfast burritos from McDonalds that he liked so much. That morning he treated himself to three of them.

He returned to the motel and slept for hours. His voices hushed and for once let him sleep.

He drove out again before it got dark for more food and a hike through the woods. Everywhere he went he smelled the acrid stench of smoke. It trailed him like a hungry dog he couldn't shake. He tried. He ran. Stumbled. Couldn't get away.

When night fell, the mud people popped out of the tree shadows and began tailing him. He escaped into his car. If he drove fast enough sometimes he could leave them behind.

He parked a short distance from the cop's house and trekked the rest of the way on foot, glancing behind him every so often to make sure he wasn't being followed. He had to be cautious walking in the dark as he didn't dare use a flashlight.

Hidden among the trees his eyes riveted to the people talking softly on the porch, he heard Frank Lester's voice. Lester, his mortal enemy, was up there with the old woman, victim number three, and another man. The other man was a cop, too. He could tell because the other man talked like a cop.

He smiled. They had no idea he was out there watching them. They thought the night, the lightless porch, and their whispering hid them. Ha. He could hear and see them fine. He had night eyes. Keen ears. Smart enough to avoid the dogs.

He wanted to hate Frank Lester, the man who'd crippled him—his doppelganger—but somehow his hate was mingled with awe . . . and jealousy. The cop had a beautiful home, family, lots of friends, and respect. Frank Lester had a good, happy life. The people on the porch were friends, all eating and drinking together. He could smell the sharp aroma of coffee and chocolate in the night air.

For a moment he longed to stride out of the bushes and join them. Be one of them. The special. The loved. The normal.

What was he anyway? A loser without friends, a job, a home, or a life.

Loser. Loser. Loser.

Don't be a fool. Lester and his friends loathe you. They want to destroy you. To them you're a criminal. Less than a man. They are your enemies. Don't forget that. They'll never understand how unique you are.

What did it feel like to be happy? he wondered. He didn't know. He'd never been happy his whole life. Not when his mother had belittled or beaten him and locked him in the basement. Not when the voices had made him do things he didn't want to. He had to obey them, but he didn't really know why. He only knew the voices wouldn't leave him alone if he didn't. That was worse than unhappiness.

And the voices returned to torment him.

Enough wallowing in the pity pot. You're not a loser, a nobody. You're famous. Everyone talks about you, knows of you. Fears you. Don't forget that. You'll live forever but how many people will remember that stupid cop? You can't stop now. Watch that cop's house and sooner or later she'll leave it for something . . . and you'll be there to grab her.

Do what you're good at.

Obey us.

They were right. He was famous. He was on television. In the newspapers. *Famous.*

Forever.

Placated, he crawled away through the wet, cold grass, got in his car and drove back to the motel. He had work to do. Plans to make. Like his voices said, sooner or later the woman would leave the cabin and when she did, he'd be there to take her. Or he'd figure out another way. If one were patient, there was always a way.

And he was a patient man—except when the voices drove him crazy or the mud people distracted him.

All he wanted was to be left alone. All he wanted was silence.

Chapter Fourteen

Frank waited until Abby and Myrtle were tucked in. "Sam, keep an eye on the house and our guests for a bit, would you? I have to go out. Myrtle said the man she saw in the woods drove an old burgundy car. Believe I'll check out the area's motel and hotel parking lots and see what kinds of cars are hanging around. Might luck out." Sam and Frank had cleaned up the dessert dishes and were standing in the dim kitchen having a late cup of coffee.

"You know I'll keep an eye on the women, Frank. But don't you think the sheriff's men will be out looking for that burgundy car?"

"Yeah, and houses fly. If I do it myself I know it's done right. And I can't sit here any longer and wait for him to make the next move. I have the feeling he's been watching us."

Sam rinsed out his cup in the sink. "I'd feel better going along with you if you run into trouble. It's dangerous, you going after him alone, Frank. You ought to call the sheriff for backup, at least."

"The kidnapper would see a posse coming. He's smart. I can sneak around better, unnoticed, by myself. And I'm only looking. If I run into our guy, I'll call for help. Promise."

"You better." Sam dried his cup and put it in the cabinet.

"You know, he could be living in his car or in an empty shack somewhere, not in a motel at all."

"I know. I'm looking for the car, that's all. Just a hunch."

"And we all know about your hunches. Go for it, I say. But be careful, partner.

"I guess I'll go watch a little television," Sam added. "Do some light reading. Stay in my clothes for a while and keep the phone close. Call me if you need me." He went into the living room.

Frank put on a jacket and slipped his old service revolver into one of its deep pockets. Walked outside. He could smell rain in the night air. "Great," he grumbled under his breath, as he pushed the truck out of the garage and down the circle driveway slowly, not wanting to wake Abby or Myrtle. He'd been keeping his vehicle in the garage in the back of his place since the trouble had begun. He wasn't letting the kidnapper see what he was driving.

There were four or five motels he could drive through that were either in or right outside town. Frank was sure that the kidnapper was close, so he could get in and out quickly and be near the news and gossip. That was his way. He reveled in the terror he was creating. Beginning at the nearest motel in town, the Blue Moon, Frank cruised through the parking lot on the lookout for a late model burgundy car.

It was at the fourth motel, Shady Rest, a twenty-nine dollar a night fleabag halfway to Chalmers, that Frank spotted the burgundy Buick Rivera. A boat on wheels. Dented and dingy. Paint faded. About an '88. It had definitely seen better days. Something about the car made Frank's skin clammy. It *could* be the one Myrtle had seen in the woods earlier. There was mud over the solitary license plate.

Frank drove his truck to the rear of the lot and parked in a spot that couldn't be seen from the rooms. He got out, gently closed his door, walked around the building to have a closer look at the burgundy vehicle and peered inside. It was difficult to see anything because the windows were dirty, but the seats seemed full of trash of some kind.

Frank rubbed at the grimy license plate with his fingers and found there was nothing beneath the dirt. No numbers on it. They'd been scrapped off somehow. Frank tried to open a door. None locked. That was like an invitation.

He slipped into the front seat, keeping an eye on the motel rooms opposite in case someone came out; shut the door quickly so the dome light would go out. With a penlight from his pocket he panned around the clutter of empty food containers, clothes and papers, seeing nothing unusual, except an abundance of trash. Whoever owned this car was a slob.

There were no weapons, ropes, or puddles of blood and no sign that the car might belong to a psychotic killer. Frank checked the glove compartment. Strange. It was empty.

He couldn't get in the trunk, unless he broke the lock, and without a warrant, that would be going too far. The burgundy car was parked in front of room number six, whose curtains were tightly drawn, though a weak light seeped out from beneath the drapes.

Frank snuck up to the window and stole a peek into the room. Couldn't see a thing. A sliver of light. No movement. A low TV hum tipped him off that someone might be inside. Carefully he tested the doorknob, his other hand grasping the gun in his pocket. Breaking into the car and the room was illegal. He knew that, but his curiosity was eating at him. Had to see who was in the room if he could.

The door was locked.

He walked down to the motel's office with another plan. There was an elderly man in a tattered baseball cap at the desk, half-asleep, who woke up sometime when Frank came in. Frank didn't know him.

"Who's in room number six?" Frank asked in a casual manner.

The baseball cap tilted up. Bushy white eyebrows curved over bored eyes a flat hazel color. "What's it to you?"

"Curious. But it's worth a twenty to you if you can give

me a description of the guy and a name. That's all. Not against the law."

"Nah, it ain't." The old guy's eyes lit up and his wrinkled hand came out. Frank put cash in it. The twenty disappeared into the man's front pocket and he shoved the check-in book at Frank. "Says his name is Fred Dwyer. Doesn't look like a Fred to me. But who am I to say. Most happy travelers, families and such, people with money, don't stay here. It's a dump. Mostly weirdos coming through here on their way to somewhere else. Hiding out. Wanting privacy. Who knows? I take their money and hope they don't mess up the rooms too much.

"Now this Fred Dwyer? I only saw him the night he checked in and didn't see him real well. He had a long jacket on and a hat tugged down over his eyes. Stood back as far away from me as he could. Only stepped up to sign the register. Pay me the money. Cash. Was out in a flash. Been here about three weeks, I'd say. Haven't seen him since that first night. He leaves money every morning in the mail slot. So the only thing I can tell you about his looks is . . . he's tall. Six-foot-five or more. Has a deep voice. Drives that purplish Buick parked out there.

"Oh, and he insisted on having room six. Said six was a lucky number for him. No problem 'cause it was empty. There you go. Sorry I couldn't give you more."

"Thanks. It's more than enough." Very tall and a deep voice. The fact that the man in room six was obviously hiding himself from the world was what Frank needed to know.

It could be him.

Frank considered asking the desk clerk for the key to the room, but he had no right. He wasn't a cop anymore, he didn't have a warrant; he didn't have proof the man in number six was his man. He could stroll up and knock on the door . . . but if it was the kidnapper, he wouldn't come out without a fight. And Frank couldn't risk losing him this time. Best to call the sheriff and they could knock on the man's door together. Have some words with him. Do it legally so there'd be no loopholes.

"Could I use your phone?" Frank asked the night clerk. "Police business." Which wasn't a lie. Exactly.

"You a cop?" The old man had come to attention.

"Used to be. I'm sort of helping the police these days."

The man hesitated only a moment. "Sure. The phone's in front of you. Help yourself."

Frank called the sheriff and walked outside to keep an eye on room six. The ugly burgundy Buick was gone and the door to number six was ajar. Frank ran to the room and pushed open the door the rest of the way and slid in, his hand on the gun in his pocket.

Someone had left in a hurry. Like the car, the room was full of discarded fast food containers and Styrofoam cups. Little else. No forks or spoons. No clothes left behind or personal accessories. No toothbrushes or rinse cups. Nothing DNA could be taken from. Not that it would help. The kidnapper had never left any physical evidence behind. Nothing to tie him to anything if they did get a DNA sample. Unless he was already in the criminal system.

Frank had a strong hunch the man who'd just left was the man he was looking for and he wasn't coming back to room six.

Somehow the guy had known Frank had found him. Been tipped off. He'd seen Frank's truck driving by or seen him breaking into his car or maybe had seen Frank's penlight bobbing around in the interior.

Furious at losing his suspect, Frank dashed outside and jumped into his truck. Hit the accelerator and flew down the highway. Breaking the speed limit because the roads were empty. Taking a chance on which way the man in room six had gone, he guessed wrong. No burgundy car ahead of him anywhere. He retraced his route and sped down the other way. No burgundy car.

He soon gave up. It was useless to drive around blindly in

the dark. Frank returned to the motel to wait for the sheriff who arrived minutes later. For once Sheriff Mearl had been at the police station, on duty, and wasn't half-asleep. He'd been catching up on paperwork on the missing persons cases and making calls about the house explosion. He'd brought a deputy along.

The three men entered room six and stood in the middle, taking in the unmade bed and left behind empty meal containers. All the lightbulbs but one had burned out. Shadows hid in the corners. Something about the room—a sense of something being wrong—made Frank's old inner cop voice tell him, *he was here. The man you seek. He was here.*

"The place is a mess, all right." Sheriff Mearl stood with his hands on his gun belt. The leather belt and holster squeaked when he moved. "You think it's our man, Frank?"

"I have a gut feeling it might be."

"Think he might come back?"

"No. He knew I was here and took off. Won't be back. That's my guess anyway."

"I'm going to put out an APB for the car. See what we can drag in," the Sheriff said.

"Good luck. He'll vanish somehow like he always does."

"Well, got to try anyway."

Frank helped the sheriff and his deputy search the room and brought them up to speed on what he'd been doing that night. The sheriff wasn't happy. "You could have gotten hurt or worse, Frank. You need to stand back and let us do our jobs. You're retired, remember?"

Frank didn't respond. He'd tried to make the sheriff understand the stake he had in finding this guy, but the sheriff wouldn't listen. He was too territorial. Frank changed tactics. "Did your forensic people get fingerprints off the mud figures I gave you or off any of the notes?"

"Sorry, no. He must have been wearing gloves. But, we've been monitoring the telephone calls coming in since Samantha started running the stories in the paper. Weeding out the crank calls. We received one from a woman who saw a suspicious car, a big plum-colored one, as she described it, a few blocks away from the house explosion this morning. Didn't belong. Said she had never seen it before. It matches your car here."

"That ties the car to the house fire. Which might tie our kidnapper to it as well."

"Frank," the sheriff sighed a few minutes later, "we'll handle it from here. Sift through this junk and let you know tomorrow what we find. Go on home. You look tired. Thanks for your help." The sheriff was taking control, but was cordial about it. "And . . . if the killer was here and he knows you were too, then he knows you're not at the cabin. I wouldn't stay away from the cabin too long."

He had a point there. For once. "You're right, Sheriff." Frank had been so excited about almost catching his man he hadn't thought past it. He excused himself and drove home above the speed limit.

As the night landscape sped by scenes from the past haunted him, fears and forgotten emotions resurfaced. When he had talked to Rebecca Brooks or the Lanstroms, their sorrow and heartbreak had been the same as the other families' from ten years ago. It was like stepping back in time or like dreaming the same nightmare over and over. Where was that monster now?

He had to get home.

It was a relief to find everyone safe at the cabin. He looked in on Abby and Myrtle, who were both sleeping. Sam had waited up and wanted to know what had happened. They sat in the kitchen and drank hot chocolate as Frank gave him a rundown of the night's adventures.

"I was *this* close to him." Frank's thumb and fingers were nearly touching as he shook his head. "If I'd broken into the room instead of going to call the sheriff, I would have had him." The frustration was strong in his voice, his eyes cold. "He blew up that house today, Sam. I know it. Killed two innocent people. How many dead does that make now in total? Ten? Or maybe more we don't even know about?

"I let him get away. When I was so close!"

"If it *was* him, Frank. Might not have been. You're letting your guilt get ahead of you. Let the sheriff run a fingerprint and DNA sweep on that motel room. Give the APB some time. See what he finds.

"And stop blaming yourself for the harm the kidnapper's done. He's not taking people because of you, but because he's warped and evil and that's what he does. It's not your fault. And we're going to get him—with God's help. It's only a matter of time," Sam comforted his friend, laying a hand on Frank's shoulder. "Believe that if nothing else."

Sam believed that kidnappers, rapists, child abusers, and serial murderers were sometimes simply evil—born evil and meant to do evil all their lives. The only solution was to find them and let justice lock them up. For the rest of their lives.

"But time is what we don't have. By my calculations he's going to take someone again real soon, Sam, unless we stop him. He's playing with us."

"I know." Sam peered out the kitchen window at the steady downpour of rain that had finally come. It was tapping on the roof, running down the windows. Inside it was deceptively warm and dry.

Frank also listened to the rain, sure that the kidnapper was out there watching, waiting, and scheming. Feeling helpless, he had the urge to get his rifle and randomly spray the woods around the house with bullets. That would flush the kidnapper out.

"Whatever you're thinking, Frank, it won't work," Sam uttered. "Give up the worrying for tonight and get some rest. Tomorrow in the sunlight things will look better, you'll see."

"You know me too well, old friend. But that's good advice. Tomorrow's another day."

The men said good night after they double-checked the door locks and the windows. Frank put his guns where he could get to them quickly and let his two German shepherds outside to run the yard.

No one would get near the cabin tonight.

Chapter Fifteen

"**I**'m going stir crazy sitting around here all day," Abby was telling Frank the next morning in the kitchen. "I know you're only concerned for my safety but how long are you going to keep me in protective custody? I can't stay here indefinitely waiting for that maniac to come after me again—if he ever does.

"He wouldn't be stupid enough to come here anyway. Too protected, this place. With you and Sam, it's like a fortress. But what will I do if you don't catch him for months? Or if you never catch him?" She hated to say that but it did weigh on her mind.

"Well, here's an idea, Abby. You could marry me and move in here permanently. Then I could watch over you forever." Frank smiled at her from the stove as he was frying eggs. It was seven in the morning and Myrtle and Sam weren't up yet. It turned out Frank and Abby liked rising early and that morning they'd discovered each other on the porch and enjoyed the sun coming up together. Neither could sleep.

The rain had stopped, leaving the world sparkling clean. *Nothing bad should happen on such a beautiful day,* Abby was thinking, until Frank told her of his adventure the night before with their elusive kidnapper. About room six and the burgundy Buick. Suddenly the day hadn't seemed as safe or bright. She was glad she had Frank.

She glanced at Frank to see if he was joking with the proposal. He wasn't. Before the I-was-only-fooling grin took over his face, she caught a flash of hope and it tugged at her heart. He knew she still grieved over Joel. Knew she wasn't ready to let go yet, but he loved her, there was no question. And she was beginning to love him. How could she not love such a good man who loved her back?

"By the way," Abby turned her eyes away and changed topics, "won't you be having more autograph signings for your first novel?" He'd had a few since his book had come out and was supposed to have more.

"No. Things have changed. I asked my publisher to cancel them for a while. I can't leave you and Myrtle alone. All I can concentrate on now is this kidnapper and this sick game he's playing. And catching him. That's more important than any book."

Life and death should be, Abby brooded. Again she thought how good a friend and protector Frank was. He was serious about his writing and had worked hard to get published. His book and its publicity were very important to him. That he had put it on hold for her safety said more to her than any words of love.

"Is your publisher angry at you for ducking out on them?" She'd downed two cups of Frank's addictive coffee and was on her third. He made the best coffee.

"No. They're ecstatic that I'm involved with this Mud People Killer. The ghouls. Since he's resurfaced, snatched two more victims, tried to snatch you and Myrtle and might have killed the Tucker women by burning down their house, the media has gone berserk. It's a *big* story. My editor has already hinted that I should write a book on it—after it's solved and the kidnapper is behind bars. Or before. They're not picky. Either way it'll sell." His first novel had been about one of his other solved murder cases from his days in Chicago and was selling fairly well. The book he'd been working on for over a year now was about the missing persons mystery he and Abby had solved the year before. No doubt his publishers thought a book on an active case would do even better.

"The kidnapper's not following the same pattern this time, is he? Failed attacks and arson."

"No." Frank's shoulders were stiff. "It's troubling. Don't know what to expect from him next. Not that it matters. We'll know when he does it."

Abby hadn't pressed Frank too much on the kidnapper's history in Chicago. Now she needed to. "How many victims did this so-called Mud People Killer get ten years ago?"

Frank stopped pushing the eggs around. Motionless, his face turned away, he replied flatly, "Six. He took six people. Three teenagers and three adults. Three females and three males. One a week for six weeks. They've never been heard from again. Never found their bodies so their families still live without knowing if they're truly dead. Those victims' families and their sorrows have haunted me all these years, Abby.

"I remember the fourth victim, a sixteen-year-old girl named Vangie Pantura. Disappeared at a family picnic on a cloudy summer day. The mother, father, a couple of aunts and uncles and their kids had been celebrating the mother's birthday at a local park. Grilling pork steaks. Vangie, an only child, went to the restrooms in the early afternoon and never came back.

"By the time this was noticed and the police were called in, she was long gone. The mother was in a trance and the father was so full of desperation to find his child I thought he was going to lose it. I still see that birthday cake, chocolate icing with pink and blue flowers, melting in the sun on the picnic table untouched.

"After the clay figure turned up in their mailbox—" Frank's voice broke. "Vangie's father went out into the woods where the girl had been taken, and stayed out there without food or water searching for her until he eventually collapsed. Turns out he had a bad heart and when we found him days later, he was sitting stone dead up against a tree.

"A few months later the mother killed herself."

Abby got up and put her arms around Frank, her heart heavy with sorrow for him. He carried so many ghosts around where she only carried one. For crimes he hadn't been able to solve and regrets for what he should have done but didn't. Did all cops carry this burden? The good ones, she imagined, did.

"It wasn't your fault, Frank. Your job was to try to find the girl. You did that to the best of your ability. You're only one man and you can only do so much. It's time to forgive yourself."

"But, Abby . . . I didn't find their daughter. Didn't find *any* of them. Now it's happening again. I don't know if I can stand it a second time. These last few years have been so good, so peaceful that they've lulled me into thinking life's supposed to be like this. It isn't."

The eggs were burning. Seeing the smoke, Frank flipped them out onto plates with the spatula. Abby could see he was in a dark mood. To have been so close to the kidnapper last night and to have lost him must be frustrating. If only Frank could have caught the guy . . . all of them, the whole town, could have slept in peace tonight. Abby would have been free to go back to her life and Frank could stop obsessing and wallowing in guilt.

"Until you, Abby, he's never missed an intended victim."

His words made her nervous. "My getting away must have made him angry. Do you think that's why he killed Selena and Connie Tucker?" Her last cup of coffee sat lukewarm in the cup surrounded by her fingers. She tilted it this way and that way, careful not to spill the coffee. Outside the window the sunlight had come into its full strength. The kitchen was bright and cheery. There were no shadows.

"Perhaps partly. Connie could identify him, so he had to get rid of her. Could have taken her, but blowing up her house was his way of sending us a message. Yes, he's *very* angry."

"You think he might blow us up, too?" Abby wondered about his beautiful cabin. With them in it.

"He could. It would get rid of all four of us easily enough. I don't think he will, though. That would end his fun. It's a matter of pride that he outwit me, steal you out from under my nose to pay me back for the pain I caused him ten years ago.

"When Myrtle mentioned the man in the purple car had missing fingers I immediately thought, I must have done that to him, along with his bad leg. He's failed if he can't get back at me. It's about control. You're still victim number three, as much as you don't want to believe it, and the kidnapper is going to try to grab you again. He doesn't give up that easily.

"And that's why," Frank's voice was stern. "You're not going home yet and not going anywhere alone."

"Well if I'm not allowed to go out alone, you'll have to come with me today to Martha's," Abby said. "Thought I'd have a look at her garden. Begin drawing it. It'll give me something to do 'cause I'm bored. Martha has photos, but I like to see the real thing if I can before I start. Photographs only give you so much. My house bills will keep on coming whether I'm there or not so I'll still need the income."

She heard Myrtle thumping down the stairs with slow and heavy steps and thought she'd invite her along. Martha wouldn't like it, but Abby felt bad about having left Myrtle the other day and the scare she had given everyone. She wasn't leaving the old woman behind today.

"Okay." Frank tone was lighter. He smiled. "I'll go to Martha's with you. But you know she's gonna draft us to help decorate for the party. I don't mind, if you don't. I'd like to see the garden's renovations anyway. She's bragged about them so much."

"What garden?" Myrtle came into the kitchen, nose leading her to the food.

"Martha's redone her garden again." Abby launched into her proposal. "Frank and I are going over there today before the party to see it. Want to come?"

"Martha's garden? Hmm. Let's see. Lots of flowers, bird-baths, and those hard metal benches that hurt my butt to sit on . . . Martha crowing about all her new stuff. *Nah.* Sounds boring to me. You two go. "I'll stay here with that handsome cop friend of Frank's and watch television. I like Frank's big screen—much bigger than mine. Can't miss my Friday court programs. Got more laundry to do, too." Myrtle had been washing the clothes she'd brought from her place. She must have brought every piece of clothing she owned. Going over to the cabinet, the old woman took out a plate and handed it to Frank. "I'll take five eggs, over-easy, Cook. Three strips of bacon. Two slices of buttered toast. Thank you." Then she poured herself a cup of coffee and sat down.

She'd combed her thin silver hair behind her ears and had clipped ten little girl's barrettes of different hues and shapes to hold it in place on each side. She'd painted her lips cherry red, wore diamond earrings and her dress, clean for once, was a wild-colored print.

Abby and Frank were trying not to laugh. It was obvious Myrtle thought she looked pretty. The look wasn't working for her, but Abby would never tell her that. She'd begun taking regular baths using Frank's bathroom supplies, his thick towels, and washcloths. She thought she smelled good because she was using Frank's cologne.

Myrtle had settled into Frank's house as if it were hers.

Sam came down a few minutes later and they ate breakfast like a family.

It was nice, Abby thought. She belonged somewhere, the same way the town and her house made her feel. She kept stealing looks at Frank and wondered what it would be like to be his girlfriend or his wife. He was handsome and smart and funny. Sexy with his narrow face, longish gray threaded dark hair, lanky tall frame, and piercing blue eyes.

He made her feel safe—something she hadn't felt since she'd been with Joel.

A long-forgotten ache fluttered inside her. She'd loved Joel as much as a woman could love a man and she wanted that kind of love again. She'd missed it. Wanted to move on with her life. In that moment, a bit surprised, she realized that she did want to love Frank.

Pushing those thoughts away, she finished eating, phoned Martha to let her know they were coming, and went upstairs to feed Snowball as Frank called the sheriff to get an update.

When she came back down Frank was off the phone. The sheriff wasn't in, he told her, and he'd try again later.

With Frank's help, Abby had brought her car over yesterday afternoon, put it in his garage next to the truck, and now offered to drive to Martha's. But Frank was adamant that they take his truck and he drive in case something happened. What he meant by that she had no idea, but she didn't argue.

Martha's house overwhelmed Abby with its beauty and size, as it always did. Embedded in a forest of trees draped in vibrant fall colors, the house was a picture postcard. Everyone in town fondly called it Martha's Mansion. Family home built with family money. A mansion furnished in a northwestern theme with open beams crisscrossing the ceilings, Indian rugs, earthenware pots full of plants, and furs hanging on the creamy white walls—this year. Every couple of years Martha changed the look. Abby had painted a couple of large canvases for her, one of them of the house itself. She'd been her first patron and had been well paid.

Martha had strawberry daiquiris ready for them when they arrived and a plate of miniature iced cakes. She took them to the back patio that overlooked the garden and they lounged in wicker chairs soaking in the sun, admiring the garden's new additions. The new gazebo, the elaborate stone benches and delicate trellises and the garden, filled with fall mums of every shade, were beautiful.

"This will make a breathtaking picture," Abby assured Martha as she studied the perspective. She got up and started snapping photographs. They could get them developed at the IGA in one hour on the way home, Frank had reminded her, and shop while they waited.

After Abby photographed what she needed, she and Frank

helped Martha decorate her house for the following night. When they were done it looked like Dracula's castle, which was what Martha was calling her house for the Halloween party. It had white spider webs hanging everywhere and open homemade coffins, fake body parts and stuffed dead bodies lying about. None of it scared Abby. Real life had become scarier.

They were getting ready to leave when the doorbell rang. Martha answered. It was the sheriff.

"You called earlier, Frank, and they said you'd be here," Sheriff Mearl explained as he stepped inside. "I guess I know what you were calling about. Sorry, no prints or DNA we could use from room six last night. The guy must have worn gloves or wiped everything down . . . suspicious in itself, if you ask me. He was a slob, but a careful slob. Scrubbed out the sink, the toilet, for Pete's sake, rinsed off everything or took it with him. We couldn't pull anything from any surface. The room was that clean. No evidence whatsoever that our boy was staying there. So far. But we're working on it."

Abby could see Frank's disappointment. "I was afraid of that," Frank said. "That's how I know it was our man . . . he was always a perfectionist. So clever. Apparently he still is."

"Come into the kitchen, Sheriff. Have some coffee and cake." Martha invited him in and the four of them made their way to the kitchen as Sheriff Mearl talked. "Nice haunted house you have here, Martha. How much you gonna charge and when you going to open it to the public?"

"A one day and night engagement, Sheriff. Tomorrow. And it's free. You coming?"

"Wouldn't miss it. I'm on duty but thought I'd spend some of it here. Where all the people are going to be anyway."

Martha smiled. "Good. The food is going to be scrumptious and the company stimulating. Bring all the uniformed officers you can spare, Sheriff. Can't have enough cops at a costume party. No masks please." They were in the kitchen and Martha handed the sheriff a plate with cake on it and a mug of coffee.

"I'll be here." The sheriff turned to Frank. "I also wanted to tell you that during the search in the woods around where Myrtle says she saw that suspicious man we found something." The sheriff's voice fell and his eyes, hidden beneath his hat, met Frank's. "We found a tennis shoe that's positively been identified by Rebecca Brooks as having belonged to Emil. The same shoes he was wearing the day he disappeared. She's sure, 'cause he only had one good pair."

"Where exactly in the woods did you find it?" Frank asked, observing the other man eat his cake and gulp his coffee. The sheriff was in a hurry.

"On the northern edge near the swamp area. We found tire tracks from a car as well. One shoe, that's all we gathered, but the men are still out there looking. I'm calling for a larger search of the woods. The whole forest."

"You looking for a body now, Sheriff?" Frank's manner was offhand but his eyes were strangely sad.

"Might be. That shoe proves Emil was back there. Alive or dead. The rest of him has to be somewhere. For once that crazy old woman gave us a good lead."

For once, Abby thought, someone had believed her. "How did Rebecca Brooks take the news?"

"Not well. She's had a relapse of that illness of hers. Can't get out of bed. Seems like she's given up. There was some social worker over there when I spoke to her. Feel sorry for those kids."

Abby did, too. And made a promise to herself to visit soon. See if she could help them in some way. Rebecca must need someone to talk to.

The sheriff and Frank discussed the ongoing investigation a while longer and then all of them left Martha's together. Frank got into his truck with Abby and the Sheriff got into his squad car and each drove off.

Sitting beside an unusually somber Frank, she initiated conversation. "We still stopping at the supermarket to drop off my film and get supplies? I need my photographs developed."

"I hadn't forgotten. We're stopping."

The IGA was crowded. It was Friday evening and people had cashed their paychecks and were doing their shopping. She dropped off the photos at the rear of the store for one-hour development and the girl promised her they'd be done on time.

They got one shopping cart between them and maneuvered through the aisles loading up on groceries. "It takes a lot of food to feed four," he grumbled, grabbing a large box of cereal. "I'd forgotten. Been just me for so long."

"I feel bad enough imposing on you, Frank." The basket was filling quickly. "The least you can do is let me pay for some of the food I'm consuming."

"I wouldn't think of it. You're my guest, Abby. Besides I have more money than you and I'm bigger than you." He winked at her, grinning like himself again. "I've enjoyed the last week so much with you, Myrtle, and Sam around. It's been nice, even under the circumstances. Gets lonely sometimes living by yourself."

"Yeah, it does. It's sweet to have friends." She put her arm through his and they finished up their shopping. He bought far more than they would need and at the checkout counter she learned why. Frank had the cashier put half the groceries aside, saying they were for the Brooks family and could the store deliver them anonymously? The cashier, a middle-aged woman with glasses and a ponytail—Shelly's replacement—said they could.

"That was kind of you," Abby told Frank on their way out.

"Those kids shouldn't go hungry," he murmured, as they walked out into the dusk with their arms full of bags. "With their dad missing and their mom sick they have enough to make them feel bad."

"Frank, you're a good person, you know that?"

"I try to be."

"Oops, I nearly forgot the photos. Be right back." Abby dropped her grocery bags in the truck and, without thinking about it, dashed back inside. It wasn't far. She stood in line waiting to pay for the pictures and glanced out the window at the rear of the store. The sun was dipping below the trees and night was creeping in. She saw a purplish car at the edge of the parking lot hiding in the shadows. A large burgundy car with a lumpy silhouette sitting motionless in the driver's seat. Or, at least, she *thought* someone was sitting there. She *thought* the car was some shade of purple. Hard to tell against the sunset.

She collected and paid for her pictures, left the store, and walked swiftly toward Frank's truck. "I think our kidnapper's been following us today," she whispered as she slid into the front seat beside Frank. "I think I saw him. He's parked in a car—a beat-up purple thing—behind the store."

Frank grabbed Abby's hand and squeezed. "I want you to lock the doors and lie down on the seat, Abby. Stay hidden while I go take a quick look. If it's him I can't let him get away this time. I'll be right back," Frank whispered back, taking a gun out of the glove compartment.

And he was gone.

She closed the truck windows and locked the doors, ducked down, and waited long minutes holding her breath and listening for any strange sounds. Night had fallen completely while she'd been getting her photographs and only the parking lot lights illuminated the darkness surrounding her. All of a sudden it was quiet outside. There was no one else coming or going in the parking lot.

She couldn't believe Frank had gone out there alone. It was dangerous if the man in the car was really the kidnapper.

Frank was gone a long time and she was beginning to worry when headlights came up behind the truck. Way too close for another shopper. She was lying on the seat as Frank had instructed her to do, terrified, her body shaking and her heart thudding. Was that another store customer or was it *him*? And where was Frank?

The headlights stayed on and with every second Abby became more desperate. She wanted to scramble out of the truck and run. She had nothing with which to protect herself. Why had Frank left her alone like this? By now she was sweating. The memory of the attack in her bedroom haunted her and she couldn't stay still any longer. The headlights were burning her skin. Something was wrong. Why didn't the person switch them off and go into the grocery store?

A car door opened and she peered over the seat. Someone was getting out of the car behind her. She could only make out a tall shape lumbering toward her. Limping. She panicked and scooted over to the passenger's side and shoved open the door. The overhead cab light blinked on and her breathing froze.

He'll see me.

She dropped to the asphalt and shut the door quickly so the light would go off, then scuttled on her hands and toes to the front of the truck as the shadow advanced. The man was coming for her and terror was a hungry animal with sharp teeth fighting to escape her body.

Where was Frank? She prayed nothing had happened to him, but she had to get inside the store. Among people. Had to get help. Get to a phone and call the sheriff. Call Sam.

Abby stood up and made a dead run for the store but someone grabbed her by the arm and spun her around. She couldn't see who it was because of the car headlights glaring into her eyes. But he was tall and his smell sent her mind spinning back to the night she'd been assaulted.

It was the same guy. It was *him*.

Gunshots rang out, the man holding her arm shrieked, and released her. She slid to the ground a few feet from the supermarket doors and scrambled through the entrance without looking back, blinking at the bright lights and people around her. *Safety*. She finally looked behind her.

Outside, a car screeched through the parking lot and beneath a street light. As it careened up onto the road Abby saw it was the burgundy one.

Then Frank was beside her, smelling of gun power, and

holding her tightly. "It's all right, Abby. I'm sorry I let him get so close to you. But he's gone. I shot at him and I'm sure I hit him. I was following him the whole time but was waiting for a clear shot. Almost had him when he got out of the car but he was moving too fast. When he went for you, I couldn't wait any longer to shoot. So I did. Chased him off."

Frank rocked her in his arms and smoothed her hair as she shook. Twice in a week. She was sick of close calls. "I'm okay, Frank. He didn't hurt me, just scared the religion out of me. Next time leave me a stick or a tire iron or something."

"As if you could hurt a human being. You rescue baby birds, for heaven's sake."

"*He's* not a human being. He's a monster. I could beat him up with no qualms."

"You could? I'm glad to hear it. You should be ready to do what you have to do to save your life. But right now . . . you're all right! Thank God. You have more luck than a horseshoe."

"Go on. Go after him. I know you want to. I'm okay. Safe in here now."

Frank was already moving away from her toward the door. "Call the sheriff, Abby. Tell him what I'm doing," he shouted to her as he went out the door. He jumped in his truck and took off down the road behind the burgundy car. *Go, Frank, go. Catch him.*

Abby made the phone call and it felt as if the sheriff took forever to get there, though it wasn't more than a few minutes in real time. After she explained what had happened, he drove off in the same direction Frank had taken. She called Sam and he and Myrtle came to get her. Sam wanted to join the search, but stayed with them. They went back to Frank's cabin.

Frank returned an hour later. The rest of them had been sitting on the front porch guarding the road. Waiting.

"Lost him again," Frank said. "I stopped by the emergency rooms of a couple hospitals to see if anyone came in tonight with gunshot wounds. No one has." Frank sighed as he collapsed on the porch. Hung his head in his hands. "What is he, some ghost who can vanish into the ground?"

"You know that's not true. He's a man like any other man," Sam countered. "And we'll get him. His luck is bound to change sooner or later. Don't lose heart, old friend."

Abby sat down beside Frank and put her arm around him. "You did your best. Saved me. I'm beginning to feel like some weakling female. Always in danger. Always being saved by old ladies or ex-cops."

Abby was depressed that her attacker had gotten away, but it wasn't Frank's fault. He'd done his best. "Like Sam says, you'll catch him sooner or later, Frank. He's going to make a mistake. There are a lot of people working on finding him."

"At least I think I shot him—twice or more. Hit flesh, I'm sure, by the sound of it. He screamed." Frank was remembering.

"I heard him. I think your bullets hit him, too." Then it dawned on her. "He lied in that letter. He came after me anyway. Do you think he'll try again?" she wanted to know.

"I think he might. I don't know for sure. I just have the feeling that our time's running out. All I know is, if he's alive, he's going to do something. Get back at us. Tonight would have hurt his pride and he can't stand being made a fool of." Frank remembered that from ten years ago.

"Or maybe," Sam offered Frank as comfort, "you hurt him bad enough that he'll go off for another ten years and hide. Or he'll hole up somewhere and die. He could be dead now."

Frank's laugh was flat. "I thought that the last time and was I wrong. Remember? It'd be too easy if he was dead."

"But," Abby said hopefully, "he could be"

"He could be," Frank reluctantly admitted, unsure.

They went inside, locked the doors and ate their supper, more subdued than usual. They all went to bed early.

"Sleep revives me and gives me a new perspective," Abby confided to Frank. "I want a new day to come. I want to start out over again and forget this one."

Frank said he felt the same way except, "It could have ended a lot worse. Thank goodness you're safe."

"I know. He didn't get me . . . again. God was watching over me."

"He sure was. I'll thank Him before I go to bed tonight."

"You do that. I know I will. Good night, Frank. Thank you for saving me." They were standing at her door and Abby couldn't help it, she leaned toward Frank and gave him a soft kiss on the lips. She had no idea she was going to do it, it simply happened.

Frank smiled. "It was worth that and more for that kiss."

For a moment they looked at each other. Besides the desperation in Frank's eyes Abby could see the love. Love for her.

But it wasn't time to talk about it yet. They both knew that.

She closed her door and leaned against it as her smile faded.

Abby didn't think any of them had much sleep that night. Too many noises outside. She woke up three times, heart ready to stop, thinking that someone was breaking into Frank's cabin.

Her dreams were worse than usual. In them, the kidnapper caught her, and there was no one there to save her this time.

Chapter Sixteen

The cop had shot him again! He couldn't believe it. Blood
everywhere. Burning. The pain was an agony he remembered well from years ago. Déjà vu.

Worse . . . he'd missed grabbing *her* for the second time.

Fleeing his enemy, screeching down foggy roads, he
pulled his car off into a grove of trees and switched off his
lights as the cop's truck barreled by. When he was sure the
other vehicle had passed he swerved back onto the road and
went the other way, then onto another street and eventually
into the woods that he'd been hiding in. He fought to stay
conscious. Denied the pain, but not his anger. Since coming
to this town nothing had gone right.

After being chased from his motel room, he'd gone to an
all-night Wal-Mart and purchased a cheap tent and camping
supplies with the last of his cash. It wasn't too cold to sleep
outside and motel rooms were too visible and cost too much.
He'd been paying thirty dollars a night for that last dump.
Camping out in the woods he didn't have to pay a penny.
Worked for him. And it was a perfect place to hide. The cops
would never find him there.

He put up his tent in a remote location that was difficult to
get to. Out in the woods where no roads led. And each day
when night fell he'd return and among the trees he'd open a

can of food he'd bought or he'd cook something on a stick or in a pan over the campfire. He had water. Snacks. Blankets. Everything he needed.

He could rinse off in the stream and liked roughing it, made him feel resourceful. Sleeping out under the night sky, being tucked deep in the forest made him feel invisible. No one could find him.

The woman was still hiding out at the cop's cabin. He'd been tailing her whenever she left the house with someone. That morning he'd been trailing them but, wary of following too closely in the daylight, lost them. Frustrated, he retreated to the trees behind the cabin and waited. As night came and they hadn't returned, he headed back to his campsite and stopped by the supermarket for more groceries.

It was risky. Someone might see his car. See him. The sheriff and his deputies were patrolling the area. Uniforms skulking around like jackals. Everyone was looking for him.

But he needed hot dogs and soda—warm canned soda tasted as good as anything if one were thirsty—and thought he could quietly slip into the store, get what he wanted, and get out. Parking behind the IGA so the car would be out of sight, he put on a jacket, tugged a cap low over his ears and pushed his long hair up under it. Hunched over as he walked in to make himself appear shorter, he hoped no one would notice him.

It worked. As if he were invisible, he was in and out and not one person looked his way. When he was in the car about to leave he saw the cop and the woman drive up and go inside. What luck, he thought. Another chance to make right what he'd done wrong. He only had to wait, observe, and if an opportunity arose, seize the woman. He waited as they went in and shopped. They parked close to the entrance. No opportunity there. Too many people around in the store. No opportunity there. And when they came out they both got in the truck. He was irritated that no chance to steal her had presented itself.

Then the woman dashed back in alone. Must have forgotten something. She looked out the store window in his direction but couldn't see him. He was invisible. Oh, how he wanted to jump out and go get her, but there wasn't enough time. In minutes she was out of the store and reunited with the cop.

They didn't leave. The truck sat there and he waited. If he drove out of the parking lot, the only way he could get to the highway, he'd pass right by them and they'd see the car. So he sat there waiting. Too long. They didn't leave.

What should I do? he asked his voices.

He's not in the truck. He knows you're here and he's coming for you. Go get her.

The cop had seen his car and was creeping up on him. Trying to surprise him.

Well, he was smarter than that. He started his car and sped around the side of the building, passing the truck. But no one was in it. They'd seen him. Were after him. Ha. He'd fooled them. He was no longer there behind the store, but in front of the store behind their truck.

The truck's door swung open and the woman bolted out. He got out and right up behind her, caught her arm, almost had her and then . . . *shot by the cop!*

He was big and he was fast, but he couldn't fight against a gun. He turned and ran like the time ten years ago. He ran like a scared rabbit.

Before his campfire that night, after he'd stopped the bleeding and cleaned his wounds, he took a handful of aspirin for the pain. It didn't help. He had two bullet holes in his side that had gone through loose skin. He hoped they hadn't hit anything important. It hurt something awful but he willed himself to bear it.

"What should I do now?" he whispered into the night air. He was sick of getting shot. Of hurting. Truth was, he was sick of taking people. No matter what the voices said, he didn't think it was right. Why did he have to do it?

His voices hissed in his head: *Tomorrow you will leave this place. Get on the road and drive to Canada. Stay there until your enemies let down their guard and forget about you. Disappear. Like you did before. If you remain here you will be caught. They know your car, they know you. Time to change your thinking. Your look. Your vehicle. Come back when they have forgotten and are no longer looking for you. Be smarter than they are. Be patient. You will have number three with time.*

It made sense, he thought, as he winced from the pain of his wounds. Leave. Take time to recover and make new plans. Yeah, like before. Canada. No problem to sneak unseen across the border. A person could hide there for years and never be found.

He would get a job to refill his wallet and he would wait. Wait until he was told what to do. The cop and his friends would be searching all over for him here and he'd be long gone. That would be funny. Let everyone twist themselves into paperclips trying to catch him when he wasn't even here.

Listening to the sounds of the night woods, he found sleep. Ignored the throbbing pain from his injuries. But he was alone. He was always alone and wondered why that was so.

Since his mother had died the voices had been his only companions. Not very good ones, either. He didn't think they even liked him. Sometimes he wished they'd leave him be.

He was so lonely.

At dawn the next morning, still in pain from his wounds, he broke camp and escaped toward Canada along the isolated country roads, staying out of the towns and cities and fighting to keep from passing out. No one saw him. No one stopped him.

I'll fool them, he brooded. *Like before. I'll fool them good. Maybe I won't even come back.*

If the voices would just leave him alone.

Chapter Seventeen

The following morning Abby was grateful to be alive. Her arm was sore where that man had gripped her but the pain didn't matter. She was smiling, having realized how lucky she'd been . . . for the second time. Frank had saved her. It was a little embarrassing owing her life to other people. But at least she had her life.

Outside the window, the morning mist rippled across the backyard in waves and the distant trees created a muted green fence. Was her stalker out there somewhere watching her? Waiting until he could finally get his hands on her? She couldn't bear to think about it.

She threw on a robe and went downstairs, leaving Snowball sleeping on the bed. Sam was making coffee in the kitchen and the house smelled like home. Looked like she and Sam were the first ones up, though it was after nine.

"Frank usually doesn't sleep this late," Abby remarked to Sam as he placed a cup of coffee before her on the table next to a box of glazed donuts.

"I know Frank's an early bird. Remember he was my partner for years. But he is up. Outside feeding the dogs. After you went to bed last night he went out looking for our suspect and afterward had a late night get-together with the sheriff. Frank drove by motels, roamed through hospital

160

emergency rooms—he was sure he'd shot him. Didn't get back until after three."

Sam met her eyes with a smile. "He really cares for you, Abby. If something happened to you, he'd never forgive himself. He was in a panic last night over that man attacking you.

"I know you and he say you're just friends . . . but, Abby, I haven't seen him care this much for a woman since his late wife, Jolene. He's really worried about you."

Frank's caring touched her, but he was sticking to her like a decal. After what had happened the night before she wouldn't be going home, wouldn't be resuming her life, not that she wanted to. After last night, she was content to stay at Frank's bed and breakfast for a while longer. To say she was scared was an understatement. "Frank didn't get him, did he?"

"Sad to say, no. As always, the man's a rat and has skittered into the cracks."

Abby rose from the table. "I'll mosey on outside and say good morning to Frank. Fresh air will do me good." She took a donut and her cup of coffee and strolled out onto the deck in the sunlight. Frank had finished feeding the dogs and was throwing a stick for them to fetch. As she stepped outside he stood to his full height and turned to her.

"How's your arm feeling this morning, Abby?"

She rubbed her elbow. Last night, after her attack, it'd hurt for a long time. "Better now. But me, I'm not so sure of. I can't stop thinking about last night and how quickly it all went down. How stupid I was to run like that. If you didn't show up when you did, he would have had me."

"That's true. But that didn't happen. You're here. You're all right. And hey, some of that being stupid belongs to me. I never should have left you alone in the truck. What was I thinking? I believed that guy was out there and I knew how devious he could be. Won't make that mistake again. I'm sorry, Abby."

"You're absolved of everything because in the end you saved me—again. I can't argue with a hero." Abby sat down on the top deck step and Frank sat down beside her as she kept talking. "I was shocked he was so close on our tail and swooped in to snatch me like he did. I thought I was off his radar. I really did. But until last night I didn't grasp how relentless he could be. I won't underestimate him again. So you're right to be overprotective.

"And if I haven't said it before, thank you for letting me and Myrtle stay here and for taking care of us." She slid her hand into his and the two of them sat there comfortably, breathing in the morning air and holding hands. The close calls had made her see things clearer. Life was precious because a person never knew how long they had. She wanted to live and enjoy it. Joel was dead but she was still there. Time she let go of the past and lived again.

"Are we going to Martha's party tonight, Frank?"

"I think we should. If we huddle in this house in fear of that creep, he's won. Our friends will be there and if we stick together, no one leaves the house alone and we're careful, I don't see why we can't go. The sheriff and a couple of his men will be there and we'll eyeball people at the door so no strangers get in. I know most people in town, and Martha knows everybody, so that should be easy. We'll patrol the grounds and keep our eyes open. We'll go armed. Martha won't mind."

"No, gun-lover that she is, she won't." Abby didn't like the idea of taking a gun anywhere, but after what had happened to her twice, she wasn't going to argue about it. "I'm glad we're going. After the last few weeks we've had we need some fun. Shake off this gloom that's been riding on our backs. And—" Abby gave him a small grin, "promise I won't stray more than five feet away from you and Sam. I'll keep an eye on Myrtle, too."

"Ooh, we have to take the old lady, do we?" he kidded, picking up the stick and throwing it again for the dogs.

"No way out of it. She knows the party's tonight. There'll be food and games. People. Can't keep her away, Can't leave her by herself here."

"Nah, I guess we have to take her," he said smiling.

"There's something else." Abby squinted up at the rainbow sky that was dominated by a glowing yellow sun. It was one of those rare, late October days when the temperature was in the sixties, the humidity was low, and the breeze was warm. The morning haze was lifting and it was a perfect day. Abby was happy to be there to enjoy it.

"I'd like to take Laura and Nick Brooks to the party tonight," she said. "Laura's sort of my protégé. She wants to be an artist . . . and she's very good. While I was working on the library mural she, Nick, and I became friends. I haven't seen them for a few days and I hear their mom's in the hospital. A neighbor is watching them until something else can be arranged. I think those two kids could use a night out and a good meal. I kinda feel responsible. I'd bring all seven of the kids, but I don't think I could handle the whole mob."

"Now that you mention it you couldn't bring all seven anyway," Frank caught her up, " 'cause I heard they've split the family up. Relatives from out of state took the younger kids. Laura and Nick are the only ones at the house right now. Nick wouldn't leave Laura and since Laura's almost fifteen, they've let her and Nick remain at the house with the neighbor and a social worker checking up on them every day—until the social worker finds a temporary home for both of them. Maybe as soon as Monday. We can swing by and pick them up tonight if they want to go."

"I hadn't heard that the family had broken up." But then she'd been busy lately and hadn't bothered to keep in touch with Laura and Nick. Hearing what Frank had to say made her feel guilty for forgetting about them. "Why did they split up the kids if Rebecca's only in the hospital?"

His voice subdued, he said, "She's in critical condition, might not make it. And, as you know, the search for Emil Brooks hasn't found a trace of him besides the shoe, that is."

"And they're looking for a temporary home for Laura and Nick? Really?" Part of her heart began to ache. She was holding her breath and didn't know it until she got dizzy.

"You interested?" Frank was studying her.

Caught off guard, she couldn't look him in the eyes. "I don't know . . . if it wasn't for my insidious shadow . . . my life's not stable or safe enough to think about taking in a kid or two. You said Laura and Nick wanted to stay together." She stopped talking, there were so many thoughts clashing around in her head she couldn't make sense of them.

"You have a bond with those two kids, don't you?" Frank could see right through her.

"Since the first time I met Laura we've had this . . . connection. The art, the way she thinks about things. It's like looking back at myself when I was a kid. I feel so awful for her—if her father is never found and now her mother . . ."

"Dies?" Frank finished gently.

"Yeah." Abby looked out over the yard and shook her head. She heard Myrtle chatting with Sam about waffles in the kitchen behind them. "As I've told you before, Joel and I always wanted kids. It never happened. Something about Laura makes me believe I'm supposed to take care of her. And now she needs me. I could reach out to her and Nick . . . except for the creature that's trying to mess up my life. Terrible timing. I can't put those kids in danger like that."

She knew Frank wanted to comfort her, say that they'd get the kidnapper, that everything would be all right and she could go back to her real life soon. She gave him credit for not doing that.

"When this is over maybe you can think seriously about Laura and Nick?" was all he said.

She nodded and stood up. "Right now I'll take it a day at a time. The party tonight, taking Laura and Nick, having a good time and eating all that fabulous food and desserts Martha's going to have. That's all I can handle for now."

"Then that's all you have to handle. You've had a rough week."

They went inside to eat the waffles Sam was cooking and whose smells were making her mouth water. In spite of everything, she was looking forward to Martha's shindig.

Looking forward to seeing Laura and Nick and their reaction to going to a Halloween party.

After breakfast Abby called Laura. She was excited when Abby asked if she and Nick wanted to come to the party. Laura said yes and told Abby what she already knew. "Aunt Bessie and Uncle Edward took William and Penny for a while. Cousin Sheila took Charlene, and Eunice went with my father's sister, Louise. Giles turned eighteen last week. He's wanted to join the Army for a long time and signed up way before Dad disappeared and Mom got so sick. Yesterday he reported for duty and is on his way to Fort Lenardwood right now. Me and Nick are the only ones left." Laura's voice sounded so miserable Abby wanted to rush over and console her.

"You have enough food? Electricity and everything still on?"

"Food? Sure we have lots of food. We got delivered a whole bunch of stuff last night from the supermarket. Someone—don't know who—sent it to us.

"And none of the utilities have been shut off . . . yet. The social worker lady made phone calls so they wouldn't and she comes by everyday to check on Nick and me. Tell us how Mom's doing at the hospital. Sometimes she or one of our neighbors—usually Mrs. Snowden who comes over everyday—takes us to see Mom. I told the social worker we're doing fine. I can take care of Nick and myself. Been doing it all my life. People are worried about us, but we're okay here by ourselves, I tell them. We keep the doors locked and don't open them to strangers, especially after what happened to our dad and Shelly. Don't know why we have to go to some foster home.

"Mrs. Betts, the social worker, says if she hasn't found us a place by Monday, we might have to go to a state home or something like that." Laura's voice fell. Abby could hear the desperation in it.

"But somebody's got to be here when they find our dad.

The house can't be empty and dark when he comes home, you know? Someone's got to make him supper and laugh at his jokes. Dad tells the worst jokes."

Abby's heart went out to her. She'd once been young and poor, too, but she'd always had her mother and father. Laura was alone with her younger brother and facing an uncertain future. Abby wished she could have put the girl's mind at rest and told her she wanted to take her and Nick in. But she couldn't offer them a home when she wasn't sure when she could go back to that home.

"How's your mom?" Abby inquired instead in what she hoped was a cheerful voice.

"Not good. Weaker every day. She can't walk no more. That's why she had to go into the hospital. She's on pain pills and talks silly. If only she could come home then my brothers and sisters could come home, too. Charlene and I can take care of the rest of them. Why can't the doctors make my mother better, Mrs. Sutton?"

"They're trying to, Laura." Abby knew she shouldn't lie to her and was as truthful as she could bear to be, but she wasn't about to tell the girl her mother was dying. She couldn't do that. "But your mother has a serious disease."

Then like any fifteen-year-old, Laura zeroed back in on the party. "Is it a costume party tonight? Should Nick and I dress up? Will there be food and games?"

"You can dress up, but no masks. And yes there'll be food, sandwiches, cakes, and candies. Games, too, if I know Martha." Abby excitedly described Martha's haunted house and the amazing food that was going to be there. She didn't say anything about her close call with the kidnapper the night before or that it had been Frank who'd sent her and Nick the anonymous groceries. If Frank had wanted them to know, he'd have left his name.

"We'll pick you both up early, about three o'clock, Laura. You two be ready."

After Abby hung up she felt better. Laura and her sorrows

having been on her mind lately, it felt good to give her and Nick a little bit of happiness.

Feeling restless, Abby helped Frank clean house and did some laundry for herself, sent some bills, and studied the photos of Martha's garden she'd rescued from the seat of Frank's truck. Some of them were really good. She could definitely get a painting out of them.

Sam was on the computer doing business with his home office and then he and Frank spent time closed off in the den plotting, Abby imagined, on what to do next. The phone rang numerous times and she could hear Frank's voice behind the door angrily talking to someone. The authorities probably. Frank was upset that they didn't have any more leads to the crimes.

A short time later a squad car was sitting outside the house. So now they had police security. It should have made Abby feel safer, but it didn't. There'd been a police car outside her house the night the kidnapper had broken in and tried to abduct her the first time. Fat lot of help they'd been then.

All of them decided to dress up for the party and lighten their mood. Abby had picked up a long black dress from her house the day before—an old costume from her Joel days— put it on and painted cat whiskers on her face and black eyeliner around her eyes. Little black paper ears on a headband. "I'm a cat," she purred at Frank. Pretending to hiss and scratch at him as he laughed and pretended to fend her off.

Sam came out looking like he usually did. Casual but classy in slacks and a nice blue shirt. "I'm a homicide detective undercover," he informed everyone with a grin. "Sorry, I never had time to pick up a costume." Truth was, Abby was surprised Sam was still with them. He missed his family so much. Seemed preoccupied most of the time fretting over them. He'd spent an hour on the phone with his wife that morning. One of his kids was really sick with the flu and Abby knew Frank felt guilty for keeping Sam away from his family for so long.

Frank made an elegant Zorro with the black mask cleverly outlined across his face so anyone could see it was him. He wore a sword at his waist and a pistol in a shoulder holster hidden under the cape. Ingenious way of going to the party armed, making it part of his costume.

Abby found herself staring at him every chance she got. He was so dashingly handsome. But Zorro had always appealed to her. Antonio Banderas in his black mask and cape with that mustache. What a hunk. And Frank could have been his twin—in the costume anyway. "You know," Abby complimented him, "you're so wickedly handsome in that get-up that all the women at the party won't be able to take their eyes off you."

He whispered in her ear as he pulled her close, "Let them look, but my heart belongs to you, Abby." He pirouetted in the living room, his cape whirling around him like a living thing, took a fighting stance and pulled his sword to make the classic sign of Zorro.

"You're good," Abby told him while she laughed.

His eyebrow went up, pulling the drawn mask with it. "I've had extensive fencing lessons, my dear. One of my many other interests. I'm quite good at it, too, if I do say so myself. Won a few matches in my time, in fact."

"An expert at fencing. Who would have guessed."

"Martha's also having music at this bash," Frank mentioned, taking Abby in his arms and twirling her around. "Hope it isn't all 'Monster Mash' and 'Black Magic Woman.' I'm in the mood to dance." He winked at her and kissed her spontaneously on the tip of her nose.

Myrtle dressed herself as a gypsy. No surprise there. Looked like her normal dress except she had on more jewelry and more makeup—if that was possible—than usual. When she sashayed down the steps, Abby had to cover her mouth to keep from giggling. Myrtle wore a rhinestone tiara on her tiny head and earrings so large she looked like a retriever. She'd drawn eyeliner around her eyes in raccoon fashion and her lipstick was a shade of flaming crimson.

"I'm Salome," she announced regally, throwing her twig thin arms up in what she thought was a provocative pose and rotating around in a slow circle. She clapped her hands together and sang a song in her high-pitched voice that sounded familiar but Abby couldn't place. The old lady seemed so happy with her appearance that everyone went along with her that, yes, she looked marvelous, and yes, her costume would be the hit of the party. Then the group filed out of the house and into Sam's station wagon. It would hold all six of them and wouldn't be recognizable to the killer if he was out there looking for them because Sam had kept it hidden in the back beneath a nylon car cover since he'd arrived.

With most of the kids gone the Brooks' house seemed strangely quiet. Laura and Nick came running out, grins on their faces. Laura was dressed in a homemade peasant outfit, which was really only one of those peasant blouses that were so popular again, paired up with a long skirt that was also in vogue. With ribbons in her hair and a tambourine in her hand, she and Myrtle could be twins. They both looked like old-fashioned gypsies to Abby. One old and one young and one with a lot more makeup and jewelry.

Nick had blue pants and an old blue T-shirt on with a red towel tied around his scrawny shoulders. He'd painted a jerky S on the front of his shirt with a black magic marker. Said he was Superman.

"Wow," Abby exclaimed, sending a look Frank's way and then Nick's. "Now I have both my favorite heroes with me tonight." Nick got a kick out of that and insisted on sitting next to her and holding her hand, acting as if he were Superman and she was Lois, even though she looked like a cat.

He was so hungry for attention it melted her. Hugging the boy close, Abby talked over his head with Laura. The kids were thrilled to be going. They caught her up on their lives and flooded Frank with questions about how the searches for their father and Shelly were going. They already knew why Abby and Myrtle were staying at Frank's. Tongues had been wagging. Apparently the whole town knew everything, and the kids had big ears. So much for keeping secrets to protect them. They were smart kids and not much could be kept from them anyway.

Martha's party was a success and most of the town was there. Their hostess was costumed as Cleopatra and Ryan as her lover, Marc Anthony. Samantha was dressed as Lois Lane, which made Nick as happy as a contest winner.

Everyone mingled, ate, danced, but was jumpy over every outside noise fearing that the kidnapper was outside spying on them. Police officers patrolled the grounds and were stationed at the doors, but nothing sinister materialized.

Abby had a great time. There were whimsical games with outrageously expensive gifts as rewards. Somehow both kids each won something. Laura won a CD player and Nick won twenty-five dollars. She and Frank danced, she and the kids danced, and she even danced a few with Sam and Ryan. She ate too much. But they all did. The food was delicious.

As everyone left, they were warned to be careful going home. Don't stop unless they had someone with them and keep their eyes open.

Abby and her friends returned to Frank's cabin safely. Abby was touched when Frank asked the kids if they wanted to go home with them and stay for the rest of the weekend.

"It's only a day or two. I have an extra room sitting there empty and I'd feel better if you two were with us anyway. I have a folding bed I can put up for Nick."

Abby knew what he really meant. The kids would be safer with them.

"Tomorrow I'll call your neighbor, Mrs. Snowden, tell her where you are, and clear it with your social worker too."

The children agreed without argument. Free food and nice surroundings? Why not?

Exhausted from the party and all the excitement, Myrtle and the kids went to bed. Sam put in a leisurely phone call to his wife, and Abby and Frank sat at the kitchen table over hot chocolate reliving how fun the party had been.

"Laura and Nick had a good time," Abby stated. "I've

never seen them that happy. Laura said she'd never been in such a beautiful house as Martha's. She thinks Martha is some millionaire now. After you, that is." Her eyes swept across the kitchen.

"She would. Seeing where she and the boy live. Their house should be condemned. Did you see all the food they stuffed in their pockets?" Frank chuckled. His face was clean. His cape and weapons and Zorro gone. "Kind of Martha to give them that doggie bag to take along, as if they need it here. They act like they're starving."

"In a way they have been. It hasn't been easy for them," Abby spoke softly.

"I guess not." Frank was looking out the windows into the night. "I've been thinking . . . I'm not taking them back to that empty house tomorrow or any other day. They can stay here as long as their mother is in the hospital or until a more permanent place is found for them. Social workers can visit them here as well as their parents' house. Two kids can't eat that much. Don't take up much space, either. I have the room. What's two more people for a while?"

"You're a generous man, Frank." Abby touched his hand and he turned to hold hers. "You have a good heart."

"Yeah, don't tell anyone, though. People will think I'm a millionaire, like Martha, and want to borrow money."

"Never thought of it that way." The silence that fell between them was comfortable.

After a few minutes Frank murmured, "No sign of our nemesis tonight, thank God. I expected him to have at least left a taunting note, a phone call or something. Follow someone home. Something." Instead of being relieved, Frank seemed perplexed. He continued to study the world outside the window as if he expected the kidnapper to be out there staring back at him. "I don't like it. He's up to something, I know it."

"All we can do is wait. Protect ourselves." Abby's hand squeezed his and when their eyes met she smiled at him. She felt safe with him. She always did.

"It's that I don't like feeling helpless like this, Abby. Feeling like I can't protect the ones I love." For a second, Abby actually thought he was going to lean over and kiss her. But he didn't. He was waiting for her to let him know it was all right.

She wanted to kiss him again. But last night had been a fluke. He'd saved her life and she'd reacted out of overwhelming gratitude. She wanted to give in to the feelings that had been growing between them for months, but she didn't. Joel's face haunted her, and reflected in Frank's eyes. She needed a little more time.

"Did Claudia tell you about the thieves in town last week?" Frank broke the spell and asked her. Claudia Mathis was a good friend of theirs, owned the bookstore in town and passed on gossip as well as Martha.

"Said she's losing books and the other shopkeepers have been coming up with missing items too."

"The hardware store's been hit," Frank added. "Someone stole a set of expensive hammers and boxes of nails a few days back. The bakery and the IGA have reported the same problems. The gift shop was robbed of a very expensive jewelry box and a crystal figurine."

Frank sighed, "Used to be such a law abiding town."

"Used to be," Abby said, thinking, serial kidnappers and now kleptomaniacs. What next?

"Well, I think we should get some sleep, Abby. It's been quite a night." Frank yawned and got up. He walked her to her room and again she thought he might kiss her, but he didn't. Instead he said good night and walked away.

When he was gone she couldn't stop thinking about him. About them.

The kidnapper seemed far away. The danger, too. The party—seeing the children so happy for once and the happiness she'd had dancing and laughing with Frank—was a more recent memory.

She had the strangest feeling that everything would be all

right now. She didn't know why, she just did. Maybe Frank had scared away the kidnapper with his bullets—had hurt him badly—and they'd never see him again.

Wishful thinking. But Abby had a feeling she was safe. Finally. That they were all safe. Wouldn't it be great, she reflected, if it were true?

Tired from all the food and partying, sleep came quickly. And that night she didn't dream.

Chapter Eighteen

Abby was finally going home. Walking through her front door, her bulging overnight bag in one hand and Snowball's cat carrier in the other, elation washed over her, not just because her exile was over but because the kidnapper hadn't made a move in over five weeks.

Life was almost normal. Almost, because the memories of her attacks lingered no matter how secure she felt. She let the cat out of her prison and Snowball scurried around the house, tail straight up, meowing like a wild thing.

I'm happy to be home, too, Snowball.

Staying at Frank's had been like a long vacation but there was no place like home. Opening the windows, chilly December air rushed in to chase out the dust and staleness. No one could tell anyone had ever broken in. Luke had done a fine job on the windows.

Abby and Myrtle had remained with Frank after the night of Martha's party and as the days went by without further attempts on their lives and no sign of the kidnapper whatsoever they began to feel safe again little by little. The townspeople began to forget. October slipped into a wet November, with weather warmer than any November Abby could recall.

"Your bullets must have gotten him, Frank," she said one November night on his porch.

The kidnapper's weekly deadline had passed and then another and another. Three weeks had gone by without anymore hate-filled letters, attempted abductions, kidnappings, or assaults to break the town's or their peace.

No more mud people in mailboxes.

"He must have been badly wounded. . . . could even be dead." There'd been hope in Abby's voice. A drizzly day after a stormy night had brought Frank and her out on the porch to admire the lightning and to feel the quaking of the thunder. They'd had on jackets to keep them warm from the rainy cold, but she loved the cool air on her face, loved the winter smells. Loved the idea that maybe their ordeal was over and they were no longer a madman's targets.

"Wouldn't it be great if he was stone-cold dead? Stuck headfirst in a ditch somewhere, wild dogs gnawing on his evil bones? Never be able to hurt another human being. I don't care if he gets a decent burial or not. Doesn't deserve one. Let the forest animals have him." Abby had been going on and on about it and it felt good to vent the frustration she'd built up.

The porch lights had been off; they hadn't been that brave yet to call attention to themselves, so they'd still talk in whispers, making Frank's face unreadable in the gray shadows. His voice guarded when he spoke. "I believed he was dead ten years ago, Abby, and he . . . came back. I can't make the same mistake. Don't know why he's laid off us so long or why he deviated from his normal method. Don't care. But I know I don't trust him. Sure . . . he could be off licking his wounds, he could be dead, or this could be some scheme to throw us off kilter again. Only time will tell."

"Well, time is what I'm talking about. Been four weeks living off your hospitality, Frank. Isn't it time I go back home? And Myrtle's acting like a prisoner ready to break jail. Don't know how much longer you're going to hold her.

Or Sam. Good thing he's been on paid leave from the job and his paycheck hasn't been docked. We've kept that man away from his family long enough, don't you think? He misses them and they miss him. Your phone bill is going to be astronomical." Living six hours away from home wasn't easy.

"Least I can do for all his help." Frank had stuck his hand out beyond the covering of the porch and let the raindrops splash on his skin. "I want to be absolutely sure it's clear before I release all the hostages." A soft chuckle.

A streak of lightning had veined through the sky, illuminating Frank's pensive expression. "One more week, Abby. See if he shows himself or makes a move. Lay low here seven more days and if there are no new developments you can go home. Though, I'm going to be sorry to see you go. It's been like having a family again. With my son away at medical school it's been lonely, I confess. I've enjoyed having all of you. It's why I built so many bedrooms in the first place. To lure people to stay."

Laura and Nick had remained at Frank's only a short time. Rebecca Brooks had passed away from complications of her illness a week after Martha's Halloween party. More like from a broken heart was Abby's belief. When her husband hadn't been found she gave up. The disease won. Laura cried for hours. Nick didn't cry at all.

After their mother died, and after a week when no one else could be found to take them, the social worker thought it best to transfer them to the county's foster care facility.

Abby had wanted to ask about taking them but she'd gotten cold feet. She wasn't sure she was safe yet and she needed time to think about it. Two kids were a huge responsibility and she had no idea how to raise children. Besides, family might still come forward and claim them. Frank would have let them stay; he wanted them to, but the social worker insisted they come with her. There were proper channels to go through.

Abby suspected the social worker didn't want the kids in

the same house with any kidnapper targets, which ruled both Abby and Frank out. She understood that. So the kids were taken away.

She and Frank visited them often at the foster care facility. Brought them gifts and homemade baked goods. They missed them. A solid bond had formed the week they'd been with them at Frank's. The foster care facility let the kids stay with Frank for Thanksgiving Day to share their holiday meal.

Frank's sister, Louisa, and her husband Michael, along with Frank's son Kyle, Martha and Ryan, Myrtle, Sam, and Abby made up the rest of the Thanksgiving table. Kyle, usually shy, made an instant connection with Laura and Nick. By the end of the day they were behaving like brothers and sister. Kyle let Nick play games on his laptop computer and the three got to know each other better over board games.

Laura and Nick returned to the foster care facility that night with full stomachs, leftovers and warm memories, Abby hoped. She and Frank kept in touch by phone and visits.

She'd finished Martha's garden picture the first few weeks at Frank's. He helped her cart over her art supplies and easel from the house and on nice days she'd sit outside on his deck and paint. Sometimes Frank stood in the doorway behind her watching.

Twilight in Martha's Garden, she'd named the painting. Martha had loved it. The money, enough to pay her bills for months, was in the bank. Abby should have been happy, but she wasn't. She'd wanted to go home, wanted her old life back—the one without a criminal stalking her and abducting people she knew. She wanted the town and her friends to be safe.

She got her wish. The weeks had gone by and the kidnapper wasn't heard from again and she finally went home. She'd assured Frank she'd be careful, lock her windows and doors whenever she was in the house, keep the club close and watch her back.

"I'll keep an eye on you, too," Frank had promised. "As much as I can."

Now she was home.

Looking in the refrigerator, Abby took stock of what needed to be thrown away and what needed to be bought. She cleared the rotten items out and made a list. She spent some time cleaning house and then went to the supermarket. It was good to be living a normal life again. A little strange not having Frank or Sam shadowing her, but kind of nice.

Walking into the store, memories of the night Frank shot at the kidnapper assailed her. *He has to be gone or dead . . . has to be . . . because we can't watch our backs, can't live in uncertainty forever.*

Shelly had never come back to work. Had never come back at all. Her manager at the IGA had put up a picture of her above the checkout counter that he'd gotten from her mother. Beneath it people had laid flowers and little gifts. It made Abby cry.

She collected her groceries and got out as quickly as she could, went home, put them away, and sat down to do bills. That night she made a pot of stew, a special recipe handed down from her grandmother, and biscuits from scratch. Baking calmed her.

The thought crossed her mind that Myrtle would have liked the stew, Laura and Nick, too, and for a moment she was unhappy that she was the only one going to eat it. That's what living in a group home for five weeks had done to her.

When the stew was done she brought a bowl out onto the porch, sat on the swing and took pleasure in the solitude. Her club propped behind her against the wall. It was warm today for December and she only needed a sweater. How long would the heat spell last? She wanted snow for Christmas. As dusk moved in, her eyes examined the edges of the yard. Some of the shadows resembled a skulking man. She got up, went inside, and locked the door.

Frank was right. It wasn't over. It would never be over.

She went to bed with the club beside her. Better safe than sorry.

The next morning as she was feeding Snowball the phone rang.

"Good, I've caught you. This is Bonnie Mowry." Bonnie Mowry? Oh, yes, the woman who worked at city hall. She was a somebody in town politics with well-to-do friends and city council connections. The elite of Spookie.

"Hi. What can I do for you, Bonnie?"

"Frank said you were back home. Anyhow, I'll get right to it. Abby, we liked what you did at the library. The mural? Liked it a lot. I'm in charge of beautifying the city hall, inside and out, and the city council has agreed to commission you to do us a mural too. If you agree?"

She didn't have to think about it. "I do."

"You working on anything right now?"

"No. Just finished something for Martha Sikeston. I'm available. What did you and the council have in mind?" Abby's heart was racing. If they hired her to do something it'd help her make a real name for herself. She'd be on her way.

"Perhaps you already know that a group of eccentrics settled our town over a hundred years ago. Unconventional bunch of adventurers and dreamers. We have old photographs of some of them and what the town looked like at the time. Those first years. We'd like you to combine the people with the town photographs. You know, a painting of the early town with people, horses, and carriages all transposed on the mural. Make the people look like the original settlers in their original dress as much as you can. Not perfect, but muted, you know?"

"Do you have a size and location for this mural?" In Abby's mind she was seeing Main Street lined with the early shops and houses and with people in period dress walking or riding in carriages. Small figures, but recognizable as original settlers.

"Our main lobby at the city hall has a massive expanse of

wall ten feet in height and, ah, about thirty or so feet in length. Do you think we could meet sometime today, Abigail—maybe for lunch—and discuss this further? We can talk payment then, as well."

"That would be fine. I'm going into town today anyway so I could meet you."

"How about 1 o'clock at Pasta Corner? Our treat?"

Abby couldn't turn that down. Pasta Corner was a new Italian restaurant on the edge of town that had been open about six months. It was a tiny place in what was once a used furniture store. The owners were a married couple, Tammy and Scott Garner, who turned their passion of making home-made pasta and special sauces for their family and friends into a business. They sold Italian food from eleven in the morning until eight at night every day but Sunday. It didn't hurt Stella's business much. Stella didn't serve pasta. If a person wanted Italian or cozy ambience the Pasta Corner was perfect. The restaurant was small, the food was excel-lent but costly. Frank had taken Abby there for her birthday in August. Most of the time, though, it was off her budget.

At lunch Bonnie produced photographs of the old town and its inhabitants and they discussed what they wanted in the mural. The amount Bonnie offered was more money than Abby would have had the nerve to ask for, but she wisely kept her mouth shut and took it.

And, Bonnie told Abby she could have as much time to finish the wall painting as she needed. Start anytime after Bonnie and the council okayed her preliminary drawing. Lunch was delicious. When it was over, Abby left with the photographs and went to take care of the errands she'd come to town for in the first place. Pay a water bill. Pick up some books waiting for her at the library. Relish her freedom.

Everywhere she went, she kept her eyes open and scanned her surroundings. Never got in the car unless she checked inside and underneath first. Her head was full of the new project, how she was going to lay it out, what color scheme she was going to use. It would be the biggest and most difficult task she'd ever tackled. Could she do it? Would they like it? And if they didn't like it, would they still pay her?

She stopped at the post office for stamps, paid the water bill, and ran by the library. Then she walked into city hall to have a look at the wall she was going to be working on, took exact dimensions and gauged the light she was dealing with. Good location, good light for a mural. Everyone who came into city hall would see it.

Driving home, her eyes on the road ahead, behind her and on the land and trees around the street, she couldn't shake this feeling that someone was watching her. Gave her the willies. She was glad to get home and lock the doors.

Calling Frank to check in, she gave him the news about the commission and he was happy for her. He mentioned he was writing again and she was happy for him. He said he would see her soon and she had no doubt of that.

That night before she fell asleep she heard his truck drive by. She knew what the engine sounded like. As he'd promised, he was keeping an eye on her and it made her feel safer.

Abby began the preliminary drawing for the city hall job. Inspired, she worked most of the night and thought it was about ready to show to Bonnie and the council, but would hold off a day or two. Couldn't look too eager or rush it. But she couldn't wait to begin painting.

That night for the first time in a long time, she dreamed of Joel. He was in the woods looking for her and she was in the woods looking for him. Never ran into each other. She awoke at dawn, heart pounding like a trapped bird to the ringing of the telephone.

Answering it, there was no one there.

Joel, what are you trying to tell me now?

Joel, as usual, didn't answer. Unable to go back to sleep, she got up, made coffee, and popped a bagel in the toaster.

At the kitchen table, nibbling on the bagel, she put the finishing touches on the city hall sketch. Today she would call Bonnie, tell her the sketch was ready. She'd decided that the sooner she got approval, the sooner she could start the job;

she was eager to begin. She was always happier when she was working.

Suddenly she didn't care how eager she looked.

It wasn't until she was on her way to town to deliver the sketch that she realized she hadn't thought of the kidnapper once all morning.

And that was just fine with her. She finally had her real life back.

Chapter Nineteen

Late that Friday afternoon Abby felt drained, but a good kind of drained. She was eyeing the mural she'd been painting and was ecstatic with the work so far. Everyone coming into city hall who'd seen it was impressed. She was already half done but loved doing the work as much as finishing and getting paid for it, so she was taking her time and enjoying herself. When she finished there'd be enough money—more than she'd ever made for one project—to keep her creditors away for months.

"What you've done so far Abby, is amazing." Claudia Mathis, owner of the town's bookstore and one of the first ones besides Martha to become Abby's friend, had come up behind her. When Abby had almost been abducted from her house, Claudia had called and offered her a place to stay. Abby had turned her down, not wanting to put her in danger, too. When Abby had been at Frank's, Claudia had called every few days to give her support and had sent her special books to read. She was a good friend, but wasn't much of a party person.

"That detail and the figures are so intriguing. I can almost see faces and expressions. Good color combinations, too. The mural is going to be beautiful when it's done. You're getting better with every job. Everyone's talking about the library mural and how gorgeous it is," she breathed. "When you're finished with this, how about you paint something for me at the bookstore? I have a wall crying out for a Sutton original."

"I'll mark you down next in my book." Pleased to be appreciated and also have another job lined up, Abby glanced at Claudia over her shoulder. She was trying to paint a few final minutiae on the mural before stopping for the day. Earlier than usual this day because she was driving to the county foster care facility to pick up Laura and Nick for the weekend. It was an hour's drive in the best of weather and they were predicting snow. She couldn't wait to see the kids.

Claudia was dressed in a cinnamon hued wool cape with fur trim and hood. She'd traveled all over the world and the way she dressed matched her sophisticated personality as her purse matched her leather gloves. She gave Abby a smile that Abby returned.

She and Claudia, lovers of books that they were, had become good friends from the first time Abby had wandered into Claudia's bookstore.

"Thanks for the compliment, Claudia. I think this project is going pretty well myself. What else are you here for . . . besides wanting me to paint on your wall? Checking up on me or what?" Abby finished a stroke or two on the historic courthouse. The picturesque long-ago village was coming to life. Soon she'd brush in the last of the people sitting on the porches and riding by on horseback or in horseless carriages. A couple of kids rolling hoops or riding bicycles.

"I got some interesting paperbacks in this morning. Knew you were over here working and thought you'd like to know. Some mysteries by Patricia Cornwall and Tony Hillerman you haven't read yet, I bet. I remember you like them."

"Thanks. I'll stop by on my way home if the weather's not too bad, or tomorrow, if it is. I *am* out of reading material," Abby said to Claudia, her gaze on the white windows.

Outside snow had started falling. Big fat flakes. "Looks like a blizzard. How bad is it really out there?" The weather report that morning had forecast an inch or two of snow by late afternoon or evening. First snowfall of the year and it was mid-December. The warm spell had broken a few days ago and suddenly, overnight, winter had slid in with freezing temperatures, sleet, and now snow. Abby loved snow. Made her think of Christmas, twinkly red and green lights and sugar cookies. The crystalline flakes cleansed the world and she thought the world needed a cleansing now more than ever. It could wash away all traces of the last few months.

It was ice Abby didn't like. Especially if she had to drive on it.

"A sprinkling of snow so far. But it's getting colder. There's ice on the trees and roads. When the sun goes down it's going to be treacherous."

"Then I'm quitting for the day right now. I have a journey to make before I head home and I want to get there and back before the roads turn into ice-skating rinks. One fender bender and they jack up your car insurance. Don't need that."

"None of us need that." Claudia observed as Abby put her paints and brushes away in a closet Bonnie had procured for her. Then she didn't have to lug art materials home at night and back everyday. "I'll walk you out," Claudia said, as Abby put her coat and woolen cap on.

People hadn't forgotten the recent scare. Some continued to be vigilant like Claudia, like Abby, even though no one had heard anything of the kidnapper in two months.

Claudia left Abby at her car and returned to work, reminding Abby not to forget the books. Abby said she wouldn't.

Pulling out onto the street and heading toward the foster care facility, the snow flurried around the car and Abby had a hard time keeping it on the road. Ice glittered everywhere. *Getting slick out here all right.* A premature twilight had fallen on the winter scene and the inch or so of ivory powder on the ground lent an eerie pale cast to everything. Abby was glad she'd taken off early. The roads were already dangerous.

Chrissie Morgan, the woman who ran the foster care facility for the county, was in her office sipping hot tea. She welcomed Abby in with a smile and offered her hand. Abby had gotten to know her on her visits to see Laura and Nick and today she was more animated than usual. "Got news for you, Abigail. The county will approve you for fostering Laura and Nick. All you have to do is sign the final papers. I have them on my desk."

The woman's gray eyes, the exact shade of her close cropped hair, shimmered. She was what in the old days they would have called a spinster. In her fifties. Never been married. No children of her own. But she treated the forty or so kids under her charge as if they were hers. Good woman. Huge heart. She'd been on Abby's side since Abby had first asked her to look into her potential for getting the kids.

Abby had been afraid they'd turn her down because she was a widow and alone. Also that she had been a target of the kidnapper. But Miss Morgan had been confident that that wouldn't matter. "Not these days and not with the ages of these kids," Miss Morgan had pointed out. "And since Frank—one of Spookie's most respected citizens—vouched for your sterling character and backed you up saying he'd help with the children, too. You were a shoe-in. They're yours."

Abby hardly knew what to say. She'd been toying with the idea of taking the two kids since their mother had died and she found out that none of their relatives could take them, but until that moment it hadn't been real. Now it was too real. "Oh, so fast? Can I have some time to think about it?"

Miss Morgan caught Abby's hesitation and waved her hands. "Give it some thought over the weekend, Abigail. I know it's a big step. Instant motherhood and two children to boot. I'm not pressuring you." Abby could see the disappointment Miss Morgan tried to hide as she closed the folder the papers were in and stood up.

"Well, anyway, the kids are waiting. They've been ready for hours. Thrilled to be going home with you for the weekend. They do so look forward to your visits and their visits with you." She ushered Abby to Laura's room, one she shared with ten other girls and Abby had been to many times. Nick was already there with his sister.

County Care was a nice facility, but still a county holding pen for unwanted children. Everything was neat and clean, but sparse. Same plain tan bedspreads on all the single beds, tasteful but simple curtains at the windows, and worn rugs on the floor. Prints of children and animals dotted the neutral walls. Bleak is what Abby would have called the place and that would have been charitable.

Most of the kids appeared content enough, some more dispirited than others, some lonelier. All were hungry for affection and attention. Abby saw the envious looks the other children gave Laura and Nick when she picked them up or brought them gifts.

She and Frank, who also visited the facility, had resolved to do something special for all the kids at Christmas. They would help, and get others to help donate to the Christmas party menu and give presents. Even if she took Laura and Nick away for the holidays she wouldn't forget the other children. The hungry hearts and lonely eyes of the others had left their mark on her and she wanted to do as much for them as she could.

Laura and Nick didn't hate the care facility, they tolerated it as children who never had much could and accepted what life threw at them without a whimper. Abby knew they missed their brothers and sisters, mother and father . . . their old life. Their sad faces haunted her all the time, though they came alive when they were with her or Frank. Abby wanted to protect them. Make life better for them. Give them things. She'd grown to love them completely.

But to have them with her everyday, all the time, and to be wholly accountable for their emotional, physical, and financial well-being *forever* was an overwhelming responsibility.

How did she think she could take care of both of them, when just taking care of herself at times was difficult enough? Miss Morgan was right, she needed to think some more about it. A little more time couldn't hurt.

Laura, thinner than last time Abby had seen her, her clothes worn and too loose, ran up to Abby and threw her arms around her. "Abby, I'm so happy to see you. I got so much to tell you!" she exclaimed. "I've made a bunch more drawings for you to look at. I've been working so hard." In her arms she clutched the sketchbook Abby had given her. Seemed so long ago now. Before her father had gone missing, before her mother had died. Was it only months ago?

Nick, as usual, stood behind them, eyes down, hands nervously clasping each other. He looked thinner, too. Weren't they eating? His eyes, when raised to take in Abby's face, were full of restrained hope. These kids depended on her—and Frank—now. Like drowning kittens, they were reaching for her to save them. Their puny overnight bags were at their feet. They had so little, Abby thought, and her heart hurt.

"Great. Laura, I'll look at your new drawings when we get to the house," Abby told her, taking the sketchbook and helping them gather their things. Outside the window the snow was a solid blanket and she was anxious about the roads and getting them home in one piece. "It's getting really bad out there and we need to get going. Are we ready?"

Both children nodded their heads, grinning like little clowns. Nick moved forward and grabbed Abby's arm. He tugged her downward and, surprising her, kissed her on the cheek. "I'll be good this weekend, I promise, Mrs. Sutton. Real good."

Abby sent the boy a questioning look. Why would he say such a thing? Nick was an angel. Well-behaved and considerate of everyone. It hit her that he was only trying to please.

Both of them were. She'd never discussed her fostering them, but kids had a sixth sense about some things. Maybe they were hoping that they could come home with her and stay. Maybe they'd been in the facility too long and they were scared for their future.

She didn't blame them. It must be frightening to suddenly be an orphan.

"You're always good, Nicholas." Abby had slipped once and called him by his full name and he seemed to like it that she did, so she'd continued doing so. He seemed more a Nicholas than a Nick to her anyway.

"Come on, you two. Have I got a supper for you. Ever have shrimp and macaroni?"

"No," they voiced in unison as she ushered them out the door, down the hallway and into the snowy afternoon. She noticed how shabby their coats and gloves looked. Nicholas was limping. He said his shoes were too tight. Means he'd grown out of them. Laura had no purse. Abby thought all teenagers had purses filled with makeup and money. That Laura had none made her sad.

The weather had worsened and all Abby could think about on the way home was staying on the road because the car was skating. Ice flakes sparkled in the darkening air and visibility was near zero. The kids, attuned to her worry, remained quiet and unmoving. They were such good kids, she thought. Couldn't have asked for better ones if she'd given birth to them herself.

Abby could have kissed the front door of her house when they arrived. She opened it and let them in. Settling the kids in their makeshift room, which was the front room, she unfolded the sofa bed and stashed their few belongings in the nearby closet.

She'd been considering—if she took the kids—the possibility of turning the back hallway that connected the kitchen and the living room into Laura's bedroom. It had enough space for a bed and some furniture, was private enough if the doors were closed. Had windows. Laura would need privacy more than Nicholas. The hallway was supposed to have been Abby's art studio someday but she'd never gotten around to turning it into that. Her upstairs loft bedroom, she thought, was large enough to section off into a bedroom and studio. It could work. Then she could give the hallway to Laura. Though eventually, she'd have to build onto the back of the house and add two separate bedrooms.

Laura was almost fifteen and Nicholas nine. They should have their own rooms.

The kids helped Abby make supper. Laura cooked the shrimp in the frying pan and Nicholas and Abby made the macaroni with extra cheese and onions. They whipped up some biscuits. Snowball got underfoot and meowed for shrimp scraps. After the salad was made and the milk poured, they sat down to eat. They exchanged stories from their week and the kids ate every bite of food. That hadn't changed. They were like termites.

Imagine what my grocery bill would be like if I moved them in? Abby mused.

After supper, they cleaned up the kitchen and Laura asked if they could sit out on the porch swing. They'd done that many a night at Frank's and it had become a ritual no matter where they were.

"But it's night, snowy and cold outside, honey," Abby warned her.

"I know. We can bundle up, wear gloves. I love the snow, you know that. I love to sit and watch it from the porch. They won't let us go out at night at the home. Won't let us watch the snow. Please?" she pleaded, pulling Abby from the kitchen into the living room.

Nicholas was waiting with their coats, caps, and gloves.

"Why couldn't I pick kids who liked to lounge before the TV at night? Simple couch potatoes. Eating chocolate bars and watching Star Trek?"

"We like Star Trek. Like watching television," Nicholas reminded her. "But we also like the porch. And we love the snow."

Abby laughed, giving up. "All right. We'll go sit out on the swing in the cold, snowy dark. But only until our fingers freeze and our lips turn blue. Then we'll come in and watch this great movie I rented."

"What movie?"

"*Harry Potter.* You seen that yet?"

Nicholas whooped, "Yippee! *Harry Potter.* I've been wanting to see that movie so badly for so long." He threw his arms around Abby. Affection, twice in one day, was rare for him.

"Why are you so good to us?" Laura pressed in a whisper, her eyes full of questions.

"Because—" Abby didn't know what to say and settled for telling them part of the truth. "Because I care for both of you. You're special to me."

They stared at her, wanting more. She couldn't give them more yet. She wasn't sure.

Abby turned away, didn't let them see her confusion, put on her coat and led them out onto the porch. They had to sweep off the swing before they could sit down. But they snuggled on the wooden slats together and contemplated the snow as it filled the night. It was beautiful.

The kids spoke of what they'd done all week at the home. Abby encouraged them to talk about their mother and father and missing siblings. They still believed their father would walk out of the woods one day and return to them. It wasn't fair, having to lose so much so young. Wasn't fair at all. Abby's attitude was that grief grew when left in the dark. Better to bring it out into the light and face it. It helped to get it off their chests and she wanted them to be able to talk about anything with her.

Laura asked if they could invite Frank over on Saturday night. She knew Abby and Frank were close friends and she liked him, too. Like Nicholas, she saw him as a father figure. Whenever he was around, the kids were all smiles.

"Sure, if he's available," Abby answered. "Tomorrow morning we'll call and invite him for supper or something."

"Can we play Monopoly afterward?" Nicholas begged. "And Crazy Eights? Like we did when we stayed at Frank's house?"

"Yep. Whatever you two want. It's your weekend."

When they couldn't stand the cold any longer, they went inside and made hot cocoa and popcorn for the movie. Nicholas played with Snowball, who became his shadow whenever the boy was around. The cat loved him and even slept with him at night.

Laura showed Abby her latest batch of drawings and Abby gently critiqued them, not that they needed much as good as they were, and encouraged the girl to keep drawing. Abby promised to take Laura the next day to see the mural she was working on at city hall.

The rest of the night was spent in Harry Potter's magical world and it made Abby happy to see the kids giggling or clenching each other's hands as Harry got in and out of one mess after another. If only life could be that simple, Abby reflected, as Harry flew around on his broomstick. Magic to solve their problems, ease their way, accomplish tasks. Magic to get rid of the unsavory characters in their lives and to protect them from harm. If only.

But there was no such thing as magic.

After the kids were asleep, and Abby had double-checked all the locks in the house, she lay in bed pondering what to do about fostering the children. She mentally tallied her assets, financial and otherwise, and came to the same conclusion she always did. To raise two kids, she didn't make enough money. Not alone, anyway. They'd need clothes, food, and medical insurance. Her insurance was expensive enough and heaven knew how much it would cost for the three of them. She still had savings, but with three people dipping into it, it wouldn't last long. Keeping those children was impossible. Just impossible. She fell asleep asking herself who was she fooling? She couldn't take Laura and Nicholas. Couldn't it go on as it had so far? Frank and her visiting them and taking them for weekend visits when they could. Wasn't that enough?

She had never asked for this. Truth was, and she recognized it, she was just afraid. Afraid to take on the responsibilities. Afraid, pure and simple.

Abby dreamed of a faceless villain who chased her through the streets and into empty houses in a deserted subdivision. She was never more than one short step ahead of him and she could feel his hand brushing her skin. He chased her all night and she awoke in an exhausted sweat, the phone ringing. Took her a second to accept the ringing had only been in her dream. Did that mean Joel was trying to tell her something but she was too stupid to decipher it?

Breakfast was French toast and bacon. Laura called Frank and he accepted the dinner invitation, but insisted on bringing the dinner. Pizzas. Around six o'clock. Sounded good to Abby. Then the three of them went into town. The snow had stopped and the roads were no longer icy, but mushy. In Abby's mind she still heard the ringing of the dream telephone; couldn't shake it or the intuition that something was wrong. She just didn't know what.

Guilt made her take the children to a clothing store and buy them both new coats and gloves. Got them off the fifty percent discount rack and a yellow tag on both of them gave them another fifteen percent off. They were a steal. Found shoes on sale for Nicholas, too.

She thought, what the heck, and from the same clearance section bought them new tops and blue jeans and for Laura a purse. Wasn't that much with the discounts. Laura and Nicholas couldn't believe she'd bought so much for them and thanked her over and over. Obviously no one had given them much in their short lives. Certainly not new clothes.

Laura liked the city hall mural. She walked its length and her fingers hovered inches away from the paint, her face glowing. "Someday," she breathed. "I'm going to paint something as beautiful. People are going to say I'm a some-body. They'll respect me and treat me like I'm special. I'll make lots of money, never go hungry or look like a poor kid again. I'll be an artist, like you, Mrs. Sutton. Someday."

"I told you, Laura, call me Abby. Mrs. Sutton seems so old."

"Okay . . . Abby."

Abby wanted to circle her arms around the girl's shoulder and promise that she'd be there to see her become some-body. Say she'd help her every step of the way, but instead she mumbled, "Someday, Laura, I have no doubt you'll be as good as me. Probably better if you keep drawing. And . . . you're already an artist." What a coward.

Abby introduced the kids to Bonnie, who was in on a Sat-urday catching up on paperwork. She showed them around the rest of city hall. They'd never been inside. The offices were empty, the workers at home, but there were a few peo-ple around and Laura was impressed that they knew Abby, said hello to them, smiled at them. Nicholas strutted around showing off his new clothes. He liked to call out in the long hallways and hear the echoes.

On their way out of town, they shopped at the IGA, picked up snacks and dessert for that night and, remember-ing Claudia's visit the afternoon before, they stopped by the bookstore.

For some reason, Nicholas didn't want to go in and Abby had to almost shove him through the door. She asked him what was wrong but he wouldn't answer. Wasn't like Nicholas to act so skittish.

"I just have to pick up a few books Claudia has been hold-ing for me," Abby explained to him. "It won't take long. Come on." He threw her a wary look and dashed straight away to the far recesses of the store where Claudia kept a table filled with refreshments.

Laura meandered over to a stand of new romance novels and started to browse through them, her head down.

"Those two urchins come in all the time, or used to before

they were sent away, and devour every cookie I have out," Claudia told Abby in a confidential voice. "Now they're orphans. I've heard you and Frank have taken an interest in them. So kind of you both. They're good kids all in all. Laura is quite a reader. Nicholas loves magic books. He's read all the *Harry Potter*s I have in the store. Astronomy. He told me once he wanted a telescope but his parents couldn't afford one. Poor things."

"Yeah, they're good kids," Abby echoed, looking over at Nicholas stuffing his mouth with cookies at the refreshment table. No matter how much she fed them they always acted as if they were starving.

"Come for your books, huh?" Claudia pulled out a stack of paperbacks from under the counter and Abby exchanged the used ones she'd brought along for them. Trading used paperbacks for used paperbacks was a cheap way to get books. It worked for her. "I meant to ask yesterday, Claudia, and forgot—you still coming up with missing items?"

"No. Strange you should ask. The thievery stopped. All of it all over town. None of the other shopkeepers have reported anything missing for weeks."

"That's great. Maybe things have taken a turn for the better." Could the town have purged itself of thieves and a kidnapper . . . was Spookie actually safe again?

At that moment Abby happened to look across the aisle and caught the expression on Laura's face. *Guilt.* She'd overheard them talking about the shoplifting and her reaction was guilt? Nicholas reluctant to enter the bookstore?

Abby met Laura's eyes and she knew. They were the thieves. Or had been. But looking at her thin face with the circles around her eyes, Abby couldn't be angry with her. They'd lost their parents and their whole life. Wanted and needed things but had no money. They'd been getting what they needed by stealing.

Sighing softly under her breath, Abby knew she'd have to talk to them when they got home, and went back to her con-

versation with Claudia. She cut it off short saying they were
expecting Frank with pizzas any minute and had to be on
their way.

The children were silent going home and Abby was wondering how she was going to broach the subject of their
shoplifting. The direct approach was best, she figured. They
walked in the front door, she turned and said to the two of
them, "I think the three of us need to talk about something.
Let's go in the kitchen. Put these snacks away first."

Laura's eyes were filled with tears when they sat down at
the table. Nicholas was looking everywhere but at Abby.
They knew each other so well already.

"You know about the stealing, don't you?" Laura wrung
her hands and looked sideways, first at Abby and then at her
brother. The look he gave her was one of panic.

"I guessed," Abby said. "Tell me if I'm right. You two
have been taking things from the local stores?" Abby had
put the groceries away. Ice cream in the freezer. Thinking
how to handle this little problem as she worked.

"Yes. It was us," Laura confessed, her face hangdog and
her tone apologetic. "But we're *soooo* sorry. And we've
stopped. We *promise*. Now that we're in the care facility we
don't get to town anymore, except with you. And we
wouldn't take anything else anyway." Genuine regret and
shame in her voice. Nicholas bobbed his head in agreement.

"Oh, boy." Abby wasn't mad because they seemed truly
sorry. She put her arms around their shoulders. "We'll work
it out. It's going to be okay. We'll make amends to the store-
owners somehow and go from there."

"Will we have to go talk to them? Tell them what we
did?" Nicholas was fidgeting, his eyes looking everywhere
but at her.

"That's right. You'll have to face every one of them, both
of you, apologize, beg forgiveness and ask them not to press
charges. Return the stuff if you can. Just tell me what you
stole and why?"

Laura opened her mouth to speak, but it was Nicholas

who answered first, "We were hungry . . . that's why we took the food from the IGA. We were alone at the house and all the food was gone. After they took Mom to the hospital and before people started bringing us groceries. I borrowed the hammer and stuff to fix a hole in the wall. The pretty glass things were for Mom in the hospital . . . to cheer her up. Laura took the books because she loves to read and we didn't have no money. We're so sorry for taking those things."

It was the most Abby had heard him say at one time.

"But we can't return all of it." His lips quivered. "We ate all the food. Gave the glass animals to Mom. Don't know what the hospital did with them."

"But we can give the hammer and the books back," Laura gushed. "They're at the house. "Not all the nails, though. Nick used some of them."

"All right." Abby put her hands up, smiling to soften the words. "Tomorrow before I take you back I'll go with both of you and you can apologize to the shop owners. Maybe the hospital still has the glass figurines. I'll check. They were pretty expensive." She paused, feeling bad for them. "What you did was stealing, children, and believe me, stealing is a crime. You can go to jail for it, so you must never do it again. Promise me?"

Laura nodded, her eyes fearful. "We promise. Don't let us go to jail. We didn't mean to be bad. Everyone else had so much and we had so little. Nicholas was hungry . . . and Mama deserved something pretty before she died. She was so sick we just wanted to make her happy. We didn't mean to hurt anyone. We were going to pay it all back . . . someday. I swear."

Nicholas nodded.

"No one's going to jail," Abby said. "The shopkeepers will understand. Talk to them and tell them the truth, like you've done with me. Say you're really sorry. It'll work out, I promise."

Their vulnerability touched her emotions. The way they

stared at her with hope in their eyes, their naivety, made her understand what was important in life and what she wanted. She wanted them to be healthy and happy and wanted to be there to guide them to that happiness. Smooth out the hard times for them as much as she was able. She wanted to take care of them.

She'd faced her first major crisis with the children and had handled it successfully. She could raise these kids, she thought. Wouldn't be easy, but then nothing in life was easy. She had to try or she'd never forgive herself. Because she couldn't imagine her life now without them. She was no longer alone. And neither were they.

She hugged Laura and Nicholas and they set the table for supper. Frank showed up with the pizzas. After supper Frank treated them to the new Star Trek movie in town at the local theater. Abby didn't mention the shoplifting episode until they were back at the house, the kids were sleeping, and she and Frank were in the kitchen sharing a cup of coffee.

It'd begun snowing outside again and the dropping temperature was freezing everything into ice. She was glad she wasn't the one going back out into it. Frank was.

She told him about the kids and the stealing. He listened and commented, "Those poor kids. We should have known they were alone at that house sooner. That they were doing without. We should have done something."

"We had other things on our mind," she replied glumly. "Remember?"

"No excuse. We should have been aware of it. And Abby, don't worry about what it costs to make this shoplifting problem right . . . I'm sure the store owners will forgive them if they're repaid for their losses. Tell them to send me the bills for whatever the children can't return. It's the least I can do. I'll vouch for them if I need to. They're decent kids and they've been through a lot these last few months. They need a break."

"Glad you feel that way, Uncle Frank." She laughed softly. " 'Cause I've decided to sign for their foster care tomorrow when I take them back to the care center. By next weekend they'll be living here full-time."

Frank's smile told her everything she needed to know. "I'm glad! I was hoping you'd do that. If you weren't going to take them, I was. And I want to say now that I'm with you a hundred percent, Abby. Anything I can do to help, anything, all you have to do is ask me. Money, time, a shoulder to cry on, babysitting services. I'll help you raise them because I care for them too."

He threw his arms around her and kissed her on the lips. A kiss that turned into another more lingering one. Abby pulled away slowly but there again was that love in his eyes, and for the first time she didn't want to hide from it or anything anymore.

"Then how about coming over this week with your truck and helping me cart back some beds and furniture for them? Martha said she had two old dressers I could have. Stella said I could borrow some unused beds. I'm turning the back hallway into Laura's bedroom and Nicholas can continue to sleep in the living room until I can work out where to put him. You can help me get her room ready and help me figure out a more permanent place for the boy."

"You got a date. I'll call you tomorrow to coordinate. I can contribute some furniture for the cause myself. I have the perfect nightstand for Laura, made by hand. It's small but pretty. Should fit in that hallway. I have desks for them too, for their homework. Let me look around and I might have even more furniture."

"Thank you." She leaned forward and kissed Frank again. The surprise on his face was priceless.

"I'd better get going," he said reluctantly, lifting his body from the chair and picking up his doggie bag of leftover pizza. He'd brought so much everyone would have lunch from it the next day. "They're expecting eight or more inches of that white stuff before tomorrow. The roads are going to be a real mess soon enough.

"I had a great time tonight, Abby. Call me if you need help getting the kids back to the facility tomorrow. My trusty truck can go anywhere in any weather."

"I'll do that if I need to." Abby stood up and walked him to the door, where they tenderly kissed one more time. It was all so new. Showing their love to each other. No longer hiding. They both understood they were taking it slow. She hated to see him leave, but let him go. After all, the children were asleep behind them.

It was almost an afterthought as Frank was going out the door, Abby asking about it, because it hadn't crossed her mind all night. "Any sign of our kidnapper, Frank? Anything at all?" A whisper as if just speaking of the monster would bring him back.

Frank was outlined in the doorway with snow as his backdrop, when he said in a voice as soft as hers had been, "Not a trace. No kidnappings. No sightings. Thank God. Not a note, letter, or a phone call. Nada." The snow was drifting in large flakes and the sky was a cobalt velvet between them. The white world outside was hushed.

His hand found hers and squeezed. The gesture meant everything. Neither one of them had the courage to say, *Maybe it really is over. Maybe we're truly free of him.* If they said it aloud they might curse themselves.

Then Frank was gone. Out into the wintry night.

Abby stood at the door and waved as he trudged to his truck, got in, and drove away. His headlights cutting a swath of light through the drifting snow.

Neither one of them saw the pale car sitting behind the line of snow-covered trees across the lane, so blended in with the landscape it seemed to be made of snow. A minute or two later it slowly pulled out onto the road behind Frank's red truck and followed at a safe distance, lights off, guiding itself by the brightness of the snow world.

The large man crouched low behind the wheel was grinning. He looked tired and there were circles around his eyes. His face was dirty and so was his hair. Looked like he'd slept in his clothes. Looked like he was sick. But he followed Frank like a shadow.

Chapter Twenty

He'd been driving for three days straight. Coming down from Canada where it was even more freezing and icy than Spookie.

His voices had told him not to stop for food or sleep, only for gas and restroom stops. They told him that he had to strike now because time was running out. He didn't understand what they meant by that, but they were insistent.

Nag. Nag. Nag. Drive faster. Don't doze off. Take this road instead of that one. No food, no cheeseburgers until you complete your assignment.

He was so hungry and his eyes burned from lack of rest, but he did as he was told. Or they wouldn't leave him alone. Wouldn't let him rest or sleep. Or eat.

The fox was running in front of him and, as all hungry wolves know, one doesn't lose the fox or one ends up with no prize. He shoved the gas pedal down, but the car would only go so fast. It was a lousy car. It stalled at stop signs and wouldn't always start again. Didn't go over sixty. Guzzled gas. It got him where he wanted to go and barely that. He'd stolen it weeks ago outside of a Wal-Mart. The voices told him to. It was the right color. Ivory white. Blended in nicely with the snow that he'd been traveling through for days. Snow everywhere. It made him invisible.

The truck was moving along in front of him, not even aware he was following it. It led him through the dark town and into the darker woods where the cabin was. He remembered how to get there but the purpose of tailing the truck was to catch the driver unaware when he got out of it next. Use the element of surprise.

He'd almost hated to leave Canada. He'd gotten a job at a burger joint making burgers and fries for people.

In the beginning no one had noticed he was hurt. He'd bandaged himself and hid his pain. Took lots of aspirins. He'd liked working there. He'd gotten all the free cheeseburgers he'd wanted, course he was supposed to pay for them but he never did.

Sometimes he worked nights and he'd be the clean-up man. They'd let him sleep in this shed behind the place. It was bare, just a cot, but it had running water and a sink he could clean up in. The owners had let him stay there for nothing because of the sob story he had given (his own idea) about being homeless since he'd been laid off his factory job.

Told them his wife (as if he'd had a wife to begin with) had run off and taken all his money. That she'd taken the kids, a boy and a girl, and he hadn't seen them in months. Another lie. They'd felt real sorry for him.

He'd gotten his hair cut short, grown a mustache and a light beard. Gotten clothes from a Goodwill. He'd liked it there. People were nice to him, as ugly and big as he was. And the voices had left him alone for a long, long time. The mud people had even disappeared for a while. What a relief. He'd almost forgot why he was there. To hide out. Lay low. He was a normal working Joe, except for the bullet holes in his side that wouldn't heal. The pain that never stopped. He had the cop to blame for that all right. The one who'd shot him. His fault.

Then the voices had come back, and the stinking mud people following him everywhere, and here he was. He hated it.

Time to return to his dream life. Wished the voices would

heal his wounds, though. He knew they could. Had before. Maybe when he'd done what they wanted him to, they'd heal him.

It was the main reason he was doing this. The pain was driving him insane and it had to stop. They could stop it. They could get rid of his shadows, too. They were every-where. Out in the snow behind the trees glaring at him all the time. When he stopped the car they'd crowd around and climb in with their dirty clothes and slack faces. Their ac-cusing eyes. He was always chasing them away and shooing them out of the car.

He had to keep driving or they'd overwhelm him.

The snow was coming down harder, which made it diffi-cult to drive. But the white stuff hid him too. This was a great plan, he thought, as the truck in front of him turned into the driveway, curved around, and pulled up behind the cabin.

He stopped his car in front, grabbed the cloth in one of his gloved hands, grabbed a tire iron—this time he wasn't tak-ing any chances—in his other. Got out and stealthily scur-ried around the side of the house, staying close to the outer walls so the cop wouldn't see him.

Hurry. Hurry. Had to catch the cop before he got into the house. Soft crunch. Soft crunch. His big feet went carefully on the icy snow. Quiet as a bunny.

He heard the rear door to the cabin open and feared he'd missed his chance. But the cop came out of the house and re-turned to his truck, the car door still open. He came up on the cop as the man was leaning over the front seat, pulling some-thing out, a bag of something—and up and down went the tire iron in the snowy night and—*Wham!*—on the cop's head.

Just enough of a blow to stun his enemy and knock him out, not kill him.

The cop twisted around as he went down and threw him-self against his attacker, his hands at the other man's throat. The two struggled in the snow, the cop strong for a dazed man, and then he slammed the wet cloth to the cop's face and that was that.

The cop went down and passed out like someone had shot him.

The larger man dragged him back to his car and threw him into the trunk, closed and locked it. He'd given him enough of the chloroform to knock out three men for hours.

He drove through the night storm, fighting his excitement at having captured his adversary and also an overpowering exhaustion accentuated by gnawing hunger and a strange weakness of his limbs. The voices were punishing him. But why? He'd done what they'd told him to.

He got where he was going and stopped the car as far into the trees as a car could go.

It was too dark and snowy to go into the woods tonight, he'd lose his way and the mud people would get him. He laid his head down on the steering wheel to rest a little, closed his heavy eyelids, and the next thing he knew he was waking up. It was late morning. He could tell by the position of the sun.

Oh, no, I've overslept.

Startled at the passage of time, he grabbed the tire iron and ran to the trunk. Opened it. The cop was moving a little, groggy and slow, and he put the cloth across the cop's mouth again until the moving stopped. But he was in a hurry and didn't leave it on long. He lifted the body from the trunk and began the slow progress to his destination about three miles farther into the woods. The body was heavy and his steps dragged. He had to halt and rest a few times; his heart was pounding like an old man's. Feeling dizzy at one point, he nearly dropped the body. Maybe he should have eaten and not listened to the voices for once.

He didn't see the drops of blood he was leaving behind in the snow.

In a hurry, he was anxious to dispose of the body and go after the woman. He'd already fashioned her mud person and couldn't wait to deliver it. But he had to do this first. His voices had warned him that the cop would stop him again if he tried to take the woman.

So get rid of the cop first and then the woman. It made sense.

Deeper into the woods he stumbled with his human burden. It'd stopped snowing during the night but the snow was deep and slowed him down. He kept moving as the sun climbed above until he broke out on the edge of the crevice by a towering tree.

He'd made it and not a moment too soon. He felt so weak, so . . . unreal. Hungry. Thirsty. So cold. Couldn't stop shaking. Silly him, he'd forgotten his coat.

Of course, he hadn't felt like himself since the cop had shot him up the last time. The wounds had never healed and were red and puffy and oozed with infection. Today the pain was worse than ever.

Wobbling, he lay the body down so he could rest.

In a minute I'll do it. In a minute I'll stand up and throw the cop into the muddy pool of quicksand below . . . just like the others. Then I'll go find the woman and do the same to her . . . and the voices will leave me alone forever. They promised. But first they'll heal my wounds and I'll be normal again. I just have to rest a minute or two first.

Chapter Twenty-one

Frank woke up in the car trunk and knew he was in trouble.

Stupid. He'd been so stupid to be caught unaware. No cop with a brain in his head would have allowed this to happen. He should have looked around when he was coming and going from his house and protected his back as he usually did.

But the normalness of the last two months had lured him into being sloppy. *I've been retired too long,* he thought. *One slip.* One unguarded moment and look what happened. How long had he been unconscious? He wasn't sure. A while. His head hurt and he was awake, barely, but couldn't make his body or limbs move yet. Must be the effects of whatever he'd been forced to inhale. Most likely chloroform.

His attacker was the Mud People Killer all right and it looked like Frank was going to be his next victim.

The car ceased moving. Lying in the trunk unable to move, terror froze his mind for precious seconds that counted out like hours.

He had to stay calm. *Think, think. What to do now?*

Then the trunk opened and a man glared down at him. Big brute with a lumpy face, short hair, mustache and eyes as dead as a corpse's. Eyes with no emotion or pity. Finally there was a face to go with the nightmare. Connie Tucker's composite had been right on the mark, Frank thought.

207

Shame she was dead. Without the long hair and mustache, it was the same man as the drawing . . . the man who'd been tormenting Frank for so many years.

It was *him* and Frank was at his mercy. Frank fought, but he could only make his arms and legs jerk like a puppet. The cloth came down again but this time Frank remembered to hold his breath . . . for as long as he could . . . until he became a little dizzy. This time he didn't pass out.

He was being carried through the woods. Holding his breath had worked and he was gaining back the use of his body. He could hear the man grunting under his weight; muttering to himself as he stumbled along. Talking to someone but there was no one else around.

Frank didn't let his captor know he was awake as he was waiting for his chance to make a move. He'd have to fight for his life and he knew it. If he was lucky he'd have at least one chance. Just one. And he'd better be ready when it came or he'd be as dead as all the others.

The man carrying him was acting bizarrely. Talking aloud to no one and almost bumping into bushes and trees. He acted as if he were running from someone. He acted as if he were ill.

Gathering what remained of his strength, Frank relaxed his body. He could almost move again and his mind was clearing. Just a few more minutes. . . .

He prayed and waited for his chance to save his own life.

Chapter Twenty-two

Abby woke early Sunday morning and showed Laura how to make waffles with strawberry topping and whipped cream. The kids liked them and ate seconds. Doing something as ordinary as making breakfast helped clear Abby's mind of the uneasy images leftover from her dreams the night before. Dreams of Joel again. Lost out in the woods. What was new?

It'd been snowing, freezing, and black, and there'd been a strange hum in the air. Joel had been a phantom figure hiding ahead of her behind the trees, with an air of frantic desperation and spikes of lightning crackling around him. She'd been chasing him but never quite catching up with him.

She could sense he was afraid for her, sense there wasn't much time for him to do whatever he was there to do. He'd left glowing footsteps in the deep snow that were rimmed with blood. He'd kept glancing down at them and pointing at her.

She couldn't understand what he'd been trying to tell her and it was frustrating. As the dream drifted away he'd given her four words: *See Frank. Ask Myrtle.*

And she'd awoken.

Joel had been desperately trying to tell her something. *Ask Myrtle what?* Heaven only knew. Abby sure didn't. And what was that about Frank? She saw Frank all the time. It was a puzzle. She pushed the dream aside and concentrated on the children and the important decision she was making that day to take the kids permanently. A huge life step.

It was about all she could think of.

She'd intended to keep the children until afternoon and drive them back to the care facility after three o'clock. But plans had changed. Outside, the snow and fog were as thick as a woolen blanket and the little man on her counter TV said the weather was going to get worse before it got better. They were going to have an honest-to-God blizzard. Ice, strong winds and a ton more snow.

She decided to take the kids back after breakfast or the roads would be impassable. She thought how sweet it would be when she didn't have to take the children back anywhere. When they could stay there with her. Not today. One last time they had to go back to the foster care facility.

Over breakfast Abby made the final leap by asking Laura and Nicholas, "What would you two say to coming to live with me here? To *me* being your foster parent?"

Both of them were out of their chairs and hugging her as if she'd just told them they'd won the million-dollar lottery.

"We thought you'd never ask!" Nicholas yelped and threw himself into Abby's arms.

"Yeah, we were . . . waiting . . . for you to say you wanted us. We prayed for it every night," Laura confessed in a choked voice. "We were so afraid you wouldn't want us and then what would have happened to us?"

"Well, I do want you. Both of you."

Like a real family they discussed what would happen next. Sleeping arrangements and schools. Chores. Laura and Nicholas were excited, though Laura made it clear that if their father returned that they'd have to go live with him.

Abby nodded and agreed without showing her doubts. Their father wasn't coming back, yet she'd never completely destroy their hope.

"I'm taking you back to the foster home early today because of the bad weather," she announced after answering their questions. Outside the kitchen windows the snow was coming down heavy and the wind was wailing. She didn't look forward to going out in it at all.

"It'll be the last time. Today I'll sign papers asking to be your foster parent. Miss Morgan says it'll take about a week or so to finalize everything. You'll have to stay there, though, until all the paperwork goes through. Just one more week or so.

"And next weekend you'll come here—to your new home—to stay."

They were grinning at her. Nicholas had strawberry topping around his mouth and Abby's face was sticky where he'd kissed it. "After today you won't have to go back to that care facility ever again."

She'd never seen Laura and Nicholas so happy. In the time Abby had known them they'd had nothing but sorrow. She knew she was doing the right thing. Call it fate, destiny. Or insanity. The kids were meant to be with her. Meant to be her family.

How odd her life was turning out to be, but how wonderful.

They cleaned the breakfast dishes and loaded up the car for the trip. Laura couldn't stop making plans for when they moved in and Nicholas couldn't stop grinning. Abby couldn't wait for next weekend when they would move in. This time next week they'd be with her for good.

The drive to and from the care facility was a horror. The roads were slippery slides covered in wax paper. Black ice glinted in patches and the winds swirled the snow into a white churning fog that was hard to see through, much less drive through.

After dropping the kids off, saying good-bye to them, and signing the foster care papers, Abby was relieved when she was on her way back home. Sooner she got home the better. She was coming near to town when Joel's words from the dream came back to her.

See Frank.

She had it. Joel wanted her to go see Frank. Right away. Now. For what reason she had no clue. But a premonition so strong she couldn't oppose it made her swerve the car to the right and take the turn to Frank's. The car slid on a patch of ice and she nearly landed in a ditch. Shaken, she continued.

Abby arrived at Frank's and parked out front. The curving driveway had too much snow on it to take the chance of driving around back, she'd get stuck. No one answered the front door so she hiked to the rear and saw Frank's truck with the driver's side door wide open. Dome light was out. Frank's bag of leftover pizza lay on the seat. *Oh, no.* He'd never go off and leave the door open like that. The car battery was dead. Nothing worked.

Frank's back door was wide open as well. Something had happened.

The kidnapper had returned. She knew it.

Oh my God! Abby rushed into the house and searched. No Frank. There was no one inside. The cabin was empty. Frank had left her house late last night but there were no signs he'd spent the night at his cabin. The dogs were going crazy inside down in the basement. Their food and water bowls were empty. Looked as if Frank had been abducted when he arrived home.

The kidnapper was here and he has Frank!

There was no other explanation that made any sense. And the terror she'd thought had left her flooded back in.

How long had the kidnapper had Frank? All night? *Oh, no.* She didn't want to believe Frank could be . . . dead. She had to act and act quickly. There wasn't any time to waste.

What should she do now? The sheriff!

She called and told Sheriff Mearl what she'd found and what she feared. He said he would alert the FBI and Sam in Chicago, gather his officers and any other help he could muster from anyone, and start searching the area around the cabin. Any place the kidnapper could have taken Frank. Look for clues to where they'd gone. Put out an APB on Frank, the kidnapper and his car. Put up roadblocks.

"The foul weather is going to hamper the hunt. The snow is covering tracks as fast as they're being made and the visibility is only a couple of feet," Sheriff Mearl cautioned her. She already knew that. "But for Frank I'll pull out all the stops. You stay put, Abigail, and I'll send out a deputy to look after you. If the suspect has returned to town, he could come after you next. He could be around the cabin watching you. Lock yourself in. Do it now!"

Abby didn't answer the sheriff, just hung up. She didn't want to be caught in a lie. There was no way she was going to sit there and wait to hear that Frank was gone forever. She had to do *something*. Even if it put her in danger. Frank would have done nothing less for her. Time might be short. Time might be gone. She had to go find him, help him. She didn't dare wait for help.

Ask Myrtle. In the dream that's the other thing Joel had said.

So she was going to Myrtle's. First she got a gun from Frank's room, went back out into the snow after locking up, and drove toward Myrtle's place.

Abby was like a crazy woman pounding on Myrtle's door until she answered.

"Hey, girlie, what's the hubbub?" Myrtle's head popped out. She looked like an awakened mummy, dark eye circles around feverish eyes and skin so white it matched the snow. "Oh, Abigail. What are you doing out in this blizzard?" She sounded like she had a cold. She was sniffling, her nose was running and she kept wiping it with the back of her hand.

Abby explained that Frank was missing and Myrtle yanked her in. Made her tell her everything. Abby described the dream about Joel and what he'd said to her that made her go to Frank's house. She explained how she found Frank's truck door and house door wide open. She'd never talked so fast because she was terrified she was wasting time when every second might matter.

"Myrtle, where did you say you saw the kidnapper in his car that time?"

"Out by Gage's Bog."

"I need you to take me there."

"I would, child, but I'm *so* sick," she croaked, her voice going out on the last word. She fell into a coughing fit and Abby had to wait for her to continue. The old woman was sprawled on her sofa, huddled in her robe and a couple of blankets. Face slick with fever sweat. She looked awful. "I've been real ill these last few days and can't hardly walk, much less stomp about in a snowstorm and ten feet of powder. I'm so dizzy I'd fall over. Sorry, Abigail, I can't take you anywhere. Wish to God I could. You know I love Frank like a son. I just can't do it."

Abby put her arm around Myrtle's skinny shoulders. She knew the woman wanted to help her save Frank but her sick old body wouldn't let her. "It's okay, Myrtle. Just tell me how to get there. Quickly."

"Well, you go behind my place and straight back about three miles. That's the shortest way. Got to walk it cause a car won't fit through the trees. You can't miss Gage's Bog because the trees will be shorter, scrawnier, and further apart. At first.

"After awhile you'll come to this humongous crooked tree, can't miss it, looks like a bent hand and finger pointing to the sky. Below the tree the bog begins, so be careful where you tread. There's a ridge running past the tree that has a steep drop underneath it. Like a pit surrounded by rocks and boulders. That's the quicksand pit."

"Quicksand? There's quicksand in Gage's Bog?" Abby had lived in town over a year and hadn't known that.

"Well, it's not exactly quicksand. More like a mud and quicksand mess." Myrtle stopped to cough. "But if you fall into it you can't get out. Can't get traction. It sucks you down. So be careful once you get to the crooked tree, Abigail. Break off a tall stick or two and test the ground ahead of you before you step on it or else you'll fall into the mud and become a mud person. People have disappeared in that bog and were never heard of again."

Something else she'd not heard about. People disappearing in the bog.

"Oh, no," Abby mumbled, as it came to her, triggered by Myrtle's words.

Or else you'll fall in the mud and become a mud person.

"I think I know what the kidnapper does with his victims, Myrtle. How he disposes of their bodies. He throws them into a quicksand pit or a bog."

"Like Gage's Bog?" Myrtle shivered under her blankets.

"Yeah, or any other kind of quagmire, mud, or quicksand pit. Swampland. Marsh. There are places like that in many parts of the country, if you look for them." Abby pondered for a moment, another awful truth forming. It was so simple. Why hadn't anyone seen the connection before? "I bet there's a swamp or bog around Chicago and he threw his victims into it. That's why bodies were never found and that's why he fashions those clay figurines and leaves them in people's mailboxes or at the houses.

"His *mud people*! Because that's what the kidnapped become when he throws them in—life-sized mud-covered people lodged forever in the ooze. Oh my God!" Abby put her hand over her mouth. She had to get to Frank. "That's what he's going to do with Frank. Kill him and throw his body into the mud!" *If he hasn't done it already,* she thought frantically.

"I've got to go," she groaned at Myrtle. "I telephoned the sheriff from Frank's, but he's not coming here. Call him and tell him *to go to Gage's Bog.* Tell him to *hurry.* I'm going there now." And she flew out the door and headed into the woods behind the trailer wishing she could take her car with the heater on. Couldn't. Instead she had to freeze on foot. No matter. She'd do anything for Frank.

The snow buffeted her body as she trudged through and in between the trees. Her face, fingers, and toes were numb in minutes. Her only consolation was that if she was having trouble getting to the bog, the kidnapper must have too.

If that was where he'd taken Frank.

Now she was beginning to doubt herself. What happens if she's wrong? If Frank was already dead? They did have a head start. Abby pushed herself to move faster, tugging her wool cap lower around her ears as her teeth chattered. She was running on fear and anger.

How dare that monster come back! How dare he take Frank, who was a good honest man who'd never done harm to anyone, but had helped so many. So what if he'd shot the kidnapper a couple of times, maiming him—the man had deserved it. He was evil, evil, *evil.*

God, Abby hoped she was going in the right direction. Wished she had a dogsled. Frank's dogs would have worked well . . . they could even have sniffed Frank's trail out.

She kept seeing this shadowy hulking figure throwing Frank into a muddy pit. She could almost hear Frank's screams and it made her want to run harder, but she couldn't. She could hardly see a thing ahead of her and she was moving as fast as she could.

Abby found a cream colored car parked among the trees, unlocked. Hood cold to the touch. It gave her hope. It had to be the kidnapper's. Who else would be out there in the middle of a blizzard?

There were fading footsteps leading from the car into the woods. One set. Deep. Someone carrying someone?

The snow was filling the footprints in and Abby was reminded of her dream; Joel pointing down at them, and she began to run tracking the faint outlines and . . . drops of blood. She bumped into a tree limb and slowed down. She'd gotten to the stretch where the trees were stunted and sparse and ahead she saw the huge crooked tree Myrtle had spoken of.

The beginning of the bog.

Breathing hard she paused long enough to break off a walking stick from a small tree and poked it through the snow into the ground ahead of her. Shame it'd been so warm until only a few days ago, or the bog would have been frozen. Just her luck. There wasn't much time. She was tired and frightened but she followed the footsteps. The blood was easier to see at times and between the two pairs of foot prints she had something to follow.

Frank might be dead.

With the pain that thought caused her she knew how much she'd grown to love him. Need him. She was crying and her tears became flecks of ice on her cheeks as she stumbled through the snow. Time seemed to drag, like her feet. She felt as if she'd been out in the woods for hours. Days.

Then she heard noises—something moving through the woods ahead of her. She tripped, wiping the snow from her face as she looked around.

Two shapes were struggling in the snow in front of her with a line of boulders behind them. Behind the rocks was the mud pit Myrtle had warned her of.

One of the men looked like Frank but it was hard to tell with all the swirling snow.

Abby screamed Frank's name but couldn't hear her voice above the wind so she rushed forward. Closer, she saw that one of the men was taller, had short hair and was wearing a sock cap—a stranger.

The other man was Frank. Thank God!

Her eyes took in the rocks and the way the land dropped into the pit behind them.

The larger man was wrestling with Frank and trying to shove him over the precipice when he wasn't yelling at something or someone that wasn't there. Or at least Abby couldn't see anyone else. But Frank's assailant was bigger and Frank wasn't winning.

The insane sometimes have abnormal strength.

Abby ran toward them—the deep snow dragging her steps almost to a walk—shouting and waving her stick, not caring if she fell into quicksand herself. *She had to save Frank.* She hadn't been able to save Joel but she darn well would save Frank!

"Get your hands off him! Leave him alone!"

Frank's attacker didn't listen to her. No surprise.

About to be thrust over the edge, Frank screamed.

Abby couldn't wait, couldn't get there fast enough, and pulled out the Beretta 9mm automatic, Frank's duty gun that she'd taken from his house, from her coat pocket. She brought the gun up and shot without hesitation at the stranger until the chamber was empty. All that target practice with Joel she'd had had finally come in handy. It came back easily.

Abby wasn't sure she'd hit the man fighting with Frank, but she prayed she had.

Is this real? I'm shooting a gun at a man who's trying to kill someone I love and I'm ready to take a life to protect him. And then another truth hit her . . . she loved Frank. She really loved him.

In a split-second frozen forever in her mind, the other man—the kidnapper—screamed in pain and stopped moving. He was staring at something in front of him and speaking words Abby couldn't hear to empty space.

What was he doing? Who was he talking to?

Frank, who'd fallen to the ground, took the opening and slammed his boots into the other man's legs, who then lost his balance and plummeted over the edge into the pit.

They soon heard the sound of something heavy hitting soft ground; a thrashing, sucking sound and then an eerie silence.

Frank knelt at the edge and glared down as if he couldn't believe the other man had gone over instead of him.

Abby stooped down and took him into her arms as fresh snow fell around them. "Frank, I'm so glad you're alive!" Bruised and bloody, but alive. She was crying but she couldn't help herself.

"Was that the man you've been searching for? Was that the kidnapper?"

"I'm pretty sure it was." Frank smiled weakly up at her. There was a bloody scratch along the side of his face. "Didn't know you could shoot a gun, much less shoot one so well, Annie Oakley. You hit him in the chest, twice, took him off guard long enough for me to push him over. Thought you hated guns." His voice was raspy and faint and he was shivering from the struggle, the bump on the back of his head, or from the cold—Abby couldn't be sure which.

"I despise guns, but I'd hate losing you more," she admitted in a husky murmur. Frank closed his eyes. He was fighting to remain conscious.

She had to keep him talking. Keep him awake until help arrived. She rocked him in her arms trying to warm him up and telling him about her brother Michael and how a gun had killed him so many years ago. "And that's why I hate guns so much."

"But you . . . got my . . . gun from the cabin . . . and used it," Frank's voice was fading.

"To save you, Frank. I couldn't fight with my bare hands. I needed a weapon. Here." Abby handed Frank the gun. "You can have it back now."

"Thanks." He took it and slipped it into Abby's coat pocket after he'd clicked on the safety. "I've got no pockets so you take care of it for me until we get home."

"The police are going to want to see it, I suppose?" she asked, aware of how weak Frank was and hoping the police would arrive soon.

"No doubt. Has Sam been notified?"

"Yes. Sheriff said he'd call him. He's probably on his way, but weather's bad between here and Chicago, too. It'll take longer than usual."

Frank peered one last time over the rim of the cliff through the curtain of snowflakes and she followed his gaze. The hole in the white blanket below in the pit had closed as if no one had slipped away beneath it moments before. A human being was down there fighting the quagmire, fighting for breath . . . dying. Abby couldn't bear to think about it and looked away.

"He went under fast, didn't he?" Frank's eyes were dazed. "Not a yell or a whimper. And now not a sign of him. As if he'd never been at all." But they knew better. He'd left a legacy of sorrow and loss behind him.

"What happened, Frank?"

"I'll tell you soon as we're someplace warmer, Abby. Soon as my head starts working again. Right now nothing seems real. Are you real?"

"Oh, I'm real."

"Hope so. Otherwise I'm already dead." There was a bruise beside his left eye and his head was bleeding. He was holding his side and when he moved Abby could see it hurt him.

"Thank God. After all this time it's really . . . over." Frank's shoulders slumped and his head tilted downward.

"It's really over." Now that the danger had passed, exhaustion had set in. She could hardly think. A sense of relief so strong it was like pure joy descended on her. Frank was okay. She was okay. No more kidnappings and no more killer. She could finally think it: *No more killer.*

She could have wept, instead she smiled and Frank was smiling back at her.

They were finally free.

There were shouts in the woods behind them. "The sheriff and his posse have finally arrived." She sighed, helping Frank to his feet. He wouldn't have wanted Sheriff Mearl to see him crumpled in the snow. "About time."

"Must have heard the gunshots. Here they come." Frank wobbled and stood straighter, leaning on Abby. "Hope they have an extra coat. I'm freezing. My lips must be blue." A slow grin.

"Good to see you still have a sense of humor after what's happened to you."

"I'm not sorry he's dead." Frank echoed what she was thinking. "He deserved to die."

"That he did. And I'm glad he's dead. too." Instead of Frank, she thought, instead of herself.

Later she'd tell Frank about her dream and how Joel had helped her find him, but it could wait. "You need to go to the hospital," she told him. "You have a nasty bump on your head and you don't look so good. How are you feeling?"

"Not bad under the circumstances. Head hurts." Then out of nowhere he leaned over, put his arms around her, and kissed her. A long gentle kiss that made her knees weak. It'd been a long time, she thought.

Abby returned his kiss and tears came to her eyes. *Frank was alive. Frank was safe.*

"I'm so happy you're all right," she said when he let her go. He laughed and hugged her close as if he was afraid she'd run away.

Abby pulled away after a few moments and yelled into the woods at the search party and someone yelled back. They had almost reached them.

Abby and Frank waited, holding each other as the snow continued to fall. It felt as if she was coming out of a long nightmare. She could only imagine how Frank must feel. But right then they were both smiling, thankful to be alive.

"How about having supper with me tonight, Abby?" Frank requested before the sheriff and a crowd of uniforms got there. "Someplace really nice and expensive. With wine, fancy desserts and the whole thing? I feel a need to celebrate."

"That sounds lovely, Frank. I'll dress up." She didn't want to tell him that he was most likely going to the hospital instead of out to supper with her. But why spoil his dream.

"Good, I'll call you for a time. I think," he was looking at the men coming toward them, "we're going to be busy for a little bit first."

"I think we will be, too. I'll be waiting for your call."

The police and dogs and men in uniforms surrounded them and soon they were too busy to think about anything else.

They both had stories to tell.

Chapter Twenty-three

"The kidnapper's name was Garrison Hegler," Frank was telling Abby as they moved Laura's bed a few feet to the left. He was catching her up on what he'd found out from the FBI since Hegler's plunge into the mud pit.

At last a name to go with the monster who'd invaded their lives.

"Papers and expired car license found in Hegler's stolen car showed he was forty-two years old, six-foot-five and until a few years ago lived in a suburb of Chicago."

That morning they'd picked up used furniture for Laura and Nicholas from Martha's and were arranging it in the back hallway. Frank had put up a door at the end of the hall so the space could be closed off for Laura's privacy.

Nicholas would sleep on the sofa in the living room for now.

She and Frank were picking them up from the foster care facility for the last time in about an hour and all of them were going to a get-together at Frank's in Abby's honor. He'd invited their friends and was telling everyone Abby was a hero and had saved his life because she'd shot Hegler.

He would have done the same for her, she said to anyone who would listen, yet it would be fun having a gathering the week before Christmas and on the day they brought the kids home. Sort of like a welcome-to-the-family party. Laura and Nicholas would love it.

Abby and Frank had never had that romantic dinner the night of the shooting and he'd been in the hospital recuperating from a concussion and cracked ribs until a few days before.

They'd finally had their celebration dinner the night before and when Abby looked at Frank now she saw his face reflected in the candlelight, his eyes laughing and the two of them holding hands. They were two lucky people, they'd told each other. They had each other and they were alive.

Abby felt bad about shooting another human being, but she'd accepted she'd had no choice. Frank would have been the one to die if she hadn't. And eventually, if Hegler had gotten away, others would have died as well. So she tried not to think about Hegler and what she'd done to him. It was hard, but Frank claimed, in time her feelings of guilt would lessen.

She hoped he was right. She'd never shot anyone and had never been the cause of anyone's death before.

She hadn't yet mentioned her Joel dream, the footsteps and blood in the snow, and how they'd helped her find Frank. Sounded too weird, even to her. Better if she kept it to herself. Perhaps she'd tell him one day.

She wondered if she'd dream anymore of her late husband. Since that last dream something felt different to her. Joel's image, his memories, no longer seemed as real. No longer hurt her as much. He seemed dead to her now for the first time since she'd found out he'd died. Maybe she wouldn't dream of him again. They'd finally completed their good-bye.

She'd never forget Joel but possibly now he'd stop haunting her and let her go on with her life. Perhaps he wanted her to be with Frank now. It was time.

"Hegler was a loner," Frank was saying after they moved the bed again. Snowball had been hiding under it and scampered beneath the nightstand, one paw playfully clawing out at them. Frank stopped a moment to play with her. "That fit the FBI profile all right. Never dated. Never let people get close. Not neighbors, not fellow workers. An underachiever who held a string of low-level jobs, but according to high school transcripts had an IQ of over 190.

"People Hegler worked with over the years thought he was crazy, talking to folks who weren't there. They said he heard voices. That would explain a lot. Lived with his chronically ill mother, Ester Hegler, all his life until she . . . disappeared about six years ago. Now the police suspect he killed her, too. And the worse thing is that the profiler believes Garrison Hegler had been taking and killing people since he was eighteen."

Abby's mouth fell open. "He *was* a monster. Good riddance. I'm glad I shot him." She meant it. She would never forget the terror and heartache Hegler had caused them. And Frank had ten more years of bad memories than the rest of them. It'd be harder for him to forget.

"One monster," Frank gloated, "who won't be tormenting anyone else ever again, that's how I look at it. It's a shame we can't retrieve his body or the bodies of his victims. The FBI would like proof he's dead and the families would like to bury their loved ones. But the pit at Gage's Bog is too deep. No retrieving anything that's fallen into it, or not easily anyway.

"Our word that Hegler went over the edge and sank, and his DNA from the blood found in the snow, will have to do. Though the FBI is looking into how they can reclaim the bodies from the bog. Good luck to them. Myrtle swears it's bottomless.

"Speaking of Myrtle," Frank added, straightening up with a grimace. His side was still sensitive from his broken ribs and Abby wasn't letting him do too much heavy moving. Just the bed, with her help. "I saw her on my way over here in the snow on the streets with her wagon. Singing Perry Como songs at the top of her lungs as usual. I invited her over tonight. She's coming. Said she'd bring a bottle of wine or two. Says she figures she's owed a party too, since she saved you that night at your house and then you were able to save me."

"Sounds like she's feeling better."

"Seems to be. Looked fine to me," Frank said. "Wasn't coughing, sniffling or anything. She says she can't wait until tonight and wants a detailed account of everything that happened after you left her place that snowy morning . . . details of the killer and all."

Everyone would. Abby inhaled sharply and let it out. As if her and Frank's adventure hadn't been splashed all over the ten o'clock news and in all of the newspapers. On the radio. They were celebrities. People should be sick of them and their stories by now, but they weren't.

"You think the news media is going to be at my party?" she teased him. "Should I wear makeup and dress up so I can look good for the photo opportunities?"

Frank threw her a dirty look. "I didn't invite them." He hated cameras and the reporters with their endless questions. They'd camped out day and night at the hospital bugging him and had tailed him home. They'd found Abby's house and had bugged her for days. Wanting interviews and photos. "For all I care they can stay out in the cold snow and go hungry. They're not coming in. Sometimes I think, if not for the media and the publicity, serial killers wouldn't have all the fame and notoriety they crave. Attention that might keep them killing."

"But Hegler's dead, and there's big money to be made for your story," Abby kidded with a sly smile. "Now that it's all over."

"Don't we know it," he retorted. "When I got home yesterday my message machine was filled with article and book offers. The money made my head spin. But I've promised the exclusive story to my publisher. This book, unlike my first one or the one I've been working on about our original adventure together, is going to garner a hefty advance and a wider distribution." Frank was humming aloud, pleased with himself, as he shoved Laura's desk closer to the wall. He straightened up, groaning.

"No more furniture moving for you today," she admonished him.

Abby also had offers to tell her side of the story to the media, but she wouldn't do it in any form for any amount of money. She just wanted to be left alone so she could get back to her peaceful life and forget.

Frank's situation was different. Perhaps the book would be a good way for him to rid himself of his Hegler demons. He had a lot more of them than Abby did.

Sam Cato had phoned and said they'd discovered a swamp fifteen miles from Hegler's mother's home in Chicago. The swamp was deep, covered many miles, and if Hegler had dumped bodies in it they probably wouldn't be recovered either. And as they'd feared, the FBI had connected Hegler to other disappearances in and around Chicago going back fifteen years.

Hegler's childhood home had been torn apart and they'd discovered an older woman's remains buried in the basement, encased in floor cement. Turned out it was Hegler's mother.

And duplicate clay figurines were found on shelves down in the basement. The same kind the kidnapper used to leave his victims. So he'd made two of them for each kidnapping. One for the victim and one for his private collection.

Each clay person had a name and date scratched in the bottom. All missing people. And the body count was escalating.

Finally, a diary, filled with confessions of Hegler's abductions, was found buried with Ester Hegler's body. There was no doubt now whatsoever that Garrison Hegler had been the Mud People Killer. He confessed to it himself in his diary.

So it really was over. Except for all the ghosts Hegler had left behind to haunt the survivors.

"Before someone else asks you, Frank, I want to invite you for Christmas Eve here. Just the four of us. Five if your son comes home for the holidays. I'll bake a ham and we'll make cookies, trim the tree and sing carols. An old-fashioned Christmas Eve at home. Laura and Nicholas are looking forward to it. Our first Christmas together. Can you come around three?"

"Couldn't keep me away. I'll brew my famed hot spiced apple cider and bring a copy of *It's a Wonderful Life*. Got to have that on Christmas Eve. And I'll bring over the Christmas presents I have for the kids. Went kind of nuts buying stuff for them."

"Yeah, I think you had too much time on your hands in the hospital and spent it, and all your money, on the Internet Toys 'R Us."

"They deserve a real Christmas after what they've been through. Besides, it was fun buying all those toys for them. Like being a kid again."

Abby rolled her eyes. Frank was an old softy. "Don't go overboard on the children, Frank. We don't want to spoil them. Not right off anyway."

"Why not? It's Christmas."

"I give up." Abby threw her hands upward. Who was she to talk? She had a closet full of presents for the kids herself, donated from Martha, Claudia, and Samantha. Among them were art supplies for Laura and a Game Boy with games for Nicholas. And new clothes for them she'd gotten on sale. She was grateful to her friends for contributing. Now the kids would have a fine Christmas.

Samantha had even run a story on the foster care facility and asked for clothes and toys for the children there. The response had been overwhelming so the children there would all have a magical Christmas as well.

"You know," Abby conveyed the news, as she set a lamp on Laura's nightstand, "Martha's giving the annual New Year's Eve gala at the mansion in two weeks, I hear. Going to be a wingding. Games for the kids, gourmet food, pricey door prizes, balloons, noisemakers, and alcohol. Taking out all the stops. Martha wants to celebrate the end of our Hegler nightmare."

"How about coming with me, Abby?"

"I wouldn't go with anyone else." They were becoming a couple and she liked it. "But I have to warn you, I have two children, sir."

"Just two?" Playing along. "That's not many. Speaking of kids." Frank glanced at the clock. "My get-together for you starts at seven. I have food to prepare. A table to set. It's time we go break the kids out of jail."

"And we can't kept them waiting. Not today. Laura's called twice already. Nicholas, too."

Frank drove them to the foster care facility and they brought Laura and Nicholas home.

Laura loved her room. With tears in her eyes and a big smile on her face she walked in and saw the bed with the new quilt on it, the desk and the nightstand Frank had made. The frilly pink curtains on the windows and the blinds for privacy. Nothing like the bare room she'd had at home or the sparse one she shared with the other girls at the foster home.

"Thank you! Thank you so much." Laura threw her arms around Abby and then Frank. "It's beautiful." She sat on the bed, gazing around the room as if it were a room in a palace.

"Sorry, partner," Frank said to Nicholas, his arms around the boy's shoulders, "you have to sleep on the sofa awhile longer. But I promised Abby that come spring we could put a room on the back of the house easy enough for you, if she wants me to. If she says yes, you can help me build it since you're so handy with a hammer." Frank ruffled Nicholas's hair.

"Ah, sleeping on the couch ain't too bad. Leastways, at night I have the front room all to myself." Remembering the facility where he'd slept in a room with lots of other boys, that seemed like a real gift. Nicholas was happy to be there.

They went to Frank's that night and the get-together was full of laughter, good friends, and good food. Lots of talk and games. Laura and Nicholas enjoyed all of it.

Coming home afterward with the kids was one of the greatest joys Abby had ever experienced. She and Frank tucked them into bed and said good night. Loving every moment.

When they were asleep, she and Frank strolled out onto the porch in their coats, sat on the porch swing, and breathed in deeply the frigid winter air. Snowball sat behind them in the window, too smart to come out in the cold.

It'd been clear all week but white flakes were falling again and the outside world was beautiful with the moonlight on the snow. Everything was beautiful now that they were safe and sound, now that Abby had a family of her own and had Frank to love.

All in all moving to Spookie, opening her life to new experiences and people had been the best thing she'd ever done. Life was good.

"The weather people are predicting three inches of snow tonight and more tomorrow. Snow next week. It's going to be a white Christmas, Frank, and who can ask for more than that?" Abby was holding Frank's hand, snuggled up against him after they'd kissed. They'd kissed a lot since that morning she'd shot Hegler. She'd never believed she'd find love again, but with Frank she had and it amazed her everyday.

"Not me," Frank whispered in her ear. "I have everything I want." He kissed Abby again. "Well, almost."

Abby knew what he meant but played dumb. He wanted their romance to grow. Wanted a commitment. She knew she was in love with him and whatever followed from that would come in time. When she was with him she was happy, felt safe and more alive than she had felt since Joel had disappeared.

Frank was a good man.

Snowball, impatient, meowed at them through the glass.

She wanted them to come in. The cat was never happy until everyone was in the house and the lights were off. House quiet for the night. Even though Snowball would sleep with Nicholas, she wanted everyone else in their beds too.

"Time for me to go home, Abby. For now, anyway," Frank sighed, getting up to leave. His truck was parked in the driveway.

Abby watched him climb into his truck and drive away through the snowy dark, a grateful smile on her lips that she had someone that special to love her again. Maybe some night they wouldn't have to go their separate ways. Her smile grew wider.

The next week was Christmas. Homemade cookies. Parties, friends, presents, and trimmed Christmas trees. Carols and spiked punch. The town all prettied up with sparkling tiny green and red lights in all the windows and on all the houses. Everybody being so kind to everyone else.

Oh how she loved Christmas.

Sam Cato was thinking of coming down for a few days with his wife and children before New Years and staying with Frank. Abby hoped they'd make it. She'd enjoy meeting the family he'd talked so much about.

The kidnapper was gone forever. The danger was past. The city hall mural was coming along well. Should be done in a few weeks. Which would give her more money than she'd know what to do with for once. Her reputation was growing and she had a slew of new commissions because of the library and city hall murals.

And . . . the house behind her was full of life.

Joel would have been proud of her. Would have been pleased for her as well. He'd been a good man too, and he would have liked Frank. A lot. In fact they were very much alike. Honorable, strong, devoted, and generous.

Her heart as full as her life, she went inside. She couldn't wait to sleep and wake up again. Fix breakfast for *her* kids. Knowing Frank, he'd mosey over sometime during the day . . . maybe for supper. Just to make sure the children had settled in. To see all of them. To share their happiness.

There was so much ahead of her, Abby thought, as she turned off the lights and went to bed. So much. And she couldn't wait to live it.